THE HIDDEN LEGION

BOOK ONE OF THE HIDDEN LEGION TRILOGY

ALSO BY
SNORRI KRISTJANSSON

Swords of Good Men
Blood Will Follow
Path of Gods

Kin
Council

THE
HIDDEN
LEGION

BOOK ONE OF THE HIDDEN LEGION TRILOGY

SNORRI KRISTJANSSON

SOLARIS

Paperback edition published 2024 by Solaris
an imprint of Rebellion Publishing Ltd,
Riverside House, Osney Mead,
Oxford, OX2 0ES, UK

First published 2023 by Solaris

www.solarisbooks.com

ISBN: 978-1-78618-976-9

10 9 8 7 6 5 4 3 2 1

A CIP catalogue record for this book is available from
the British Library.

Designed & typeset by Rebellion Publishing.

Printed in Denmark

To Steini,
I think you'd have liked this one.

I

HISPANIA

DEATH HAD COME to Aemilius, and it stood before him, and it stared him in the face.

And though he had spent a great deal of time thinking how he would face death, how he would carry the honour of his ancestors, how he would speak poetry and be remembered for his nobility, his fearlessness, and above all his Roman pride, all he could think of was—

Not like this.

They had been heading back from the village, like they'd done a hundred times before. Racing across the plain, up the hill, around the three big rocks. He had been about to shout at the boys to wait up, when Marius's horse had reared and thrown him. Moments later the other three mounts had lost their minds as well, eyes bulging with terror, bucking and thrashing, screaming in protest.

Not like this.

Lucan had gotten off unharmed and tried to grab the reins, only to have his mare half twist her head off as she tried to bite him before bolting off the path, into the scrublands. Without the horses, they would not be home until sundown, and they'd get an earful for their troubles. After the initial shock, Vincius had complained, as he always did.

And then... the... thing had appeared.

It seemed to come out of nowhere. Lucius had been trying to convince them again that he'd been trained as a hunter and it was okay because he could track the horses, and his uncle wouldn't be annoyed. And all the while as they argued as to what had caused it—wolves, big cats, snakes—none of them had thought to look *up*. Aemilius tried to remember his training, but the swordmaster had prepared him for shield walls and formations—for combat against human foes—and thought little of his talents. He had done his best, but always hoped that death would come to him nobly, like it had done to the men in his family before him.

Not like... this.

He couldn't even rise to his knees. Everything was too much. The ridge of red rock was suddenly painful to look at. The sand was rough and warm under his palms, but despite the evening sun he was cold with sweat.

It had finished Marius off quickly, in a spray of blood and gurgled screams.

Lucan and Vinicius had put up more resistance, shouting for him to join, to come on, to fight. And he had watched them, watched the thing rise to head-height on powerful wings that beat the stink of it towards him, watched its talons shred their flesh, with a sinking weight in his stomach.

It looked so horribly effortless. One moment they were there, waving their swords, shouting and shrieking like you would to scare off any normal animal.

The next, Lucan was sinking to his knees clutching an arm reduced to strips of meat, hanging limply from his elbow. Stricken by his cousin's fate, Vinicius took his eyes off the creature for a moment and his face *disappeared*, sending him spinning to the ground with the force of the blow.

The... thing knew, too. It knew exactly when there was no threat anymore. It landed gently, almost tenderly, and turned. Slowly, painfully slowly, it turned to look at him, and having had only a side view thus far, Aemilius now saw the whole of the thing.

He wished he hadn't.

It stood maybe four feet tall, on three-pronged talons dripping in the blood of his cousins. Powerful legs feathered in blue and grey carried the torso of a bird, out of which the pallid flesh of a child rose, like a careless sculptor had changed his mind midway through. Wings like a bird of prey's extended wider than a man's arms, ending in claws that looked like ragged human fingernails.

But the face was the worst of it.

It looked like someone had de-boned the skull of a young girl and stuck it on a ball of spite. The... thing grinned at him, and none of the muscles in its face moved right.

"...Harpy." The words were out before he knew it, whispered to no-one. "You are a harpy. You're... not real."

The harpy hissed at him, and Aemilius felt the contents of his bladder running down his legs, and realised he was crying.

Not like this.

He was supposed to die in battle a general. Not slaughtered on a country road in Hispania by a monstrous apparition that only existed in tales to scare children.

He was supposed to reach his fiftieth year a hero, like in the stories. Not to die in his fifteenth, pissing himself.

He was supposed to be buried to the wails of mourning by family and followers. Not a bloody irritating... tin whistle?

The harpy screeched and rose from the ground in a flap of wings, shaking its head and squeezing its beady eyes shut, but the whistling persisted. Its eyes flew open again and Aemilius recoiled. Gone was the cold, smug superiority; they glowed with hate and fury, hotter than any furnace he'd ever seen.

And still, weaving in on the thin air, the tin whistle sounded.

"Look straight ahead," a deep, calm voice said somewhere behind him, in learned but accented Latin. "And whatever you do, don't move."

Aemilius nodded, eyes wide open. He saw the harpy's gaze waver, then turn to look to his left. To his side, an odd-looking woman was emerging from the scrub. She looked like someone had stuck a dead shrub on a dead tree, all wrong angles and long limbs and a serious face, with the unruliest head of hair he had ever seen. She held a tin whistle, swaying gently from side to side and hitting the wrong notes with almost surgical precision.

"Good," said the voice behind him. "Look at the whistler. Try not to listen, if you can." There was a hint of a smile in the voice.

The harpy hissed, spat and tried to fly towards the woman, but something seemed to be wrong with its wings. It thrashed harder, and whatever invisible chain was slowing it down seemed to shatter. A triumphant shriek—

And Aemilius saw the movement out of the corner of his eye just before he heard the heavy sound of wood on bone.

The harpy dropped like a stone.

Behind it stood a rotund, happy-looking man, holding a simple, studded cudgel the length and thickness of a butcher's forearm. "Gods, but I love that sound," he said, looking affectionately at the pool of blood forming at his feet. "Bird's cooked."

The tin whistle stopped. "It is the only music you make, barbarian."

"Who are you calling barbarian, you upstart twig? I haven't seen you eat anything that isn't a root or an abomination. I should—"

"Be quiet, the both of you," the voice behind Aemilius rumbled. "We need to get going. Taurio—get the bag."

"Why do I always have to get the bag?" the fat man complained, pulling out a stubby knife from his belt. "I'm not the one who is going to be rooting around in its guts."

"He might try to eat them on the way," the woman said.

"Prasta—horses," said the voice. "Pick up the strays, if you can."

The woman turned smartly and loped off, disappearing into a gap in the shrubs that Aemilius could not see. With both of the others occupied, he finally dared turn to look at the source of the voice.

Rising up out of a hiding place in the bushes was a house of a man, standing easily a head and a half taller than him and seeming utterly unruffled by the events just passed. Gilt robes, in a fashion Aemilius vaguely guessed might be North African, flowed around his broad shoulders in a vibrant crimson. Bald and dark-skinned, he had a ready smile and a twinkle in his eye.

"Who... are you?" he stammered.

"My name is Abrax," the man said in his deep, accented voice, "and we are your friends. You are coming with us."

"Where? What? Why?" Aemilius found that his voice was rising, and he could do nothing to stop it. "No! No. I can't. They're all dead. And there was a harpy. A *harpy!* I have to go home. The horses bolted! I have to find them. Father must know. He'll—"

And that was all Aemilius said.

The man named Taurio caught him when he fell, dropping the cudgel as he did so. It swung from a loop in his belt.

"You didn't have to hit him," Abrax admonished, bending down to examine the fallen youth.

"Answer me this. Is he a Roman?"

"Yes," Abrax sighed.

"Then he deserves a smack on the head."

The woman named Prasta reappeared, holding the reins of five horses. One whinnied and another stamped when they scented the dead harpy, but none pulled on the reins. She took one look at the fallen boy at Taurio's feet. "Oh, for the love of Maponus," she snapped. "If you've cracked his skull—"

"I haven't!" Taurio adjusted the heavy bag over his shoulder. "Unlike some, *I* know what I'm doing."

"If he's broken, she'll roast you on a spit."

"Oh, shut up. He's fine." Taurio prodded Aemilius with a toe, ignoring the fact that the boy didn't move.

"Again," Abrax rumbled. "Both of you. The boy will live—or you should hope so, at least. If you have damaged him, Prasta is right. She will *not* be happy." He bent down, picked up Aemilius's fallen form easily and slung it over his shoulder. "Let's get back to camp. The sun waits on no-one."

Fading hoofbeats left behind three dead bodies and long shadows on a silent road.

ATOP A HILL plateau bordered by a semi-circle of boulders, looking down on a gentle slope running down to the Iberian plain, three horses grazed next to an unconcerned donkey, a stone's throw from a plain-looking two-horse cart. In between large rocks, tucked away well out of sight from all but the most dedicated observers, two women were deep in conversation.

Rivkah leaned back against a flat slate, linking hands behind her head and stretching her legs. "...And *I'm* saying that's nonsense." She regarded the woman opposite her with barely disguised contempt.

Sitting cross-legged and straight-backed opposite her on the ground, Livia smiled and gently moved a lock of stray blonde hair from her eyes. "Say what you like. It's just what I've heard."

"I've heard the rumours too. And she looks a mean old bitch, I'll give you that. But sixty? That's a *number*." The short woman paused and sat back up. "Although, saying that, your lot would know about assassinations."

"What do you mean, *my lot*?" Livia replied coldly, giving Rivkah an icy stare.

It was Rivkah's turn to smirk. "You know. The rich. The powerful. The wealthy. Our betters." She rose gracefully and executed a mocking bow from the waist. "...Your Exalted and Most Noble Highness."

"Oh, go shove a cactus up yourself," Livia snapped. "You know exactly how much that annoys me."

The wolfish grin on Rivkah's face said as much as she stretched and limbered up, rolling her hips and her shoulders.

"Fine. If you don't believe me—let's ask Hanno, shall we?"

Rivkah swore in Hebrew. "He smells of mould."

Sitting half a stone's throw away, Hanno the Wise's voice was almost too quiet to register. "I can hear you. With my ears," he added, keeping his eyes trained on the contents of his tin cup.

"You were meant to hear me," Rivkah said. "And you *do* smell."

"I do," Hanno replied. "But that is not the worst a man can do." He lifted a slim, long-fingered hand and moved it in an intricate pattern over his tin cup.

Rivkah sneered, then grimaced. "Hey! Stop that. You're doing it on purpose, and you know it gives me aches. No—I mean it. Stop it, or I'll smash your face in with a stone."

Hanno looked up, brown eyes looking almost too big in his diminutive head, and blinked. "I apologize, daughter of Abraham. The moon whispered to me."

"Whatever, you freak. The Queen has a question."

Livia scowled. "We were talking about Cassia."

Immediately, Hanno's face twisted in discomfort. "She is black water in a dark cave, that one."

"We know *that*," Rivkah said. "But Princess here said she'd killed sixty men, and I said that sounded high."

"Thirty-seven that I know of—" Hanno said.

"Hah!"

"—but the real number is probably quite a lot higher. Triple that, I'd say."

Livia smiled graciously. "Thank you, Hanno."

"How would you know about that anyway, pond frog?" Rivkah snapped.

"The moon—"

"Don't," Rivkah interrupted. "force me to take your teeth out one by one with a very small hammer."

"She's so *violent*," Livia said, voice laced with mock concern. "Is that what"—she relished the words—"*your lot* is like?"

"It's all this sitting! We're not *doing* anything!" Rivkah squirmed, as if the words themselves were uncomfortable.

"We're waiting," a gruff voice rumbled from underneath a horseman's helmet. "Favourite pastime of—"

"—the mighty Roman soldier," Livia and Rivkah finished in unison.

"We hear your wisdom, O ancient one," Rivkah continued, pacing and effortlessly leaping up onto a stone, pushing off and into a backflip, landing and spinning instantly to face the supine form of Quintus Aurelius, formerly Primus Pilus of the Fourth Legion, now lying with his head resting on his saddle and fully unimpressed.

"Go do a handstand if it calms you down." At no point did Quintus move a muscle, not even to lift the brim of his helmet. "And Hanno is messing with you."

"Hanno!" Livia said, with mock outrage.

"The old stump speaks the truth," the small man said, grinning. "I am messing. I know nothing."

Rivkah sneered. "Why'd you speak, then?"

"Because you also know nothing, and I thought we could be together in ignorance. It is good to share."

"Well, you…" The dark-haired girl arched her back, stretching her arms out until she tipped over an invisible axis point and fell backwards, feet lifting effortlessly until she caught her weight on her hands, balanced in a perfect handstand. Smiling and breathing a little harder, she shifted her weight until she could slowly lift one hand. Like a puppet on a string that had just been cut, her body then folded in on itself as her feet hit the ground and she rose, cheeks flushed. "...are an idiot. But I'll let you live."

"You are kindness and light." The small man smiled and turned his attention back to his tin cup. "They're coming," he said softly.

"How far?" Quintus still didn't move.

"Five turns of the waterman's wheel. Or a small drop of the moon's tears, if that's easier."

"In all our years of travelling, my friend," Quintus said, propping himself up on his elbows and adjusting his helmet, "I still don't know what you're saying half of the time."

"But the other half is good, though," Hanno said.

The soldier rose with the care of someone who had learned the hard way to conserve energy. "Half of the time," he said, smirking. "No time to waste. Let's get up and"—he grunted—"right."

Rivkah, already seated on a saddled and snorting mare, raised an eyebrow. "Come on, old man. Every day I see you die a little more. Do you have *any* life left in you?"

Quintus thought about this. "Not sure," he said, whistling once, sharply. A mahogany bay standing separate from the other horses pricked up its long ears, ceased its grazing and trotted over, nuzzling the Roman's hand as he whispered soothing words in its ear and stroked her short mane.

The horse whinnied.

"Yes, yes. I know. But literally anywhere we go is better than here for that, and so we'll be on our way."

The mare nudged him gently.

"If I ever meet a woman who wonders whether it is a good idea to drag an old soldier to their bed, I'd tell them to go look at how you treat that horse," Livia said as she saddled a chestnut mare.

"And what do you think they'd say?"

"I think they'd see you're already taken," she said.

"A soldier who doesn't love his horse—"

"'—is a dead soldier,'" the women finished.

"The stump may look finished and useless," Hanno the Wise added as he stroked the muzzle of his donkey, "but he has strong roots and is hard to get rid of."

"...thank you?" Quintus said, swinging into the saddle.

Hanno nodded gravely. "You're welcome."

"I see them," Rivkah said. "They're going easy."

"I wish I had your eyesight," Livia said.

"No, you do not," Rivkah said. "I have to spend it looking at all of you." She laughed and pointed. Down on the plains, three riders had come into view, growing from tiny specks on the horizon to moving figures, closing in at a brisk walk.

"Heron!" Hanno exclaimed.

"What?"

"I've been trying to figure out which animal being eaten by a ravenous hog your laugh sounds like. And it sounds like a heron being eaten by a ravenous hog." The African clapped his hands in delight and smiled from ear to ear. "This is a truth, and it makes me happy."

"You are so lucky my mother told me it was a bad thing to torture small animals," Rivkah said.

The riders had reached the foot of the hill and the

front-rider raised his arm in greeting. Quintus responded in turn.

Rivkah looked over at Hanno, who was suddenly grimacing and writhing. "Hey. What's wrong with the frog?"

"Hanno…?" Livia said, concern in her voice. "What's…?"

"Bad," Hanno said through gritted teeth. "Sense it. Taste it. Bad, bad, bad." He took a quick sip from his flask, swishing the water around his mouth.

Quintus nodded towards the riders, now visible. "They've got cargo."

As the three moved closer, Rivkah's horse tossed its head. Soon Livia's mare followed suit, stamping at the ground. Hanno leaned forward, stroking the neck of his donkey. Quintus's mount snorted once and twisted its neck as if to get a look at its rider, but held fast. The soldier muttered half-words as he sat, stock-still.

When the groups could see eye to eye, Abrax smiled, moving smoothly in the saddle as his horse picked its way over rocks and the desiccated remains of plants. "We got him," he said.

"Good," Livia said.

"What's in the bag, fat man?" Rivkah shouted.

"Your dinner," Taurio replied cheerfully, patting the stained bag draped over the back of his horse. "Or your sister. Not sure which." He thought for a moment. "Could be both."

"Was it as we thought?" Quintus interrupted.

"It was," Prasta replied.

"And *your* saddle-sack, Abrax?" Livia said, pointing to the unconscious youth slung over the big man's pommel.

"He's out," Abrax replied.

"Taurio hit him too hard," Prasta added over her shoulder, busying herself with the cart.

"Come on, man," Rivkah said. "Every time."

"Hey!" Taurio threw his hands up. "I cannot be held responsible for the consequences of the actions of the Roman Empire." He grinned, until he saw the expression on the cavalryman's face. "What's the matter, old man?"

"Nothing," Quintus said curtly. "We need to move. We've got work to do." Grabbing the reins, he guided his horse down towards the lengthening shadows. Livia and Abrax shared a fleeting, quizzical look, then followed. Moments later all six were following him, heading down the hill, riding south.

AEMILIUS SQUEEZED HIS eyes shut, trying to push away the thundering headache. He tried breathing and found that he was most likely alive. Moments later he regretted—deeply—having taken his first conscious breath through his nose.

The stench drove through his nostrils and felt like it would coat his brain. He gasped, and it forced itself into his mouth like a fist. The bile rose up in him and came out, despite his best efforts, in a cough and a splutter. After spitting and hacking, he became aware of voices.

"Did no-one plug the boy?" someone growled behind him.

"Thought he'd be out for a while longer," someone else replied. "He's got a thick skull."

"*You've* got a thick skull. You hit him too hard."

"Shut up, twiglet!"

"Both of you," the first voice snapped. "Taurio—help him."

Aemilius considered his options. His arms and legs felt weak, but he was not bound. Which was not to say that escape was practical; the way his head was thumping, he was absolutely not sure he'd be able to stand up without falling over. He eased his left eye open just a crack—and found himself looking at the vague shape of a short man, lit by flickering torchlight.

Taurio's eyes twinkled. "Good morning, sunshine," he said in accented Latin. He looked up at the sky. "Good night, actually, but I thought that might be confusing. I bet your head hurts, hmm?"

Aemilius's reply was a guttural attempt to push the contents of his stomach—and his stomach itself—up through his throat.

"Yup. The smell will do that to you. It's mostly Quintus. Horse boys never wash."

"Still smell better than a Gaul," the first voice said somewhere in the dark.

Taurio smiled indulgently, rolling something between his fingers.

"Cow shit and horse shit is both shit." A woman's voice from further away. Loud. Another accent. "Just sort him out, will you? The sounds he's making make me want to punch him in the throat."

Aemilius took a deep breath and swallowed sour spittle, just as a warm, firm hand with thick fingers took hold of his jaw. "Hold still—" Taurio said, voice soothing... and waves of calm filled him. His stomach settled immediately, and he felt his mouth water. Thoughts of his nursemaid came to him, thoughts of safety and happiness. He opened both eyes, to take in the sight of Taurio looking at him, smiling. "It's good stuff, no?" he said, with a grin.

Stunned into silence, Aemilius reached up and touched his nose. It felt... full. Stuffed. "Simple. Cloth, soaked with oil and some of my nice herbs. Your head doesn't like bad smells, so why let them in? Now, if you'd allow me..." The short man gently put a bandage over his entire nose, then tied it firmly behind his head. Aemilius winced. "Sorry about that," Taurio said earnestly. "I maybe hit you harder than I had to."

"Or at all. You are an untamed forest-pig." At the edge of the torchlight the lanky woman he remembered playing the tin whistle stood, a sneer of disapproval on her face. She eyed him suspiciously. "I am Prasta." Another accent.

"She says she is a famous singer and bard," Taurio said. "I say she has the voice of a cat caught in a wagon wheel, and a selection of mysterious instruments that are all somehow worse."

"Shut up, lardbucket," Prasta shot back. "And do his ears, so he won't have to listen to you."

Taurio nodded seriously. "That is wise. So you are not due to say anything worth listening to again for... about seven months?" Grinning, he rummaged in a pouch on his belt and pulled out two thick cloth pads. "Lean forward—" He inched Aemilius towards him. "You are going to want these." With quick, sure movements, he shoved the pads under the bandage, covering the young man's ears, and then positioned himself in front of Aemilius's face. "Can you hear me?"

Aemilius blinked. "Yes. But why are you whispering?"

The fat man grinned. "I'm not," he said, moving his lips in exaggerated motions. "Your hearing is cut by half. Your eyes will need to work twice as hard."

"Why? What's—?"

And then Aemilius remembered.

The talons.

The blood.

The eyes.

"...oh."

Taurio smiled again, but now there was less mirth in it. He turned around, and Aemilius just caught sight of him mouthing, *Boy's done* to the outline of another man, moving slowly in the gloom. The man held still for a moment, and Aemilius had the sense of being *inspected*. Then the man turned away, and suddenly the torchlight vanished. He was abandoned in the dark. Gingerly, vaguely aware of his head thumping behind Taurio's assault of smells, Aemilius looked around.

The first thing he noticed was the stake. Half again the height of a man, it stood straight in the air, a taunting monolith. Threaded upon it like a common duck was the body of the harpy. It had been staked through the chest, its stomach sliced open and innards pulled out to form a grisly curtain, reaching almost to the ground. Even in death—and Aemilius kept his eye on the harpy for a long time to be sure—it seemed furious at the world. Flaps of skin, no longer animated by muscle, hung limp from its misshapen form. Something in his head struggled with what he was seeing—and then he realised. It was the middle of the night, and he could neither hear the crackle nor feel the heat of a campfire. Keeping his eyes trained on the horror, he tried to figure out where the light was coming from... There! He blinked, because looking at it hurt a little—but hovering in mid-air, close enough to the harpy to be a little hard to distinguish, was a small globe, suspended in mid-air, a flame trapped within it. Looking closer, Aemilius searched for supports or ropes… but there were none. He squeezed his eyes shut again, but the point of light kept dancing before his eyes.

What was this nightmare? And where was he?

Looking down to regain his night vision, he looked for the borders of the light and searched for outlines. He thought he could maybe see… four? Four pools of shadow, shifting in the darkness in a vague circle around him, but none of them was the giant he'd seen just after—

Unbidden, the images of his cousins' bodies, slashed to ribbons, came to him again, and he retched. He slammed his hand down and felt the sand under his palms. Soil and gravel, tufts of grass. *Hills.* The picture of a hill came to him, a rocky trail somewhere, and Aemilius cursed the darkness. He tried to scent the air, but all he could feel from his nose was a dull tingling sensation. Feeling very carefully around where he had lain, his hand touched rough cloth. A sack of some sort. Prodding it, he found metal… and handles. *Weapons.* On reflex, he drew his hand back. His father's voice rang in his ears. *Don't ever touch another man's weapons.* He remembered his father—the Governor's mansion—the warm embrace of his mother—

And then the storm broke through his thoughts.

There was no warning.

The night had been still, with no movement to speak of—and suddenly, a gale force wind blasted him, pressing him to the ground and knocking the breath out of him. Gasping, Aemilius looked up to see demonic shadows fluttering around the harpy on the stake, shrieking and clawing.

A shouted command somewhere—and a brilliant light burst from the globe. Blinded, Aemilius clasped both hands to his face. He could just about hear himself making noises, but there were no words. An urge to survive forced him to move the hands away from his face, blinking to move the white in his eyes, get some shapes back into the darkness—

Which was gone.

Instead, he was stood in a circus bathed in a ghostly glow, shadowed by the torn form of the first harpy.

Down on the ground, battle raged.

Breathing rapidly, heart thundering in his chest, Aemilius tried to get his bearings. Right in front of him, two harpies flapped at head-height, clawing at a man in a worn cavalryman's uniform. He was holding them off with a light, rounded horseman's shield, moving with the tired economy of an old soldier. One of the harpies lunged and slashed at him, hissing when the claws hit his breastplate, and received a gladius in the leg for its trouble. Standing about ten feet behind him, a slim woman in tightly-wrapped grey clothing wielded a composite bow swiftly and calmly, loosing arrow after arrow at the hovering harpies on all sides. On their flank, Taurio and Prasta stood side by side, wielding club and staff. The lack of sharp blades did not seem to bother them, and the harpy they'd engaged had no luck getting close. Moving gracefully, Taurio stepped to the side and drew the monster's attention while Prasta delivered a bone-crushing blow to its shin. The flying beast reeled and the big man pressed the attack, swinging his club with fury. The creature shrieked as an arrow lodged in its wing.

Panic flooded Aemilius, and he realised he had been looking in one direction for too long. He whipped round just in time to see three harpies flapping around...

something. They shrieked and howled, thrusted and slashed—but none of them could hit it. He felt his jaw slowly sink as realisation settled in.

It was a girl. Maybe half a head shorter than he was.

In between the monsters, she spun, jumped, ducked and swerved in an impossible death-dance. Dark blood erupted from the neck of one of the creatures, spraying in an arc behind the girl's left hand. His gut lurched as another harpy rose, triumphant and malicious, behind the dark-haired girl, beating its powerful wings, snatching at the outstretched hand. The dagger went flying, and Aemilius saw the girl's face for the first time.

Her fury more than matched that of all the harpies combined.

In one liquid movement, she dropped to the ground, under the swing of a claw, and rolled towards him. She locked eyes with him and her mouth was moving and she was saying something and then there was a creature behind her, closing in and rising, claws out, and the rage in her eyes froze him to the spot and then he was struck in the chest just as a blast of heat pushed the harpy off, and he fell just in time to see her snatch up the bag, rip out two short swords and spin back towards the harpies, screaming something at the top of her lungs as she launched herself back into hell.

Remembering that there was something—something important that he needed to do—something *really* important—Aemilius gasped for breath like a drowning man. Whirling round, he saw the Roman standing over two of the harpies' corpses, stabbing down in the easy manner of a man finishing a day's work. To the side, Taurio and Prasta seemed to be arguing as to who had delivered the killing blow to a pulped mess of a creature.

Then he was spun around, a hand firmly grasping his shoulder, and again death had come to Aemilius and stood before him, staring him in the face. This time the face was that of the girl, breathing heavily. Her dark hair, tied back in a bun, was flushed and glistening with vile fluids from the harpies' wounds. Lightning-quick, she thrust the point of a short sword at his head and flicked, and the bandage came off his head, dislodging the earmuffs.

"You little *shit!*" She threw the sword down.

"Wh-what? I, uh—"

She shoved him in the chest. Hard. "Why didn't you just stab me in the back? Huh?" She shoved him again. "Speak. You runty little weasel. *Speak.*"

Aemilius reached for the words, but none came. Instead, he found his eyes filling with tears.

The girl looked at him in disgust. "That's it. I'm gutting him. He'll be bait for something."

"But Cassia—" someone said.

"—can eat a hot plate of horseshit," the girl snapped. "She can come for me if she wants, but I'll be wearing this lily-livered little boy's balls as a fetching necklace." She looked at him with undisguised hate. "If they've dropped yet, that is." A dagger appeared in her hand, faster than a blink. "I might have to"—the end of the sentence was growled—"rummage round a bit."

"Rivkah." The word sounded like the crack of a horse whip.

"What?" she snapped back.

Not daring to take his eyes off the furious girl, Aemilius felt rather than saw the old centurion approach.

"Step back and calm down. Your blood is up."

"But at least it's still *in*, no thanks to this—" A word followed, in what Aemilius thought must be Hebrew.

He didn't need to know the language to understand the meaning. "He was standing on the bloody *weapon sack*, and I am going to teach him that you *do not do that*." She stepped closer and Aemilius instinctively stumbled back.

It happened very quickly.

The girl—Rivkah—launched herself at him, and something darted in between them. There was a thud, and he thought he saw her land on the ground, only to spring back up almost immediately. The stocky frame of the Roman soldier almost completely blocked her from Aemilius's view.

"*Ohhh*," she purred. "So *that*'s how it is." She shook herself and rolled her shoulders, like someone enjoying a delicious sensation. "Come on then, Quintus Aurelius, Primus Pilus of the Fourth. Let's see what you—"

A flick of a hand and the shield was flying, hitting her in the stomach. The old man was on her as she flinched, grabbing a handful of her tunic and kicking hard at her calves, sweeping her legs from under her. Even airborne and off-balance, she still almost twisted out of his grip, but when she landed on the ground he went with her, pinning her down.

"The kid got smacked on the head, woke up in the middle of a fight and didn't know what he was doing," the older man snapped. "And you are not going to carve him up until we have had a chance to teach him what to do, and how to do it. Understood, soldier?" He spoke easily, but with finality.

Lying on the ground, the girl cackled. "Not bad, old man. Not bad. I'll leave your precious toy alone for now. But if he does it again, I'll feed him to your horse. And it'll take *weeks*."

The Roman held on for a couple of breaths longer. Then he glanced at Aemilius, and back at the prone girl. "Two weeks, max. If I feed her human flesh for longer than that, she gets the shits." He stood up, offering Rivkah his hand.

Grinning, she propped both hands on the ground behind her head and vaulted up to a standing position. "You fight dirty."

"Against you? Always." The centurion smirked. "You will note that I am still alive." His tone changed, turned complimentary. "I saw your work. Pretty impressive, even for you."

The girl looked away. "They were—"

"Stupid," the woman in grey finished.

A murmur of agreement from the group.

"I agree," Abrax said, from a distance. His hands glowed like metal in a forge. "There is much to talk about."

"But first we sleep." Prasta spoke like a matron who would brook no argument.

"Always with the sleep," Taurio chimed in. "Don't you know the fun always happens after sunset?"

"Prasta's right," Quintus said. "We need rest."

"If it's all the same to you, I'd prefer not to sleep in harpy droppings," the woman in grey said.

"You aristocrats with your high standards," Rivkah said, smirking. "What's next, your highness? Shall we summon your silken carriage? Build you a palace? Call for your *uncle?*"

The woman looked at her with calm patience. "I know your lot regularly sleep in bird shit. But I fear *my* darling mother rather missed out on that part of my upbringing."

Rivkah hissed.

"Livia…" Abrax said.

"What?" the woman in grey said, still smiling. "She keeps on talking about my family, so I thought I'd mention hers—oh." She feigned upset. "Oh, I've said too much. May the gods smite me."

"Happy to do it for them," Rivkah snarled.

"Sleep!" Prasta said, like she was breaking up a fight between siblings. "We can dig a hole for the bodies, and they will be none of our own. Abrax…?"

The big man made a non-committal noise that could have been half a yes.

There was the crunch of shovel breaking ground, and Aemilius turned to see Quintus already at work. Without comment, Livia disappeared into the darkness, only to return soon after with another shovel. A silent agreement seemed to have been reached, and Taurio moved off towards the feathered corpses on the ground, dragging them towards the rapidly-forming hole. Rivkah muttered protests as Prasta saw to her, batting away any and all attempts at conversation in favour of figuring out whose blood was where. Abrax kept his distance from the group, holding his hands away from his body. The glow had cooled from white-hot to a gentle amber. Aemilius looked at him, willing him to look his way, but he just stood as if in a trance. There was the hint of movement somewhere close in the darkness, and a horse whinnying softly. The rhythmic sound of digging blended in with the occasional command, most often from Quintus.

Very soon, a shallow grave had been dug for the harpies. All six of them were laid out ready. Kneeling over the bodies, Taurio grunted with the effort of removing parts of their intestines.

Abrax approached, and the others took several steps back. He grunted, flicked his wrist—and a small flame sprang to life, sailing through the air and landing on the body in the middle. Unlike a normal flame, it didn't sputter and die; it just… burned there, like a candle, until a tendril of smoke snaked its way up into the air. Fire blossomed at its root and spread out across the corpse like a circle in a pond. The air turned grey and greasy.

"Flip it."

Quintus, Taurio and Livia moved in and tipped the burning harpy onto its stomach with their shovels. Smoke drifted up from underneath it. Without words, they started shovelling earth onto the pile. Aemilius watched, transfixed, as the harpies were covered with gravel and sand, and still the smoke kept coming.

"They call it 'deadfire.' It stays alive."

He jumped nearly out of his skin. Rivkah had appeared next to him.

"Whu—?"

She looked sideways at him. The fury was gone, replaced with a calculating look. It was not reassuring. "The flame. You're wondering why they're shovelling on top of it."

Amongst other things, yes, Aemilius thought.

"It stays alive as long as Abrax keeps his mind on it," she said, nodding to the smoking cairn. "And it spreads, and it burns through things. Turns them to ash. Pretty nasty stuff," she added, grinning.

"Why… didn't he just set them on fire earlier?"

Rivkah shrugged. "Magic. I don't know how it works, but from what I gather it's hard. Think of this as throwing a pebble into a pond. Setting fire to six flying harpies would be throwing a rock into a water glass from a hundred yards."

"Uh, I see," Aemilius said, not really seeing anything. "So is he...?"

"A magus. Yes," Rivkah said. "Any more questions?"

The words were out before he could stop them. "Who... *are* you people?"

The girl fixed him with a twinkling eye. "At the moment, we are the only thing keeping you alive. That's all you need to know. Now do as you're told and get some rest, *boy*. You're going to need it."

II

HISPANIA

AEMILIUS OPENED HIS eyes and choked on a scream, producing only a weak, stifled squeak. Inches away from his nose a strange face hovered. Taut, black skin, impossibly large eyes, a broad forehead tapering to a pointy chin.

The stranger smiled at him.

He scrabbled backwards, gibbering incoherently, hands slipping and scraping on the gravel, and looked around in a panic. The faint dawn light cast long, deep shadows, creeping ever so slowly across a camp that only barely deserved the name. He struggled to make out the boundaries, even from within. Bodies lay strewn about like abandoned carcasses. "Hanno," one of them mumbled sleepily. "Leave him alone."

"But he is new and shiny, like a tadpole," the man said, in an odd, sing-song voice. "Full of slimy promise. I like him."

"Well, you can keep him," someone else said. "He's useless. Boil him down for stock or something."

"Oh, but we can't," Hanno said, grinning. "For he is important. Im-port-ant," he repeated, savouring the word.

"Much more so than you, old friend." Aemilius recognised the voice of the Roman soldier from the night before. "So leave him alone."

Hanno pouted and scurried off. "Fine," he huffed. "Never get to have any fun." A smattering of muttered swears followed the slim figure through the camp. Aemilius watched him scamper up onto a large rock and then—disappear.

He blinked.

No—the small man was still there. He was just absolutely immobile, as if he'd been frozen in place, perched on an outcropping.

Forcing himself to breathe slowly, Aemilius tried to regain his sanity. It felt like holding water in his fist. Almost like he wasn't there, he listened to the heart thumping in his chest and tried to remember a time before, when none of these people existed and he knew that he'd have a bed to go to. It seemed utterly unreal but served to slow his heartbeat down.

Training his eyes to make out shapes in the slow light of the morning, he established his position. What had looked like a haphazard collection of bodies was actually arranged in a rough circle—around him. There would be no escape, even if he wanted to. A small voice within whispered that that also meant he was protected from threats, but he ignored it. The campsite, which in hindsight might not have been chosen entirely without thought, was protected from wind by a line of scrawny-looking trees in front of a ridge of hostile-looking rocks. To the side, the deeper, shadowy forms of horses seemed to gather around a cart.

Taking in his environment calmed him down and gave space for some of the events of the night before to come back to him. Waking up with a headache. The attack of the harpies. The scent—no, the stink—no, the *reek* of lavender in his nose. The girl named Rivkah nearly slicing his head off. He remembered standing, mute and confused, as the weird collection of... What were they? Mercenaries? ...dug holes for the harpies and then simply went to sleep as the smell of burning feathers drifted away on the wind, as if nothing out of the ordinary had happened.

A stone's throw away, one of the bodies stirred. A quiet, muttered curse in a language Aemilius didn't know—and then Taurio clambered to his feet. The fat man shook himself like a wet dog and rubbed his eyes.

Without glancing over, he spoke. "Good morning, boy! You are awake nice and early. I like that."

"Aemilius."

"Pardon?"

"My name. I am Aemilius."

"Ah. Yes. Of course. And I am Taurio."

"Shut your flappy mouth, Gaul." A throaty growl.

"And good morning to you too, Rivkah," Taurio replied with a widening grin. He turned back to Aemilius and winked conspiratorially in the gloom. "Would you like Prasta to play the flute to wake you up? I'm sure you wouldn't have to ask all that nicely."

"Don't you *dare*—" A jaunty, tooth-jangling tune weaved its way through the camp. Rivkah groaned through gritted teeth and another of the lumps got up, this one much faster than the first. "I hate you. I hate you all."

"She doesn't," Taurio said.

"I *do*," Rivkah said, stalking off towards a fallen boulder and disappearing behind it. Moments later Prasta's flute was joined by the unmistakeable sound of a bladder being emptied, accompanied by a groan of relief.

Taurio stretched again. "Make yourself useful," he said over his shoulder and moved off towards the cart. Aemilius looked behind him, but there was no-one. Somewhat less gracefully than he wanted, he started picking his way after the broad-backed Gaul.

When he got to the cart, Taurio was kneeling on the ground over a bundle of wood. "Any good with fires?"

"Uh—no. We always had—"

"Any good at learning?" The bundle clattered open, spreading across the stone.

Aemilius faltered. "Uh."

"Any good at talking?" Taurio said, grinning. "Or do you just 'uh'?"

A tiny flame of pride flickered in Aemilius, and he knelt down beside the big man.

Taurio glanced at him, and seemed about to say something, but changed his mind. "Build a little house of the small twigs."

"Why?"

The big man nodded. "Good. Questions are good. A fire needs two things. Food and air." Working quickly, he built a cone of twigs. "Next, bigger sticks." He glanced up at Aemilius, searching for the question in his eyes. Satisfied, he continued. "The small ones burn, then break. The fire builds, then falls in on itself. Hand me the right sticks." Scanning the selection, Aemilius found the smallest sticks left and handed them to Taurio. "Good. Keep building until you have a good house with a solid roof. We'll do a small fire now, because we have places to go."

Very soon after, the big Gaul was content. A cone-shaped stick tower stood before them, with a flattened top, and he had a fistful of dry grass pulled from the gravel. "And now—fire." He produced a curved steel from the folds of his tunic and struck it on his knuckles. Aemilius winced, then noticed the ring with the black inset.

Sparks flew towards the grass—and caught. Carefully, sheltering the smouldering blades with one hand, he knelt and poked the tinder into the base of the cone.

"And now we feed it a little more, like a precious little screaming baby," Taurio muttered, kneeling down until his face was nearly in the bundle of sticks, and blowing gently, ever so gently…

A hair-thin tendril of smoke rose towards the morning sky, quickly joined by another. The two merged, and moments later there was fire.

"Good. We'll see what we can feed the troops, shall we?" Rising to his feet with a muttered old man's complaint, he looked at Aemilius. "There is no shame in not knowing—if you learn." He bustled over to a cart and bent over the side into the bed. There was the sound of rummaging.

Aemilius nodded. This sounded very much like what had been drilled into him, for as long as he could remember. *Always learn.* He thought for a moment about his servants—the faceless shapes that had flowed into and out of rooms, making fire, removing clothes—and shuddered with the strangeness of it all.

"Any good at cooking?" Taurio said, half buried in the contents of the cart, emerging with a small kettle and a sack before Aemilius had managed to offer the obvious answer. "Then watch and learn." With impressive speed, he placed the kettle on the growing fire, emptied a skin of water in the pan, produced a knife and chopped a fistful of vegetables. "This—is important." Out of the sack he pulled a tiny bag, tied close with a string.

"Is that... magic?" Aemilius stammered, feeling instantly like an idiot.

"Green magic," Taurio replied, face absolutely serious. "Taste." He reached in the bag, and came away with a pinch of something, which he put in Aemilius's outstretched hand, motioning for him to put it in his mouth. Reluctantly, he did what he was told—and the dried flakes in his mouth yielded flavours that grew stronger and stronger. "Herbs," he added. "An army marches on its stomach, and we've all eaten Roman army food, so when we *can* do better"—he lowered the bag into the kettle, tying it tenderly to the handle—"we do." Content that he had imparted great wisdom, the Gaul produced a wooden spoon and gave the contents a loving stir, devoting all of his attention to the food and none to Aemilius.

After waiting for a while for him to say anything, the young man turned away. Around him, the landscape was changing with the rising sun. A couple of the huddled forms were now grumbling and climbing to their feet. One or two had already disappeared. He could make out the shape of Quintus in amongst the horses. Abrax was standing by the top of the slope, looking out towards the plain. The woman in grey stood next to him. Neither of them was talking, but there was an ease to their stance, like nothing needed to be said. Aemilius tried to make out what they were looking at—There. A figure, running hard uphill. He had to fight an urge to take a step back.

It was Rivkah, pounding the ground with each step as if the hill had personally insulted her.

As she reached the top where Abrax and the woman stood, she charged past them, around the side of the camp and towards a towering rock formation. Picking up speed, she leapt at the wall—and clung to it like an insect. Her arms and legs started moving, pumping, pushing, clawing and scaling the rock face. Aemilius watched as she rose almost as fast as if she'd been walking on solid ground, then vaulted over the edge, twenty feet above their heads.

"Hey, fish face!" she shouted. Across from the camp, Hanno sat on his own rock, still as a statue. "Why didn't you go up here? The view's much better."

Hanno did not move. "With age and wisdom comes the right to climb smaller rocks," he said.

"Right," Taurio said. "Food's up."

"And also," Hanno added, "it looked much more fun to climb up than down." With that he rose and jumped, landing with grace on the ground.

Up on the cliff, Rivkah muttered something that was not meant to be heard and started making her descent, rather more slowly than she'd climbed up.

AEMILIUS SAT AND watched them, feeling numb. He'd stood like a pillar while the strange crew had approached Taurio's pot and dipped their bowls in, making appreciative noises. He had sat down, awkwardly, as the others did so, and now he felt that all of them must surely hear his stomach rumbling.

"Why aren't you eating?" Rivkah snapped.

He felt the heat rise in his cheeks. *Because nobody offered? I didn't know how to ask? I don't have a bowl?*

No answer seemed anything less than bowel-twistingly embarrassing, and he wished he could just go home. But regardless of what he wished, she was still watching him like an annoyed cat would a mouse that had stopped being fun to play with. "Eat. Or you'll be even more useless, if that is possible. Taurio!"

"What do you want, hell-cat?"

"How did you imagine our guest would eat your..." Rivkah made a show of searching for words. "Is this... soup?"

"It is a *broth*," Taurio sniffed. "And I am already feeding two Romans. You can't expect me to feed three?"

Aemilius saw eyes rolling around the group.

"Give the kid a bowl," Abrax rumbled.

"Pardon *me*." Taurio rose from his seat and went to the wagon. A moment's rooting, two bursts of clattering and he emerged with a small wooden bowl. "Here you go, spawn of the Empire."

"Uh... thank you?" Aemilius said, taking the bowl and glancing at Abrax.

"He has a problem with Romans," the big man simply said. "The Empire murdered his entire family. But he makes damn good soup."

"*Broth*. Why do I feed you?"

"Because it makes you feel important," Prasta said. "And if you're at the pots, nobody tells you off for eating too much."

The two fell to bickering as Aemilius sipped his broth, a string of rapidly-traded insults that had a familiar feel to them. Then he remembered his cousins, and the food was suddenly a lot less interesting. He looked up—to find that he was being studied by Abrax.

"Ask," the big man rumbled.

Aemilius looked around and tried to tell himself he wasn't looking for an escape route, but the more everyone looked at him, the harder that became. His heart sped up again, and he could feel the colour rising in his cheeks. *Ask? I don't know what to ask! What's the right question? I don't know what to say!* "Who... are you? And why did you save me?" When the words had escaped his mouth, he felt stupid and squeaky.

But Abrax smiled, and Aemilius found that it made him relax. "Who are we?" He turned to the group. The bickering had stopped. "Who are we, really?"

"Liars," Prasta said.

"Cowards," Taurio added helpfully.

"Disgraced and discarded." Quintus touched his finger to his forehead.

"Shame," the woman in grey added.

"And trouble. Lots of trouble." Rivkah grinned.

"We are dead and we are gone." Hanno looked serious.

Abrax looked at Aemilius, and even though the sun was at his back, the young man felt cold. "We... do not exist. Rome does not want to know us, and they certainly do not want to believe us. They turned their backs on our brothers and our fathers, and if they knew that we exist they would hunt us and kill us. We... are the Hidden Legion."

It was as if every single mad thing that had happened since last afternoon descended on him at once, and Aemilius made a sound midway between a laugh and a yelp—and once the first laugh had escaped, he found he couldn't stop.

"What is so funny?" the big man said, frowning.

"You're—" he burbled, still chuckling. "Uh, you're—ahaha—fairly few for a legion." Wiping the tears from his eyes, he noticed that the seven watching him were not laughing. "Oh." He blinked. "You're… serious." None of them responded. "The… Hidden Legion? Are you, like, criminals or something?" A few of them exchanged glances.

Rivkah sighed. "Someone explain it. I'm going for another run."

"Please stay, daughter of Abraham," Hanno said. "You might help him understand."

"Only way I'll help him understand anything is with a rock in a sock," she spat, but remained seated.

"Who wants to go?" Taurio said.

"The water, the life of—"

"It is probably best that you don't, old friend. It doesn't always make things more clear," Quintus said. Hanno looked mildly disappointed. "First—let's introduce ourselves. I am Quintus Aurelius, formerly of the Fourth Legion."

"Chucked out for answering a question," Rivkah said with glee. "Rather forcefully. I'm Rivkah. They picked me up from a travelling show."

"She was tumbling above a pit of alligators," the woman in grey said. Her Latin was flawless, and Aemilius immediately found himself wanting to bow. "My name is Livia, and I chose this life."

There were at least two audible chortles from the group. "Like hell you did," Quintus said.

"Princess here—"

Livia made a face at Rivkah, which didn't even slow her down.

"Princess here pissed off her entire family because she didn't want to be a broodmare."

"And she also stabbed a man in a pub fight."

"Only the one?" Livia said, grinning.

"A fatal fascination for the seedy part of town," Taurio said. "A woman after my own heart."

Livia threw him a beaming smile, and for a fleeting moment Aemilius had no trouble imagining her at a banquet with the mighty and the powerful in Rome.

"I am Taurio—I come from the most beautiful part of the known world—"

"Lies!"

"Shut up, string bean. I hail from Gaul, a proud and independent region—"

"—that has been under Roman rule for a hundred years," Prasta countered.

Taurio looked sour. "You just love saying that, don't you?"

"Yes, I do." She turned to him. "Our pot-bellied friend spoke rather too loudly at a town meeting, and—"

"The Empire did what it does," Taurio added, darkly.

"I am Prasta of the Isles, truth-sayer and sooth-singer. I know all stories worth knowing, and all tunes worth playing—"

"—badly—"

"Hush, boar. I joined this fellowship because I believe in their mission."

"And rightly so," Abrax said. "You know who I am, and you have seen what I do. We share a common enemy."

"We all do. I, also, am Hanno the Wise."

"That's debatable," Rivkah interjected.

"As are all things," Hanno replied, unperturbed. "The river flows, and so do I."

There was a silence after his statement, and Aemilius found himself wondering. Was it his turn to speak? When he couldn't wait any longer, he stammered, "And what is your mission? Who is the common enemy? And what is this…" He forced himself to say it: "Hidden Legion?"

Abrax smiled indulgently. "What we are about to tell you is not common knowledge."

"By which he means that you will not be able to tell anyone," Livia added.

"Or we—"

Aemilius interrupted Rivkah. "Or you'll kill me?"

Rivkah made a face at him, but the lack of a snappy comeback gave him, for the briefest of moments, the rush of a small victory.

Abrax continued. "Do you know about Teutoburg?"

Before he knew he was speaking, the words tumbled out of Aemilius and he reflected briefly on the value of having had a history master with a stick. "In the thirty-sixth year of the rule of Augustus Caesar, the traitor Arminius brought together several tribes of barbarians who ambushed Publius Quinctilius Varus as he led three legions to their death in a valley in Germania. This was an important defeat for Augustus, and led to—"

"We know the history," Quintus cut in.

"But *you* don't," Taurio added. "There's more to it."

Aemilius frowned. "No, there isn't. Varus was an old fool, Arminius was sly and three legions were wiped out."

"Three whole legions?" Abrax prodded gently. "Three entire legions of battle-hardened Roman fighters, who had survived year after year and got all the way into thickest Germania?" He looked at Aemilius, calculating. "Didn't you ever think that sounded a little bit…"

"…suspicious?" Taurio finished.

Aemilius became uncomfortably aware of everyone looking at him, and suddenly he found himself questioning the lesson he had just repeated by rote. "Uh," he offered. "Varus led them through a narrow valley, and they had no time to set up formations..." The more he repeated, the less he believed. "And the barbarians, uh, hid in the forest..." He looked at the seven, who looked back at him, clearly enjoying his squirming. "I guess a lot of things had to go just right for the barbarians," he offered meekly.

"And they didn't," Quintus said.

"There weren't several tribes, for a start," Prasta said. "Just a band of heroic rebels, fighting a much bigger power—"

Taurio coughed, glancing over at Quintus. Prasta checked herself. "Forgive me. Bard's instinct. It's a good story."

Quintus waved dismissively.

"The barbarians were far fewer than anyone cared to say," Abrax continued. "There were just about a thousand of them."

Aemilius scoffed. "That makes no sense. They wiped out the Seventeenth, the Eighteenth *and* the Nineteenth! That's, what? Eighteen thousand men?" There was no response. They all just... looked at him. Waiting. "All right," Aemilius said, surprised by his own irritation. "Fine. *How* did they do it, then?"

Abrax spread his arms out, as though to address an audience. "It was a morning just like any other," he began. "Varus met with his commanders, and the orders passed down the chain nice and quick. You can say much about the Roman army—"

"Not if you are a Carthaginian, you can't," Quintus interrupted.

Abrax brushed the comment away. "...but they are efficient, and they never lose their lines."

"But the camp followers—" Aemilius began.

"There *were* no bloody camp followers," Quintus growled. "Just because that lying old bastard Tacitus said so, everyone believed it. But it was a *lie*."

"We know," Livia said, soothing. "We know. And the soldiers weren't young and untrained, either."

"Some day you should ask the old bear exactly how he lost his position in the Fourth Legion," Rivkah said, smirking. Livia scowled at her.

"The Seventeenth were tough as old boots. Along with the Eighteenth they had defeated Marcus Antonius and ripped through Gaul. The Nineteenth had been stationed on the Rhine for years, knew the territory and could smell a barbarian at a hundred yards," Quintus said. "Untrained troops, my arse."

"Grant you—it's not that hard to smell a barbarian at a hundred yards," Prasta said. "Taurio has taught us that."

Lounging next to her, Taurio nodded and smiled. "What can I say? My musk is strong."

"And before long, the legions were on the march," Abrax continued. He seemed resigned to telling the story at whatever pace the others would allow. "Tacitus was not entirely wrong…" He gestured for Quintus to be patient. "They did go through a narrow, forested valley—and that is where they got hit. But…"

He paused, relishing his account. Aemilius stared at the big man, waiting.

"They were fine, more or less," he said, with a shrug. "They were well trained, their lines formed almost instantly and they pushed the barbarians back as the Seventeenth charged forward onto open ground."

Again, Aemilius got the sense that he was being observed and evaluated. "So the story of the gaps in the lines was… another lie?" he ventured.

"See? The kid gets it," Quintus said.

Livia nodded. "Correct."

"And Arminius knowing Roman tactics and pre-empting the orders?"

"Also a lie. Think about it for half a moment. It is not as if 'Roman tactics' were a mystery waiting to be solved: you get a couple hundred big lads with heavy shields, line them up and stomp over everything. Does it make sense that Armenius somehow 'figured out' what most of the world has had to deal with for the last two hundred years?"

"No," Aemilius replied. "No, it doesn't." He chewed his lip. "So then what happened?"

Livia glanced at Abrax, who nodded. "They broke through the forest and onto a plain," she said. "Within moments they'd set their formations and prepared for an onslaught—but the barbarians didn't follow."

"They just stood at the tree line," Quintus said, a faraway look in his eye. "Just… watching."

"Waiting," Taurio added.

"Waiting? For what?"

"For hell," Abrax said with finality.

"And hell came to them," Quintus continued. "The ground shook, and trees fell, and all manner of creatures appeared and descended on the legions. An army of monsters. Terror swept the lines, and it took almost no time to slaughter fifteen thousand soldiers."

Livia continued. "When Germanicus went back to rain fire on them, they came to Teutoburg and found piles and piles of bodies, armour and weapons—all Roman. Tacitus noted, but did not write down, that there were no barbarian remains."

"What—*none?*"

"None to speak of," Quintus said. "Nobody wanted to know. Those who thought this suspicious—I think one or two senators asked about it—were told by 'veterans of the German front' that the barbarians always collected their dead. Which is horseshit. There weren't any to collect. One of them…" He frowned.

"Barbus," Livia offered.

"Barbus, yes, was the father of a commander in the Eighteenth. He protested loudly and demanded to know the truth."

"And," Livia continued, "mysteriously, a tavern erupted into a brawl just as he was passing by. He was the only one who got his head stomped. Died two days later. Nobody knows who did it."

Aemilius shook his head, as if to dislodge the idea. "But—What? This can't be true. Monsters don't exist." Taurio caught his eye and glanced pointedly at the mound where they'd buried the harpies. "I—yes," he added, blushing. "I mean—you obviously know—but… how?"

"What do you mean?" Quintus glared at him.

"How *do* you know all this?"

"My brother fought in the Seventeenth," Livia said. "He came back under cover of night. My parents hid him in an old woodsman's hut near our house—the shame of it all. He lived for a week, and I sat by his bed as he rambled."

"I was born in Carthage," Abrax said. "Taken in off the street by two wonderful old men who ran a house for those who were lost. They sent five to the legions—three to the Seventeenth, two to the Eighteenth. One came back."

"A legion is six thousand strong," Prasta said. "And every one of those men had connections. Family, friends, lovers."

Livia continued. "The survivors—a horrifyingly small number—came back to Rome, one by one or in small groups. They tried telling their story, but no-one in power would listen. We know that some were killed by those in Rome who did not want to admit that we were not all-powerful." She smiled bitterly. "Eventually the Vestal Virgins stepped in. The priestesses know a good lie when they see one—and they never questioned the truth of Teutoburg. They quietly took them in, nursed them to health, and the Hidden Legion was formed."

"Our aim is to hunt down any and all monsters that threaten the Roman Empire. Monsters whose existence cannot, in these enlightened times, be acknowledged," Abrax said.

"But—there *are* no monsters!" Aemilius protested.

Hanno smiled. "We are good at what we do."

"But what about me?" Aemilius said, rather more squeakily than he'd liked. "Where do I fit in?"

"A fair question," Taurio said.

"We were told to go get you," Quintus said.

"By whom?"

The old soldier ignored him. "For the last ten years it's been quiet. Just the odd stray creature here and there. But at the turn of the year... something changed."

"More and more sightings. We've been on the road for months," Livia added.

"Something is happening," Abrax said ominously.

"But—why me? You haven't told me why—or who sent you—or what I am supposed to do."

"Stay alive," Rivkah said, making it very clear that she considered it unlikely and unreasonable that he would.

That seemed to be the last word on the subject, because

on some unspoken signal, the seven soldiers rose and moved towards the horses and the cart.

Aemilius thought to say something, but gave up. This, it seemed, was as much as he would get out of them, for now. He'd have to think carefully before he asked the next question. It would need to be a canny question, something to lure the information out of them. Set them talking. Make them let important information slip. His father had once, in his cups, told him that he had been named Aemilius because they could trace their bloodline to the Aemilii, one of the Maiores. It was time to live up to the name. Trailing behind them, he very carefully clenched his fist and furrowed his brow in determination. He could not out-fight or out-run his captors—but he could darn well out-smart them.

"So where are we going?"

"If you ask me again I'll smack you in the mouth so hard you'll know Greek."

"But I already know Greek."

"So I can smack you in the mouth, then?"

"...no."

The late morning sun beat down on their file, their horses picking up heat with every hoofbeat. They were away from Caesaraugusta, but not far. The names of cities rattled around in his head—Pompelao, Osca, Clunia—but all he could really remember was the desk in his room and the dust he'd drawn rude pictures in while his tutor droned on. He had been a reasonably good student when the subject matter interested him, but for the first time in his entire life, Aemilius wished he'd paid more attention to his more boring classes.

Abrax rode up ahead with Livia, followed by Quintus. Behind them, Hanno sat in the cart, flanked by Prasta and Taurio. Rivkah seemed to feel she'd drawn the shortest straw, riding next to him. She looked as comfortable in the saddle as she did on the ground, swaying effortlessly with the motion of the horse. Aemilius, who had never distinguished himself as a rider, thought of the increasing tension in his buttocks and hoped wherever they were going wasn't too far away.

"Umbria," Prasta said.

He nearly fell off his horse. "*What?* All the way back to Italy? But that's *months!*"

"Depends," Quintus said. "You could do it in seven days."

"Seven? Hispania to Umbria? That's nonsense. You'd kill your horses," Livia said.

"I did it in five, once," the old man said, smirking. His mare neighed as if to confirm. "But we won't go at that kind of pace. It'll be three weeks, maybe. Give or take."

Aemilius sank back into the saddle and his arse hurt double just thinking about it. Three weeks on horseback? He couldn't remember much about travelling from Italy—he had been very young—and what he did remember, he didn't much like. Besides which, three weeks with this collection of madmen and wild women did not sound like anyone's idea of fun. "Why Umbria?" he managed.

"It's the closest we have to home," Prasta said. "The Legion has a camp in—"

"He'll know soon enough," Abrax interrupted.

"Always hiding the truth, magus," Prasta shot back.

"Knowledge is power," the big man rumbled. "And right now, he doesn't need to worry about where we're going." He glanced at Aemilius and smirked. "It looks like he'd be better served learning how to ride a horse."

Aemilius became uncomfortably aware of being assessed from all sides, and felt his cheeks turn red to match his arse. The urge to speak didn't come with any words to say, so he just stuttered, almost missing Rivkah nudging her horse out of the line to make way for Quintus. The old horseman looked Aemilius up and down. "Relax." He seemed to be speaking less to him than the horse, which smoothed out its gait under him.

"I *am* relaxed," Aemilius said, wincing at the sound of his own voice.

"Mm," Quintus murmured. "You're carrying tension in your calves, your knees, your thighs and your arse. You can continue 'relaxing' like that if you want, but if you do you might want to consider skipping the middle steps and just sit down straight in the fire tonight. It will *hurt*."

Aemilius took a deep breath and bit down the urge to tell the soldier to go ride off a cliff. Grabbing onto the words, he thought—*tension in the calves*. Moving down his body, he found his calves and tried to think them less tight.

"Good," Quintus murmured to him. "But you'll feel that in your knees." Sure enough, Aemilius's knees twinged. "Ease them down." *What does that even mean?* But still—even though he had never eased his knees down from anything, he tried, and was soon rewarded with a burning in his thighs. "Very good," the old man said, a note of surprise creeping into his voice. "And now, straighten your back—good—and allow yourself to sink into the saddle. Don't worry about your horse. He can take your weight." The old horseman looked him up and down again. "There you go. How does that feel?"

"Better," Aemilius muttered. He wanted to thank the man, but his words caught somewhere in his throat. Without any movement that he could see, the old soldier's horse picked up its speed ever so slightly, drawing Quintus out of the way.

Then Rivkah was back in her slot next to him, speaking seemingly without thinking. "You learn fast, for a drooling idiot."

The words escaped without asking for permission. "You're kind, for a yappy bitch."

Behind him, Taurio burst out laughing. "Oho! I see now. This one is ours indeed."

Heart thumping, Aemilius hazarded a glance at Rivkah. She looked straight ahead, but there was the ghost of a smile on her lips.

"What do you say, magus? How hot is it going to get? Shade and rest?" Taurio called up to the front.

Abrax seemed to sniff the air for a moment. "Not a bad idea." Scanning up ahead, he pointed to a gently rising hill, marked with curves and pockets of shadow. "We'll find shelter there."

The troop nudged the horses towards a ridge of rocks at the foot of the hill. Aemilius had gotten used to the Hispanian rhythms—waking up, making the most of the morning and then retiring from the blazing heat of the sun, to re-emerge when you could no longer feel your skin puckering and crisping like a spit-roast pig—but he'd never had to think about anything much longer than half a day's ride on horseback. Down to the village, up to the villa. Anything longer than that and they'd take the covered carts, complete with escort and a tent for breaks.

Thoughts of the life he'd now seemingly lost kept him at a steady level of misery as the horses took their time getting to the place Abrax had identified. It turned out to be an almost completely flat rock at the base of a high cliff.

"Good spot," Rivkah said. "Going to be a hot one. Has anyone checked on the frog?"

"Thank you, daughter of Abraham," Hanno the Wise said from the cart. "I am alive."

"Shame," Rivkah said. "I was hoping a bit of proper sun would dry you out. I need a new saddle bag and would happily flay you."

"She loves me," Hanno said to—Aemilius could only assume—his donkey. "With a fiery passion."

"You wish, toad," Rivkah said, ending the exchange by leaping off her horse and somehow landing with the reins in her hand. She clucked at the beast, leading it deeper into the shade.

Aemilius watched as the seven soldiers dismounted and tucked their mounts away. Quintus had a horse-brush in hand immediately, setting to the care of the animals. Taurio went to the wagon, emerging with an armful of fist-sized cloth parcels he proceeded to throw wordlessly to the members of the team. None of them needed to be told, plucking the missiles out of the air with a deftness which would have done a travelling group of tumblers proud. Before Aemilius could think to dismount, the seven were more or less horizontal, in the shade and eyeing him curiously.

"Do you think he intends to make a break for it?" Prasta said.

"Nah," Rivkah said. "He's just a bit thick."

"Sits a horse properly now, though," Quintus said from under his helmet.

"Leave the boy alone," Livia said. "He's had a big day. What he needs now is a bit of rest from you lot, and no surprises."

And that was when the ghost of a Roman centurion walked out of thin air and Aemilius fell off his horse.

III

HISPANIA

THE FIRST THING Aemilius saw, when he came to, was the side of Prasta's head.

"No, you oaf. He's not dead."

A voice he didn't recognise said something, and Prasta snapped back: "No—it is *not* thanks to you."

The new voice said something else—for some reason he was having an awful time hearing it—but clearly whatever he said went down quite badly with the bony woman, who almost hissed, "Get him to shut up or I swear I will find a way to kill him. Again."

She turned to look down at him. "Oh. You're awake. How many fingers?"

"Three," he muttered, squinting at her blurred hand.

"Water," she said. A skin of water appeared next to her, and was summarily tipped over Aemilius's head. "How many?"

He sputtered, coughed and groaned. He was lying on something massive and painful, and reached for his head.

"I wouldn't do that," Prasta said conversationally. "It won't hurt any less. How many fingers?"

"Uh, two," Aemilius whimpered.

"He's fine," she said, standing up and letting the blazing hot sunshine pelt down on him.

He winced, twisted away and groaned even louder as pain rolled over and through him. Tenderly feeling for the source of it, he discovered a throbbing lump the size of his fist, just behind his left ear.

"What happened?" he managed to croak.

The thick hand of Taurio appeared, near enough for Aemilius to reach, and he was hauled up onto his feet. "You met Felix," the Gaul said merrily.

"Felix?"

And then his brain allowed him to notice the creature standing next to Quintus and Abrax, and whatever he had intended to say next left him entirely.

"Recruiting seems to have hit a new low," the apparition said. "Does this one's mouth ever shut?"

Aemilius tried to understand what he was looking at, but he couldn't make the pieces add together in his mind. The man... the man-shaped thing—stood almost as tall as Abrax, but was rake-thin and gaunt, almost like a dried-up...

"Deliver your message, Felix," Abrax snapped. "We have no time for this."

...a dried-up corpse.

"If you only knew how little time *you* have for anything," the man they called Felix sneered back. "You disgust me, with your soft flesh and your swirling robes and your—"

"—pulse," Rivkah interrupted, to chuckles around the group.

Felix looked down at her as if he had just discovered something on his sandals. "Oh, look. The little rat is still here. I'm surprised no-one has stomped her yet." Rivkah made a face and a rude gesture at him.

Slowly, agonisingly slowly, Aemilius wrapped his head around the vision in front of him. The armour looked expensive, and Roman—a centurion's breastplate— and about three hundred years old. It was in pristine condition, except for the back of the helmet, which had a dent in it from a massive blow by a club or a rock. Abrax stood in front of the centurion, flanked by Livia. Quintus stood behind him—and Aemilius had to spell this out for himself, but he could see the old horseman.

Through the centurion.

He was looking at a ghost.

A talking ghost.

Named Felix.

He almost physically held down a panicked giggle, and felt his eyes go wide as the truth of it tried to escape out of him. *You've already seen harpies and a magus,* he chided himself. *Be calm!* With super-human effort he managed to instead tune in to what they were saying.

"—but we were told to bring him back as quickly as possible," Abrax said.

"And you will. And you will bring him back in one piece. But you will go to Benasque first."

"It will slow us down," Livia said.

"Yes," Felix replied, as if he was talking to a child. "We understand that. You"—he gestured vaguely at the group—"people are quite… limited."

"Whereas you could absolutely pick up a dagger if you wanted to," Taurio replied.

"The only manners a Gaul ever has, have been beaten

into him," Felix shot back. "Did your mother never teach you to not speak ill of the dead?"

"Oh, she did. But she was a sensible woman, and if she'd ever met you she'd have told you to immediately find the nearest cow and crawl up its arse."

Felix made a show of ignoring Taurio, and continued. "The signs were unclear, but apparently an unusual amount of livestock has been disappearing."

"Thieves. Not worth our time." Quintus looked unimpressed.

"You overestimate what your time is worth, Primus Pilus." Felix somehow managed to make the title sound like an insult. "This is not up for argument. Go to Benasque, find out what is happening and add that to your report. You are all disappointingly alive, so I gather you didn't have too much trouble with the harpies."

"As suspected, they were young," Abrax said.

"Well," Felix said. "Lead your troops into battle, Carthaginian. That has gone well for you in the past. I assume you are in charge?"

"No, and you know it. We make decisions as a unit."

Aemilius didn't think Felix could look more disdainful, but the ghost made an effort. He looked like he'd stepped in ghost dog shit. "A chicken without a head does not live long," he sniffed.

"And yet," Hanno the Wise chimed in, "here we are, breathing air and pumping blood, and you are doomed to walk the cold lines."

"I'd forgotten about you, swampling," Felix said. He looked around. "Quintus Aurelius. This is quite the travelling circus you tarry with. You must have thought about re-enlisting?"

"No," Quintus said. "Some time has passed since your day, but the Roman Army sadly still has men like you in it." There were smirks from the group, and an 'ooh' from Rivkah.

"Suit yourselves, misfits," Felix said. "I have told you where to go and what to do, and as I cannot do it for you, I will depart." He turned on his non-existent heel, swished his cape around him and walked away. Three steps in, the air around him seemed to shimmer and open into a crack, and he somehow slid out of existence.

"The beautiful isles that I call my home," Prasta began, "have a long and proud tradition of singing the truth—and we have a phrase that sings the truth of that man."

"And what might that be?" Taurio twined his fingers behind his head.

"He is what we would call a shite-bag."

Taurio nodded his approval. "See," he said to Aemilius, ignoring the mild panic on the youth's face. "If you stick with her for long enough, she does hit the mark."

Behind him, Prasta smiled.

AN ALTOGETHER TOO short a while later, they were all in the saddle and painfully aware of the noonday sun. Livia, Abrax and Quintus rode up front again, and did not care who heard them.

"Ridiculous," Abrax said.

"Menial," Livia agreed.

"And he enjoyed it all too much," Quintus finished.

"Which does make me think it's real." Livia looked as if she had bitten into a rotten apple. "Absolutely not what I want to do."

"Hopefully he steps in Cerberus's shit in the

underworld. Now—will one of you explain Felix to the boy before the idiot falls off his horse again?"

Livia glanced at Rivkah. "Why don't you do it? You seem to enjoy taking him down a peg or two."

"Fine," the girl scoffed, then turned to Aemilius. "Can—you—hear—me?" she half-shouted, in the voice one would use for a senile relative.

"Yes," Aemilius muttered. "I'm here, aren't I?"

"Excellent," Rivkah said, exaggerating every syllable. "Now. Did you see something? Just now?"

"Yes. I saw…"—he hesitated—"Felix."

"And?"

"He looked like a Centurion from the Pyrrhic wars, or possibly the Punic. His uniform was very well kept, except for a big dent at the back of his helmet—"

"—which is—" Rivkah interrupted.

"Which *suggests*," Aemilius continued, talking over the girl, "that he was killed by a missile, or a stone in a hand, and that it may have come as a bit of a surprise."

He risked a glimpse of Rivkah's face, but rather than looking angry at his boldness, she seemed quite pleased.

"Still makes me happy to think about it," she said. "And…?"

Aemilius threw up his hands. "I suppose he is a ghost. Is he a ghost?"

"Bloody annoying, is what he is," Rivkah said. "But yes. He is a ghost."

"And you should definitely not call him a fancy messenger boy," Prasta added, smirking. "He hates that."

"He carries orders through the underworld for the Legion," Rivkah continued. "I don't know how it works, but he can get to us within a day, regardless of where we are. Magus?"

Abrax turned in the saddle. "Obviously all we have are the old tales, but it is thought that the underworld is laid upon our own world, like a skin. Felix can pass between here and there."

"And sadly, we cannot follow him," Hanno the Wise said.

"What are you *talking* about, you mad frog?" Rivkah spat. "Follow him?"

"Yes," the little man said, matter-of-factly. "I would rather like to go. I think the water of the River Styx would be... quite something."

"The stories say there is only one way to enter the underworld, and that there is no coming back."

"But what about the story of—?" Hanno began.

"Did you forget to tell us that you are a legendary poet?" Rivkah said, voice dripping with scorn. "Because you do not look like one."

Aemilius thought for a moment. "Fine. Felix is a ghost. He travels the underworld, but we can't. That's... in keeping with the day I've had. But," he added, frowning, "why is he bringing you orders? And where from?"

A ripple of reactions up and down the line—some half-smiles, a smirk, rolled eyes.

"Hogsbreath," Rivkah said. "You tell him. I cannot talk about both Felix and... her... in one day."

"With pleasure," Taurio said. "Back at our humble home, we have a tower. At the top of that tower sits Flaxus, staring at the birds, and making great proclamations as to the will of the gods. At the other end of the courtyard, close to the kitchens, sits Egenny. He slaughters animals and reads their entrails. The two of them never agree on anything, but they report—separately, as a rule—to Cassia, who has a network of spies, if not nearly as many as there used to be. Cassia, in turn, gathers together the intelligence from both our seers and her spies and brings it all to her, and she picks the tidings that sound most believable and sends her orders out accordingly."

"And we jump to do what she says," Rivkah spat. "Like little dogs."

Aemilius hesitated, but there was no further explanation coming. "Who is... 'she'?"

"*She* is Mater Populi," Abrax said. He glanced at Rivkah. "And we do what she says because it is the right thing to do."

The girl huffed and did not reply.

"Isn't knowledge great?" Hanno said, turning on his donkey to stare at him with anticipation.

"...Yes," the young man muttered. Hanno beamed.

Aemilius's head swam with names, and details, and animal entrails, and ghosts, and the smell of burning harpies, which still lingered in his clothes, on the horses and in his nostrils. He pushed back the rising tide of panic, and tried to order his thoughts. What did he *know?* He was sitting on a horse. He knew that. He had ridden for longer than he ever had before, and he forced himself to remember what Quintus had told him, begging his muscles to ease off and relax. He knew that there was more in the world than he had thought there was. Much, much more.

It also seemed like fate had something quite different in store for him than he'd thought. Why did they want him? They hadn't said. And what was this Hidden Legion? It seemed they had a base, and a mission, and a connection to the Teutoburg Massacre. But was it true? Half-distracted, he noticed that the landscape was changing. They were drifting down from the hills, towards the plains that lay beyond the ridge. He had heard his father talk of this region once, of its dull inhabitants who would be born, till soil, eke out a living and then die, leaving no mark upon the world.

His father hadn't had much love for his subjects.

There had been a lot of whispered half-truths about how the noble Marcus Livius had found himself the Governor of Caesaraugusta, but Aemilius had never heard the true story. It was to have happened on his sixteenth birthday, he remembered ruefully. That was the day when his father was supposed to sit him down and bestow upon him the full knowledge of how his family came to be so far from Rome, why every decision his father made had to be verified and reported, and why it felt like his mother was waiting for an Imperial Guard to show up at any moment, blades drawn.

What will they think of this? Aemilius found himself wondering. Would they think he'd been taken by enemies? A thought popped into his head and he half-giggled with the madness of it. Would they think he'd murdered his three cousins and bolted for Africa?

No. They'd probably think their only son had been abducted by a band of madmen, and that, he reflected, looking around his travelling companions, would be fairly accurate. Maybe they'd send out a search party. Or maybe they'd just grieve. He picked at the thoughts of his family, imagined their reactions, wondered about his future and tried his best to remember his past as the horses trundled past endless rolling hills, the mountains gradually rearing in the distance, above an ocean of tufty bushes on gritty plains, feeling the sunshine beating on the back of his neck.

And suddenly, Benasque was... there. It nestled in

the foothills of what looked a gentle mountain range, though not trivial to pass.

"There we are," Abrax said.

"Call that a town?" Quintus said.

"We're not here to shit on the locals," Livia rebuked him. "We go in, ask people some questions, find whatever we need to find and go away."

"Would it not be easier to capture one of them in a field and cut him up a little?"

"No, Rivkah," Prasta said. "We have already talked about this. How did that go last time?"

"How was *I* supposed to know she was a squealer?"

Aemilius watched Prasta glance at Taurio, who sighed. "We are not arguing about this again. Admit you were wrong."

"Nothing wrong with the *idea*," Rivkah said sullenly.

"Everything wrong with the idea," Hanno said.

"Who asked you?"

"No-one, which felt like an oversight."

Rivkah shook her head and spat. "You are all old and stupid," she muttered.

"And alive," Quintus added. "We ride in nice and calm, show that we are friendly and ask questions." The procession inched on. Above the mountains to the west, the sun continued sinking.

When the first of the field workers noticed them, Aemilius felt uncomfortable. He had been taken out to visit the villages by his father, but they had not received looks like this. The farmers at home knew to be deferential; two hundred years of Roman rule had weeded out those who didn't.

But the Legion? The *kindest* eyes on them were suspicious; most were hostile.

A boy was sent sprinting up towards the houses, dust flying as his feet pounded the ground.

"Here we go," Rivkah muttered.

"The water flows, much as it always does," Hanno agreed.

"Remember—nice and friendly," Quintus said.

"I'm not a horse," Rivkah snapped. "So don't use that voice with me. I hate the way they stare, and I will tell you that I hate it. And you should see it as a personal favour from me to you that I don't open up the first potato-humper that looks at me wrong."

Aemilius glanced at Quintus, who was as ever utterly unmoved by Rivkah's outburst. The others were if anything even more relaxed in the saddle, betraying no signs of concern.

Up ahead, the road opened out into a square of sorts. Already, people were gathering.

"It looks like a child's drawing of a town," Livia muttered. "And a stupid child, at that. Remind me again why I am here?"

"Because you were young, stupid and drunk, and you gutted a man like a fish in some flea-infested shithole on the docks, and that is not a nice thing for a young noblewoman to do," Prasta said gently. "Especially when he turns out to be a senator's cousin."

"Mm," Livia said. "He deserved it, though."

"Most of them do," the rangy bard agreed.

At the front of the line Quintus had nudged his horse up alongside Abrax. A silent negotiation flickered between them, then Abrax inched up ahead. Before long, the horses slowed to a walk, then a halt.

These people can't afford to lose anything, Aemilius reflected. The gathering mob were a sorry sight: forty or so, huddled together for courage, clinging onto farming equipment that could be pressed into use as weaponry. The leader, a gaunt and hard-faced man with more than a little in common with Hanno's donkey, stepped forward. "Well met, travellers," he said in hesitant Latin. "We have little to share."

"We do not intend to impose on your hospitality," Abrax replied smoothly. "We are simply here to search."

"What for?" a sallow woman at the back of the crowd shouted.

"We have heard that you have had livestock going missing," Abrax said, with tactful sympathy.

The effect on the townsfolk was almost comical. "How do you know that?" their leader snapped, raising his voice to quell the murmurs and stop the accusing looks in the gathered crowd.

"The Governor heard of your predicament and offered us some coin to find your... cattle?" Abrax lied smoothly.

"Aye, and my sheep!" a skinny old man shouted. There was a tussle and a sharp rebuke. The young man suppressed a smile. It seemed like the peasants assumed none of the outsiders understood their particular dialect. He craned his neck slightly, ignoring the leader's halting Latin and started listening for other things.

"WELL, THAT WAS about as much use as a pigshit toothbrush," Prasta muttered.

Abrax looked over his shoulder at the town, receding into the distance. "Now, now," he said. "They didn't expect us, and I don't reckon they get many visitors."

"Wonder why."

"Why does *this* little pile of nonsense get to you so

much, twiglet?" Taurio rocked back and forth in the saddle.

Curling her lips in disgust, Prasta spat a phrase in her language and said no more.

"And where does that leave us?" Quintus said, gesturing to the miles of hills around them. "Start on the left and work our way round?"

"Maybe there isn't a problem?" Livia added hopefully. "Maybe the information from Cassia is wrong, and Felix is full of shit."

"Wouldn't be the first time," Rivkah added.

"Eight head of cattle, twelve head of sheep. Went missing up in the red hills north-west of town," Aemilius said.

"I'm just sick of always chasing—" Prasta had begun, but she caught herself in mid-sentence and turned slowly to look at Aemilius. "Say that again?"

"They've lost eight head of cattle and twelve head of sheep, and I think a boy went missing. There was something about red hills, and the reddest are to the north-west. Happened two nights ago. Someone said something about three sheep going missing a week earlier."

There was a brief silence, as the seven hardened mercenaries looked at each other, then back at Aemilius. For a while, no-one knew what to say.

Then, Taurio smirked. "See? I taught him. He's a quick learner, this one."

"Sneaky little bastard," Rivkah said, looking at Aemilius like he was almost forgiven for existing. "And they didn't know you speak the language because you don't look like them, and didn't think to watch you listening in, because you're obviously harmless."

"Plenty of good people been killed by harmless things," Quintus added, nodding approvingly.

"So that's settled, then," Abrax said, sounding cheerful. "We loop around there"—he pointed towards a rise in the landscape—"go slow and allow them to settle for their supper, then make for the hills and see if we can find tracks by the last light. Camp safe, then search from dawn."

Aemilius watched as the group set their course. No-one spoke, or had to wrangle their horses—it was almost as if the beasts understood them. His mare followed suit, and for a moment he felt almost like he was one of them.

GRAVEL CRUNCHED UNDERFOOT, and the gentle incline pulled at tired muscles. The horses walked behind Prasta and Taurio, whose bodies tensed and strained like hunting dogs. They seemed completely unaware of the riders behind them, trading in a staccato stream of half-sentences.

"No hooves, no hooves."

"Little to break."

"Too dry."

"Sand. Sandy." Sounds of spitting.

Sniffing on the wind. "Something…"

"Aye. Fear."

They both veered sharply to the left, keeping their distance, crouching low.

"Found it." Prasta was frozen in observation, her voice triumphant.

Taurio cursed in Gallic, exactly like he'd just been beaten at dice. "I make that four to two for me."

"Four to three, oaf," Prasta shot back.

"Never mind the score," Abrax said. "What have you found?"

"Path," Prasta said. She knelt. "Four sets of footsteps."

"Leading…?"

"Up."

They looked up into the hills. The setting sun turned already reddish soil the colour of a throbbing wound. Glances were exchanged.

"Anything coming back?"

A short pause.

"No."

"Tomorrow?"

"Tomorrow."

"Tomorrow."

A QUICK SEARCH revealed a depression at the base of the hill leading to a crevasse. By some unspoken agreement, Abrax and Rivkah dismounted and moved on ahead, the glow from one of the magus's light orbs throwing a pale glow around them, then quickly disappearing out of sight.

They reappeared moments later.

"Safe," Abrax said. "And space for the horses," he added, almost deferentially, to Quintus, who looked thoughtful but nodded.

"Bit of luck," Rivkah added. "Nice little bolthole. They probably cleared whatever lived here out a while ago."

"Any of your kin?"

"Shut up, Gaul."

Aemilius listened to the trading of barbs. It had started to take on a soothing tone to him already—there was no malice in it. Speed and wit was rewarded with inventive swearwords. References to mothers, farm animals and unspeakable acts bounced back and forth as they went about dismounting, handing the horses over to Quintus and Prasta and laying out the camp for the night.

Abrax and Livia disappeared into the setting sun, carrying blankets.

"Tracks," Taurio said. The Gaul's face brightened at Aemilius's absolute lack of comprehension. "We have been trying to keep the cart on mostly rocky ground, but there will be some tracks. Drag a blanket over 'em and they won't stand out. Anyone looking in earnest will find them, of course—but they'll have to look." He looked at Aemilius with what could have been sympathy. "You've done well, sapling," he said. "Now you should stop thinking for a while, have some food and get some sleep. You have a lot to learn."

"This is true," Aemilius managed to mumble, managing to sink to the ground without falling. The realities of it caught up to him again. A day ago he had been heading home for an easy meal and a comfortable bed. Now he was somewhere in the western mountains, sitting with his back against a rock wall, far away from his family, about to sleep in a cave with a band of... maniacs? He found it hard to form an opinion of the Legion, and tried to remember what he had seen.

Taurio felt like the closest he had to a friend in the group. He was the only one who would bother to explain things, where the others ignored him at best. The memory of the fat Gaul's glee as he struck the harpy from behind was still lodged in Aemilius's head, though, and he made a mental note to not dismiss Taurio as harmless.

There was no risk of that with Rivkah, either. He couldn't quite decide which had scared him more—the spitting, hissing harpies out to gut him, or the spitting, hissing girl with the mad eyes and blood-soaked knives, who had also been out to gut him. *The only real difference is that she can't fly*, Aemilius thought, then added... *I assume.* At this point, he would be entirely unsurprised to find that that was also wrong.

In front of him the group picked their way back and forth, laying out bed rolls, quietly negotiating shifts and sharing information. Taurio handed out small chunks of bread and cheese. Here, they seemed just like a normal band of scouts, like fighting men he'd seen over and over on his father's travels. Once they had a task, there was a military rhythm about them. Even with the occasional quip, there was no time wasted. In a way the normality of it all was even more uncomfortable. It forced him to accept that the Hidden Legion—or at least this band of seven, with their strange story—were real. And if *they* were real...

He thought back on the story they had told him. It sounded plausible, but it suggested that Rome was not infallible, and that did not sit well with him. His father, ever the loyal soldier, had never said a bad word about the Emperor, and had frequently and severely disciplined those who had. Something about that now niggled at Aemilius, but he couldn't quite figure out what it was. He pushed the thought away. He had been brought up as a Roman, and as one destined to be a great Roman at that. His family was proud, noble and true to the Empire, and while he was unclear on the details, he had been given to understand that once his father had done enough in Spain they would go back to Rome, robed in glory.

Something sharp nudged him in the back, and he started awake. Sitting up straight and hoping no-one had noticed him starting to slide down the side of the cave wall, his eyes rested on Abrax.

The tall, broad-shouldered magus, flowing robes lit by the evening sun, moving with confidence, grace and ease, erased the image in his mind of himself clad in his father's glory. Just at that moment, a pebble-sized orb of light popped into existence over Abrax's hand and hovered up towards the roof of the cave. A pale gleam wiped out the encroaching shadows from the setting sun. Aemilius found that he was gawping. He could still not quite wrap his head around the fact that he was looking at an actual spell-weaver. The magi had been consigned to folk tales and children's stories, along with, well, harpies. But Abrax was real, and the fire in his hands was real, and that meant that monsters were real. He had worked hard to push down the image of the beast that had slain his cousins, and the flickering shadows of their night-battle with its sistren had seemed more like a fever-dream—but they were real. It was *all* real. And if that was real... then what were they searching for now? What had taken the livestock? Fear sloshed around in his guts like cold water, and he found himself beginning to sweat despite the night cold creeping in. Desperate for distraction, he followed the pale light of Abrax's orb.

Livia stood by the magus's side, talking quietly. Aemilius had yet to see the graceful woman with a hair out of place, and she looked like she could, with one flick of her wrist, shake off the travel dust and look presentable for the Emperor. Out of all of them, she looked the most perfect, and the most perfectly out of place. He tried to remember what they'd said about her—that she'd killed someone? Looking at her, he could absolutely believe it—and that she'd do so without a moment's pause.

Prasta moved past them, weaving nimbly around the rocks. When no-one was watching, the tall bard seemed incredibly efficient, and Aemilius was reminded of his father's steward. That or a flitting insect of some sort, moving with unknown purpose. There was a marked difference between this and her demeanour when people were watching. *This is what it means to get to know people*, he suddenly thought.

Quintus came into the light behind her, interrupting his thoughts. Where Prasta made an effort to not disrupt, the old Roman horseman seemed not to care at all. Aemilius caught something about the horses, quick and functional. Abrax nodded, and with that Quintus was off to his corner. He never looked back, did exactly what was needed. Aemilius had seen men like that before, and clutched at the familiarity of it like a drowning man at a rope. Quintus was someone he understood.

And Hanno the Wise really wasn't. Out of the corner of his eye he saw the shape of the slim man jumping up into the cart and disappearing from view, and that was that. Abrax did fire and Quintus did blades. Taurio hit things and Prasta healed them. Livia fired a bow and Rivkah delivered non-specific death in general.

But what did Hanno do?

So far, he'd only seen the tiny African hiding in the cart, climbing a rock and looking miserable, apart from the time where he'd frightened him half to death. Maybe he was...

But before Aemilius could think of anything else, sleep took him.

IV

HISPANIA

WHEN AEMILIUS WOKE up, everything hurt.

His back ached. His hands were numb. His feet were cold, and his head pounded. He could vaguely sense movement around him, and when his eyes adjusted to the half-light, he surmised that somehow, he had survived the night.

"Up you get and meet the morning, kid," Prasta said, poking a toe at his ribs. "You'll miss the best part of the day." *If this is the best part of the day I would rather you kill me already,* he thought, but wisely kept it to himself, remembering what Rivkah had thought of being woken up the day before. Instead, he clambered to his feet as gracefully as he could and tried to look like he belonged.

Something felt... different about the group this morning. There was a hush about them, a purposeful silence as they packed up their modest camp. It did not take them long to saddle up, and Aemilius almost missed the point where Taurio shoved a roll of bread in his hand.

"Eat this," the Gaul grumbled, muttering something about cold breakfast and offending the Gods on a hunting day as he sidled past.

Aemilius blinked in the harsh morning light. The group was gathered outside the mouth of the cave, waiting for Prasta and Quintus to manoeuvre the cart back out. The morning sun glared at them across the plain, throwing a golden blanket on the mountainside.

Once they were ready to go, Hanno emerged from wherever he had been hiding in the wagon and sat in the driver's seat. Next to Abrax, he looked like a child. Taurio and Prasta moved to the head of the line and through nods and looks nudged their horses to the north, towards a gentle incline.

Up. The thought filled him with dread, and the haunted faces of the villagers came back to him. Given that the Legion hunted monsters... What could do away with that amount of cattle? And what sane person would go *towards* it?

THE FIRST HOURS of the morning passed slowly, and Aemilius fell into a rhythm. Nudge the horse. Stop the horse. Watch Taurio and Prasta argue. Watch one of them win. Nudge the horse. Stop the horse. He had absolutely no urge to find whatever they were searching for, but still he found himself growing impatient—but the others seemed utterly un-touched by the slowness of it all.

In the end, it was Rivkah who spoke. "It's always like this," the girl said.

"What?" Aemilius tried not to think about the parts of his legs and buttocks that hurt.

"The tracking," she said. "Takes forever. But it's better to go slow."

"Why?"

"Because whatever we're looking for tends to kill things, and you want to have time to think about it." Up ahead, Taurio suddenly spurred his horse on. "And in the end we always find something," Rivkah added with cold satisfaction.

Despite Taurio's rush, nobody else seemed to be in any haste. The Gaul was off his horse, kneeling by a lump of something. He gestured at Prasta. "Dismount," he snapped. "Look for tracks." He held up a thick hand to signal to the others to stop, which they did on the spot.

Prasta vaulted gracefully from her horse, landing softly and immediately sinking to one knee.

Aemilius stared as the tall woman's nose twitched.

"Piss."

"Lot of it, too," Taurio said. From the folds of his tunic he had produced a stick, which he was using to poke the lump he had found. With a swift movement, he flipped it over. "Hah!"

"What?"

"Teeth."

"Let me guess. Lots of them?"

"Yes," the Gaul replied grimly.

"Close together?"

A short silence. "Remember Agistri?"

Prasta's shoulders sank. "Shit. Shitting, shitting *shit*."

"Tracks?"

"Now that I know what to look for…" She sank back down to the ground. "Yes. Oh. Well. That's…" She whistled. "Come have a look."

Taurio rose and walked over to where the Celt kneeled. She pointed, and he scratched his head. "Have you ever seen that?"

"No."

A glance back to the group, and Abrax and Quintus walked their horses forward. The four engaged in a quiet back-and-forth, which ended in Prasta and Taurio re-mounting and pushing their horses into a walk.

"What's happening?" Aemilius turned to Rivkah.

She looked him up and down, and the pity in her eyes stung him. "We'll see," she said. "Just try to stay alive, will you?" Looking down, he caught sight of the lump Taurio had been studying. It was the leg of a cow, the end of which looked like it had been attacked by a drunk carpenter with a hacksaw.

BY THE TIME the sun was halfway to its zenith they'd found three more piles of remains. Pools of blood, a smashed skull, more legs—and always, the saw-marks.

Prasta kneeled by a chunk of mangled meat and bone the size of a man's torso that looked like it had been on the losing end of a dogfight. "It's... not big," Prasta offered, after the third one.

"Big enough," Taurio countered. "Absolutely big enough."

Around Aemilius, the rest of the group listened.

"Are we sure?" Abrax offered.

"Yes," Prasta said with finality. "Agistri all over." She pointed at the ground. "You can see a tail sweep over there. It's been all over the place."

Rivkah spat some words in her own language that Aemilius was glad he didn't understand.

Summoning up almost all of his courage, he leaned over. "Isn't Agistri... an island in Greece?"

"Well done, *scholar*," she hissed. "Now shut up harder. Even when you're not talking, I can still hear you whining. It must be the wind going through your nostrils or something."

"We're almost sure," Taurio qualified, as he hoisted himself back up onto the horse. "Almost."

"Right," Abrax said. "Let's move on. I suspect the tracking will become easier as we go."

"Why do we always have to go *towards* the bloody things?" Taurio muttered, as he tapped his heels to the horse's flanks.

BEHIND THEM, THE valley slowly fell away and faded. The colours changed, too—the scraggly bushes on the bleached, gritty ground were gilded by the midday sun.

The brook, if that was not too grand a name for such a piddling stream, was almost invisible.

Almost.

Aemilius was startled by the swift movement as Hanno vaulted out of the cart and shuffled towards the water. The small man crouched by the bank and gently, ever so gently, held his hand over the stream.

Aemilius remembered to breathe again, and blinked to clear his vision. The measly stream was *rising* towards Hanno's outstretched palm, like a trained snake. He looked to either side, but none of the others seemed surprised in the slightest.

Not just fire, but water.

Not one magus, but two.

Two!

Like an overloaded donkey buckling under the weight, Aemilius's brain struggled—but coped, braying all the while. He made a note to think about this later, and possibly come up with some questions. As discreetly as he could, he moved his hand up to his face and closed his mouth manually, as his jaw muscles seemed to have stopped working momentarily.

The small man grimaced. "Yes," he said. "Agistri." He spat—and then squeezed his eyes shut, gritting his teeth. "But worse."

"Oh for—"

"How?" Livia snapped.

"Tell us all you know, friend." Abrax's voice was measured.

"Blood," Hanno said. "And fury." He turned to Taurio with pleading eyes. "I will require your strongest scents for this one, my brother."

The big Gaul only nodded.

Looking around at his fellow riders, Aemilius felt a sinking dread. It seemed like Hanno's confirmation had brought home the reality of something, but no-one had yet thought to inform him.

These were seasoned monster hunters. What on earth could 'Agistri' mean? And what was worse? Nothing made sense anymore.

But then again, it seemed he was travelling with two magi, so maybe that was as it should be.

Ahead of them, Prasta was kneeling on the ground. Wordlessly, she pointed towards the hills.

Up.

* * *

IT WAS WITH weary resignation that Aemilius noted the group was slowing down. Nobody had told him anything, but he was getting used to that. He didn't want to enquire when Livia and Taurio started rummaging in the cart, producing rolls of linen wraps. He watched as the fighters all lined up, silently, to wrap their hands and forearms tightly, watched as they produced thick but flexible leather vests and bracers, watched them turn into what could almost, if you peered through half-closed eyes, be called soldiers.

They looked nothing like legionnaires, of course. There was nothing gleaming, no cohesion to their pieces, no armicustos to rap them with a stick if their uniforms were out of place.

But this, Aemilius noted with more of a tremor in his hands than he'd liked... looked a touch more serious than their encounter with the harpies. He thought back on how the fighters had shrugged that one off, how easily they'd disposed of five of the disgusting creatures.

None of them looked overly happy about what they were walking into.

"Hey, chosen one," Rivkah snapped at him. "Go see fatty and the granny."

He dismounted without any grace whatsoever, his left buttock seizing up underneath him as he landed, and fought hard not to grimace. When he reached the cart, Taurio looked him up and down, then turned to the cart and rummaged, muttering to himself, eventually producing a battered old leather jerkin.

"Put this on."

Aemilius shrugged into it, wincing as a hard corner dug into his shoulder blade. "That face you're making? It's what keeps you alive," Taurio said in chatty tones.

"A hard corner tells you that there's toughness in the leather. It tells you that whoever treated it meant for it to go tough when you sweat, and when you bleed. And sometimes," the Gaul added, pulling Aemilius's forearms towards him and starting to wrap them in linen. "It helps you get lucky."

"How?" Aemilius stuttered.

"They miss," he smiled. "Or they get their teeth—or their claws or tentacles or whatever it is they have—stuck in the leather, and it gives you a chance to kill them." He inspected his handiwork. "Or in your case, to run away and hide."

"And who should I hide behind?" Aemilius said, feeling a little wounded.

"Me. Or Quintus. Failing that, anyone else. You can try hiding behind the hell-cat"—he motioned towards Rivkah, who was engrossed in inspecting her knives— "but you'd have to be fast." With practised movements he slapped bracers on Aemilius's forearms and tied them quickly. "These are not a great fit, but I don't think it matters in your case. We're keeping you alive, not dressing you for the arena."

"What are the wraps for?"

"Again—keeping us alive. They are covered in some of Prasta's stinky creams. Smells like bull crotch, but stops bleeding faster than anything I've seen." He grabbed two short spears from the cart and threw one to Prasta, who snatched it out of the air.

"Get moving," Quintus said. There was a hardness to his voice that Aemilius had not heard before. He looked at the old Roman, but his face had turned stony. Shuffling inside his oversized jerkin, Aemilius tried to look like them, carry himself like a fighter—and realised he lacked a crucial detail as he clambered up into the saddle.

He had no weapon.

"THAT'S IT. HAD to be somewhere." Prasta stood in the stirrups. *Like a hunting dog*, Aemilius thought.

"How many?" Quintus slowly scanned the hills above them. The sun had passed its peak, and shadows were starting to appear.

The slender woman jumped from the saddle and stalked towards a small depression in the landscape. "Three," she said over her shoulder. "Maybe four. Been gone for a while."

Looks were traded around the group. "So..." Rivkah said. "That's not good."

"No," Abrax said. "Not good at all. And where do we think...?"

Prasta scanned the hills—and pointed. Up ahead, a scowling mouth in the rock face. Something about it spoke of misery, which passed easily onto the faces of the group.

"Go," Livia snapped, urging her horse up a slope. "They're coming."

As one, the group followed, the cart rattling noisily in the rear. Bouncing along with the group and fighting the urge to look back, fearing what he might see and worrying that he'd fall and break his neck, Aemilius marvelled at the reaction. *None of them asked about who, or where, or what. They just trusted her.* Up ahead, Livia pushed the horse towards the sharp, craggy corner of a big rock and disappeared from view. One by one they rounded the corner and held on to their horses, awkwardly making space for the cart when it arrived.

"How many?" Abrax asked.

"Fifteen, maybe twenty," Livia huffed. "The dust will settle. We'll need a lot of luck."

"Hanno."

"I go and snoop!" The small man bounded up out of the cart and bounded towards the top edge of the rock wall, stopping in mid-climb as he found a crack to peer through. "She who is wise in all things is wise in this as well," he whispered down. "I count eighteen, on horses and donkeys, and they're angry."

"They know exactly where they are," Prasta sneered. "Idiots. If they'd only told us…"

"Then what?" hissed Rivkah. "We could all have gone in singing happy songs?"

"Shut up, kid. We could have—"

"Don't call me kid, you shrivelled old hedge-fart."

Prasta snarled something that Aemilius couldn't understand, but he also noted Taurio inching closer and placing a hand, almost out of sight, on the woman's shoulder. *Calm.* Rivkah seemed equally tightly wound. They looked like two fighting dogs ready to be let loose.

Gently, like a deep, rumbling whisper, the sound of hooves rolled over their hiding place.

"They are so busy looking forward," Hanno whispered, "that none of them are looking down."

"Peasants," Quintus muttered.

"Normal people," Abrax rebuked him. "They don't do what we do."

"No-one does," said Rivkah heavily.

Her words seemed to settle and sharpen the group. Abrax dismounted and moved very slowly to the edge of the rock wall. He stood stock still for a while, watching.

When he turned, he looked like thunder. "They're going straight in."

"Into what?" Aemilius blurted out. "The cave? Should we stop them?"

He regretted his words immediately. All eyes were on him, and he felt like a fool.

"Think it through," Livia said. "There's about twenty of them. They've had all day to get their courage up. Step out in front of them now—and we'll become the targets." She looked around. "And while that would not be... a problem... I'd rather not murder more people than strictly necessary."

Aemilius felt a heat in his cheeks that burned in the cold in the shadow of the rocks. "I see," he mumbled, pointlessly. He had been dismissed already. They could hear the riders clearly now, thundering up the slope, shouting at each other. He could make out the occasional word, but they made little sense to him. The tone, however... It was fear. These poor souls were terrified of whatever they were going to go fight, and they were still going.

He couldn't help but admire their courage.

At the moment he felt brave enough to shit out his insides, have a big cry and then sleep for ever.

The drumbeat of hooves on hard earth slowed, and then stopped. The echo of a fiery speech, given by someone who was neither used to nor good at them, drifted down to the Legion's position. The speech ended, a battle cry was given, and then—silence.

"They're in." Abrax moved to his horse and saddled up. "Get ready."

Ready for what?! Aemilius wanted to scream at them. No-one had seen fit to explain to him, to tell him what they all seemed to know.

And then the screaming began.

Around him, the horses whinnied and snorted, but held firm. The same could not be said of the villagers' horses, bucking and tearing at their leads. More than half had bolted already and were striking out downhill, putting as much distance as possible between them and the cave, and the screams.

A very small part of Aemilius's mind calmly and rationally thought that they sounded like quite normal screams, at first. Loud, surely, but normal. Good, solid human screams, unlike the harpies. But behind the screaming echoing up out of the cave mouth were other sounds, disturbing sounds. And following them, the screams started to change—from mere battle-fury and fear into mindless terror. The larger part of Aemilius's mind, the one that wanted to follow the horses, was much more attuned to the sounds of those screams.

"Now!" Abrax shouted, spurring his horse on.

Around him, the rest of the Legion jolted into action and Aemilius found himself borne on a wave. Too late, he realised that he couldn't turn his horse around if he wanted to. Taurio was behind him, and he was flanked by Rivkah and Livia. He instinctively leaned forward, breathing in the horse-smell of his mare, seeking comfort in the thunder of hooves on the ground, trying not to look too hard at the cave mouth.

The movement still caught his eye.

Two men, bursting out of the cave, covered in blood, running for their lives.

Something—wrong—behind them. In size between a huge dog and a small horse, on thick and powerful legs, but—

Snapping like a whip, the first head lunged towards the

man on the left, maw open, closing on his shoulder with a crunch.

The second head lashed to the right and down, scooping up the other man by the ankle.

"Hah!" Taurio shouted behind him. "It's a baby!"

Hydra.

Aemilius felt the comforting warmth of his bladder emptying into his trousers and onto his saddle as he stared blankly at the monster. Five heads, each the size of his horse's, busy shredding the two villagers, fighting over the soft bits, swaying around each other on long, thigh-thick necks. Green-grey scales over a swollen belly, legs like pillars ending in vicious lizard-claws.

So now I die. We die. We all die.

He giggled, bug-eyed, relishing his last breath.

It took him a moment to realise that the reins were no longer in his hands and he was veering to the side. Flailing, he reached for the straps, saddle pummelling his backside, just before Livia stopped her horse and grabbed his reins herself, yanking back. He half-jumped and half-flew out of the saddle, tumbling to the ground; before he had stumbled to his feet, Livia had her bow out and was taking aim.

"Stand still, keep low and get ready to mount up and move," she hissed, not sparing him a glance.

I'm fine, thank you for asking, he thought, cunningly refraining from saying it out loud. About thirty yards up ahead, the Legion had spread out in a neat half-circle around the monster. The hydra reared up, hissing and snapping at them, but torn between targets.

The screech curdled Aemilius's blood.

Rivkah screamed back at it—and everything happened. The beast lurched towards her, heads snapping and whirling, but this target was a fair deal harder to catch than two panicked villagers. Dimly aware that Quintus had turned his horse and galloped the other way, Aemilius yelped as he watched Rivkah dive towards the beast, rolling on the ground once then somehow finding her feet for a leap towards what his screaming brain chose to label its chest. He made another half-sound as he watched the heads snap in towards the girl, who suddenly seemed quite frail and little. The hiss of bared teeth changed to howls of fury, as gouts of blood spurted from two of the monster's necks.

"Blood and fire..." The words just about dribbled out of him. She had somehow pushed the necks aside and used the two daggers, still wedged in to the hilt, as hand-holds to pull herself up onto the monster's back. The outer heads followed her, snapping at the air as she slid over and around to stand behind it. Moving in perfect rhythm, Taurio and Prasta closed in with their javelins, stabbing at anything that threatened to come close. Confused, the beast stomped and tried to turn to face Rivkah while sizing up this new threat.

The thunder of hooves was one distraction too many for the hydra, as Quintus and his horse charged towards it. A moment's hesitation cost the beast a head, which spun, tongue lolling, until it hit the ground with a satisfying thump. Aemilius pumped his fist and shouted as the neck went limp—

—only to shove his fist in his mouth and scream as the headless neck, hideously, twitched back into life. The blood-spurting end bulged monstrously and a new set of teeth emerged from the wound.

An orb of fire exploded into life around the stump, and the other heads wailed and thrashed in pain. A safe distance away, Abrax stood in his stirrups, robes billowing and snapping in a wind that seemed to touch him and him only, face set in stone but eyes blazing. Sensing their opening, Prasta and Taurio surged forward, burying the javelins deep where they could and drawing short swords, hacking at anything and everything with a fury. Quintus had charged past the monster, barely slowing, and swung his horse round its rump. Now he galloped past on the other side, lopping off another head, and this time, the ball of fire appeared instantly. The head in the middle writhed, trying to fight off Rivkah, who had climbed back onto the beast and was playing with it like a mad cat wrestling a giant, murderous mouse.

And then Taurio, who had somehow managed to pin one snake-neck down using the javelin in its throat as a foothold, was removing its head with workmanlike determination. He did not wait for the fire to start to leap over to Prasta, laying into the beast on its blind side.

A bowstring sang next to Aemilius's ear twice in quick succession, and arrows smashed into the back of the hydra's middle head as it lashed at Rivkah. The beast twisted around, blind with fury, only to miss Quintus as he raced towards the kneeling forms of Taurio and Prasta, pulling his reins at precisely the right moment and jumping across to decapitate the last head. Within moments, the Legion had all jumped free of the smouldering corpse and regrouped in front of Abrax.

Aemilius looked at Livia, who still did not so much as glance in his direction. "That—was—*incredible!*" he said, only belatedly realising that he was probably screaming. He felt his pitch rising as he gabbled, and he found himself unable to care. "You just killed a hydra!

That was a *hydra!* An actual one! And you killed it! That's legendary! Everyone needs to know about this!"

Livia didn't reply. She just stared at the mouth of the cave. "Abrax…" she said, tension in her voice.

"I know," the tall magus replied.

Around him, the legionnaires all stared at the cave, and Aemilius realised that there was movement in the shadows.

A lot of movement.

And hissing.

Without taking his eyes off the cave, Abrax called over his shoulder, "How are you feeling, old friend?"

"Not great," Hanno replied behind them. "But not dead. There is not much for me here."

"Do what you can."

The words had just left Abrax's mouth when two more of the creatures burst out of the cave mouth, covered in blood and powered by fury. *They can smell what we've done.* Aemilius felt the familiar cold sweat breaking out and his left knee buckling under him.

The bigger of the two charged forward, only to be wreathed in a ball of roaring fire that exploded on its chest and almost stopped it in its tracks. The smaller hydra, close on its heels, shrieked in frustration as it sank into the ground, clawed feet mired in knee-deep mud that seemed to have appeared out of nowhere before solidifying around its legs, leaving it stuck in place. Glancing over at the reedy shape of Hanno, Aemilius was struck by the power in the little man's stance. His limbs flowed like water, pulling, pulling—and even in his terror, Aemilius saw the mountain brook that had been prattling along next to them start flowing again.

Another.

He didn't have time to finish the thought.

The big hydra seemed to shake itself free of the fire, but the distraction had given Quintus time to wheel his horse and thunder past again. This blow was not as clean, but a half-severed neck was not much use to the monster. Aemilius watched in horror as another of the hydra's heads reached over, teeth closing around the neck, holding it in place as the flesh re-knit itself before his eyes.

Taurio screamed something in Gallic, wading in and swinging his club. The crunch as wood met skull sent shivers down Aemilius's spine. "No, you bastard! That—is—not—*fair!*" the big Gaul screamed, smashing his club into the two heads, working side to side. Another head swivelled to attack him, only to thrash back as Rivkah's knives plunged in on either side of the neck.

"Rivkah!" Prasta screamed—but too late. A head struck, lightning-fast, and a spray of blood gushed from the girl's leg as she launched herself away, drawing a crimson arc in the air.

"Scaly bastard whoreson shit-bucket!" she screamed, landing and toppling over.

He was four steps along before his brain caught up and started screaming at him. *What are you doing?* Very calmly, with his heart threatening to burst through his chest and leap out his mouth at the same time, Aemilius decided not to think about that question. He focussed on not breaking his ankles running across the hillside to the fallen girl, who was swearing a blue streak and pushing down on her leg.

The bigger hydra was thrashing now, three heads down and twitching this way and that under fire from Livia. Aemilius paid it no heed. *If I die, I die,* he thought as he approached Rivkah. When he saw her face, he thought for a fleeting moment he might be safer fighting the hydra.

"If you get yourself killed," she hissed through gritted teeth, "I swear I will kill you again, and then die so I can find your ghost and kill that too."

"Shut up," he said as kindly as he could, kneeling to offer his shoulder. "You're bleeding."

"And you're annoying," she snapped, leaning on him and casting a glance at the scene. "Go slow." When she saw his reaction, she burst out laughing. "We'll live. Did you think you were going to outrun it?"

Looking back, Aemilius blinked. The bigger hydra was dead, and the legionnaires had encircled the smaller one, still stuck in the ground.

"I told you," Rivkah said, wincing as she hopped towards Livia, who had already packed away her bow and produced a healer's bag. "We're good at what we do."

V

HISPANIA

A HYDRA. A Hydra. *I just killed a hydra.* No. We *just killed a Hydra.* No. Three *Hydras.* No. They *just killed three Hydras.*

A *Hydra. I just killed a* Hydra.

The words rattled and spun in his head, losing sense with every repetition. He could hold the image of the first monster, the snapping heads on the sinuous, twisting necks, the thick claws and the pounding of feet on dry ground—but then the other two crowded in, and his thoughts became one writhing tangle of snakes and teeth and death.

He looked at the others, hoping wildly that any of them was as overwhelmed as he was.

They were not.

Wearing thick leather gloves that covered them up to the elbows, Taurio and Prasta worked away at the carcasses, trading their strange shorthand. He could pick up the occasional word, but not enough to understand what they were saying. A lined crate lay open on the ground next to them, and occasionally parts of blackened meat would land in it with a thud.

Quintus was seeing to the horses, soothing and feeding. To the side, Hanno and Livia spoke quietly, pointing at features of the ground around them.

"Talk," Rivkah said. "You're staring so hard your eyes will fall out if you don't open your mouth."

Aemilius blinked and squeezed his eyes shut. Mouth. Snap. Jaw. Blood. Opening them again, he saw Rivkah sitting on a stone, leg elevated, looking at him steadily. She raised her eyebrows slowly, as if he wasn't really worth any more words.

"I, uh," he stammered. "That…" He gestured weakly towards the carcass. "That's a hydra."

"Yep."

"And… that's not… important to you?"

"I'd say it is. Shitty little beast took a chunk out of my leg."

"But—you—" Aemilius flapped his arm at the work. "None of you—you haven't even—it's a *hydra!*" he wailed.

Rivkah sighed. "Yes." Her eyelids drooped and she seemed to think for a moment. "Sit down," she said, eyes still closed. "I said—*sit down.*"

Without thinking, Aemilius obeyed.

"I forget." She sounded weary.

"Forget what?"

"I forget that there are people that aren't them." She waved at the Legion. "And there are people who don't know." She held up her hand before he could ask. "I've not been with them for long. Two years, maybe. And I'd lived a lot more than you have before I joined. No, you don't have to talk. Just say yes."

"...Yes."

"They found me in the middle of winning an argument, and decided to adopt me."

"What kind of argument?"

Rivkah opened her eyes and smiled like a cat with her paw on a lame bird. "The kind that involves a bastard, a knife and a lot of blood. They decided quickly that I was in a lot of trouble and could be useful, so here I am. Within three months I had seen five things I thought were just stories to scare children. A walking corpse, a fire-lizard, a lion with a beak. All they had in common was that they were trying to kill us. Which, considering we were trying to kill *them*, is fair enough, I suppose."

She paused for a moment. Across the stream, Taurio and Prasta were busy sprinkling something on the meat in the crate, which was now almost full. At Livia's and Hanno's feet a deep, wide hole had appeared, and Quintus was leading two of their sturdiest horses towards it. A faint light from the cave mouth suggested where Abrax had gone.

"Now, two years in, I don't really care. I know what I can do to help, and I do that to the best of my ability. Same goes for all of us. We're all just trying to not die."

A succession of questions tumbled through Aemilius's head. He settled on the third one and pointed to Taurio. "What are they doing?"

"Salting the bits. They have a list in their head of... ingredients to bring back to the Fort." She looked at him. "Not going to ask?"

"Not sure I want to know."

She smirked. "For Egenny, for auguring. Mostly. Some of it also goes to Salura, for creams and ointments. And some goes to Cassia, and you better hope you never get a taste of any of her brews." Her eyes rolled up into her head and she made a throaty noise that sounded horrifyingly like someone choking on their own vomit. When she saw his disgust, the smirk blossomed into a full grin.

"How bad is it?" Abrax's voice made Aemilius jump almost out of his skin. The big magus had somehow just appeared right behind him.

Rivkah scoffed. "Sore. I'll limp a bit for a couple of days, but everything is still attached. Would have been a bit worse if my hero here hadn't swooped in and rescued me." She bowed her head and gave a flourish of mock gratitude with her hand.

Abrax smiled. "See? He's useful."

"So is horse shit."

"Can you ride?"

"I can talk, and I can sit. What more do I need?"

"Then ask your hero to help you into the saddle. We ride once they're down and burned."

"See?" She turned to Aemilius. "No sympathy, no love. All I am to them is a tool."

"Oh, no," Abrax said. "You are so much more than that. Bait, for a start." Smiling, he swayed to the side, neatly dodging the pebble thrown by Rivkah, and walked off. "Rise, daughter of Abraham," he said over his shoulder, "and heal quickly. I have a feeling that we'll need you soon."

They were delivered with a smile, but the words filled Aemilius with dread.

COMPARED WITH WHAT Aemilius had now come to think of as the hunt—the search for the next source of death and misery—the ride back downhill was slow and dull. Once they were down off the hillside they took their bearings and headed due north. Nobody said anything. All he could hear was the gentle thud, crunch and click of hooves on the ground. And still, the questions pressed. He tried to put them out of his head, but the moment he did that, other things came rushing in.

His cousins, dying in a gout of blood with a disgusting harpy hovering over them.

The flock of nightmarish creatures descending in the night, hissing and clawing.

The screams from the cave and the unnatural form of the hydra bursting out into daylight.

Finally, after what felt like years but was maybe half of the sun's journey towards noon, he nudged his horse towards where Taurio sat on the cart.

"Why didn't we bury the bodies?"

The Gaul looked up at him, surprised. Before he could answer, more questions tumbled out. "And why didn't we go back down to the village and tell them? And why did we hide and burn the hydras? And how did they do it? And—"

Taurio held up a beefy hand to silence him. "In my country we have a saying: 'The child who asks too many questions ends up asking only one.'"

"And what is that?"

He mimicked a scared child. "'Why am I at the bottom of this well?' And the answer to that is 'Because Mummy and Daddy thought you were very annoying.'"

Aemilius blinked and looked around. "There are no wells here, though."

Taurio nodded appreciatively. "Your wisdom grows, young one. That being said, if I answer your questions and all I get in return is more questions, I am sure we could find a deep enough hole somewhere." His eyes twinkled. "But if I have understood your squawking, you were wondering about what happens... after."

"Yes."

The Gaul smiled, rattling along on the cart, back wedged up against the side, as comfortable as a prince being driven in his carriage. He looked Aemilius up and down once, evaluating. "So I reckon what you'd want to do... would be to take the bodies, or what's left of them, down to the village and tell them in some detail that a couple of bastards brought monsters to their hills, but that now the monsters are gone and it only cost more than half of all the working men in their village. Is that about right?"

Feeling suddenly less sure of himself, Aemilius nodded.

"Mm." Taurio paused, allowing the image to hang in the air. "Now take your excellent, young, sharp mind to the other side of that conversation. You live in a village. You rarely see guests. You're born, you toil, you raise children, you age, you die. Suddenly something unusual happens—and in your village, *nothing* unusual ever happens. You know everything, and you understand everything. When the crops fail, it is because of the weather, and the weather is because of the gods. If a cow turns lame, it's because she stepped on something stupid, or a wolf bit her. Nothing in your world surprises you.

"And then, half a flock goes missing. But you know about that too, because you've heard of cattle thieves. Bands of riders roaming the land, stealing cattle and killing honest, hard-working folk." Taurio looked him in the eye, just to make sure he was still following. "Just after the flock disappears, a band of riders shows up and then disappears again. You send your best and strongest men to find the cattle thieves. And then they are gone for a while… and *then* the band of riders shows up *again*, with the mixed remains of your brothers and your husbands and your uncles and your cousins, and tells you that *your* men were killed in *your* hills by… monsters that no-one has ever seen and have only been heard of in legends? And old, shitty legends at that?"

The Gaul smiled. "How would *you* feel if that was you? Would you invite the strangers to your table? Would you give them half of what you own and thank them?" He paused for effect. "Or would you get every man, woman and child of the village together, give them every single sharp thing you could find, and get your revenge one way or another?"

Taurio's smile had gone cold.

"But—if we showed them the—?"

"If you show them the monster, they will very quickly find an explanation. The monster wasn't there. Then you came along. Then the monster was there. *Ergo*," he almost spat, "you brought the monster. The monster was your fault. And because they can't get at the monster, you are the next target. And poor old Taurio only has one neck, and one head—"

"Thank the stars for that," Prasta interjected from her saddle. "I would not want to deal with twice the horse-crap."

"Oh, but think of the fun we could have," Taurio shot back. "You could listen to me argue with myself!"

"You do enough of that with one head. Start by adding a whole brain to it, before you start growing heads."

Taurio scoffed. "She knows nothing."

"He's not wrong, though," Prasta added, to Aemilius.

"I take that back," Taurio said. "She is wise as a wild hedge."

"We've tried, occasionally," Prasta went on, ignoring him. "It never goes well. People don't want to know about monsters."

"They want to go to sleep at night and feel like they will be able to understand almost everything that happens to them in the morning," Taurio added.

"So—what? You swoop in, kill the monster and then slink away again?"

"…Yes?" Taurio said "That sounds about right."

"But—nobody *knows!*" Aemilius wailed. "Nobody knows that hydras still exist!!"

Taurio sighed. "Yes. We talked about this. They don't want to know. And if they did know—What would they do with it? 'Here, peasant. Your life is hard. But don't forget that there are things out there that will rip you to pieces, and they may at any point appear in your hills and terrorise your village. May Caesar protect you—and he may, as long as you pay your taxes. Goodbye and good night!'"

"Taurio!"

Aemilius glanced over at Prasta. Snapping at Taurio was entirely in keeping—but there was an unfamiliar giddiness to her voice.

"Taurio!"

"What, you insufferable bean sprout?"

"It's—I think it is…"

"The Lord and Lady!" Livia shouted, triumphantly—and in an instant, the leisurely trudge of their caravan became a headlong sprint. Aemilius held on to the reins for dear life and tried to peer through the cloud of dust kicked up by their suddenly very excited horses. The shouting of the riders did not help, and he found himself tossed this way and that for a short lifetime until, as suddenly as they'd sped up, the horses slowed to a canter, and then a walk.

As the dust settled and he suppressed the rising bile in his throat, he saw what they had been galloping towards.

A covered wagon, brightly coloured with what looked like a mast on top, a sail neatly rolled and bound to it. Two magnificent horses standing by, patiently looking into the distance and absolutely ignoring their headlong dash.

In front of the caravan, a large table had been set out, around which a slim man bustled, laying out plates and goblets and filling them from a large glass decanter.

As the horses halted, Livia dismounted. The breath caught in Aemilius's throat: suddenly the woman who he had seen digging holes, loosing arrows and riding horses was transformed.

Like water flowing over silver, she executed an elegant bow. "We are honoured by your presence, my Lord," she intoned.

The man looked up at her, eyes twinkling. "Oh, none of that, m'dear. It's good to see you too. Drink?"

"I thought you'd never ask." Livia beamed at him.

All around him the Legion dismounted, jumped off, clambered down and carefully lowered itself cursing to the ground, before striding, skipping and hobbling to their seats at the table.

The man Livia had addressed as 'Lord' looked up at Aemilius. "I could *throw* you a plate if you want, but I think you'll be more comfortable sitting with us…?"

Shaking his head and blinking, Aemilius dismounted, remembering a little too late that his legs and arse were still not used to being in the saddle for the best part of a day. He caught himself before he collapsed to the ground, but still felt a flush of embarrassment. In the face of the Lord he saw nothing but a genuine smile—and an outstretched hand, holding a metal goblet beaded with moisture.

Just as he started reaching for the drink, his training kicked in. "We praise our host and humbly ask for a seat at the table," he recited.

"A Sardinian!" the Lord exclaimed. "Delightful. And well-educated, too." The old man examined Aemilius's face. "Vaguely... familiar. Remind me to ask you some questions, young man. Now—could I invite you again to sit at our table?"

Having had orders barked at him non-stop over three days, Aemilius was almost confused by the civility. The Legion were already seated, and conversing like they'd just spent the best part of the day at a tavern. A seat was ready for him, and Aemilius made his way to it.

The moment he sat down, a cheerful woman with short, grey hair emerged from behind the caravan, holding a large plate. As one, the Legion rose and bowed their heads, and Aemilius scrambled to follow.

"Oh, *honestly*," she chided them. "Sit down. And shush!" She glanced at their host.

"Should have seen them," the Lord said. "Livia did me a proper royal curtsy. And this one gave a good old-fashioned Sardinian greeting!"

"Sardinian? Delightful! He looks familiar. Make sure you ask him some questions. Here!" She unceremoniously shoved the plate in the Lord's hands and disappeared again behind the caravan.

"Right. So. Before anything else happens, I am going to get this right."

Realising that he was staring, Aemilius forced his gaze back to the Legion, and had to stop himself from bursting out laughing. As one, the grizzled monster-slayers, hydra-killers and harpy-burners stared at the thin man like excited children about to be entertained by a tumbler.

"Francian prawns on fresh bread, with butter and garlic," the lord announced.

As the plate was placed before them, the Legion murmured around him.

"Oh…" An appreciative moan from Livia.

"Shit, yes." Rivkah approved.

Abrax rumbled in delight, like some kind of giant cat. Quintus glanced to the sky and muttered something looking and sounding like a prayer. Hanno grinned from ear to ear, teeth glinting. Prasta stared at the plate like a hawk, assessing and counting.

Taurio sniffed. "I love them so much," he whispered quietly, one big tear rolling down his cheek as he reached for the first, palm-sized disc of bread heaped with glistening shellfish, slathered in butter and drizzled with herbs. The smell of it settled over the table, and with it the quiet of a temple.

First bites consumed, they found their voices again.

"I had forgotten…"

"This—is life."

"I would murder for this."

"To be fair, you would murder for a lot less."

"Fine. I would murder a *lot* for this."

Without thinking, Aemilius sipped the wine and felt fresh, cold joy spread from his throat to his fingertips. Road dust forgotten, he felt alive again, and took another bite of his bread, this time with more gusto. He glanced over at Taurio and had to suppress a smile. The big Gaul looked oblivious, like he had found his one true and long-lost love, holding the bread delicately in his big hand and looking at it like it was about to burst into song. Tenderly, like a lover, he took a bite and chewed slowly, savouring every moment.

The sight brought a smile to Aemilius's face. There was something so genuine and pure about the big man that he didn't notice the Lady until she spoke.

"It is good to see you, friends."

"Oh, and you too, Lady," Quintus said, deference in his voice.

"Felix told us you were nearby," the Lord added. "He thought you might need a bit of nourishment."

"He wasn't wrong," Livia said.

"What did you find?"

"Three Hydras. Forgive me"—Livia took another bite of the bread—"I, mph."

The Lady smiled benevolently as she chewed.

"Seventeen years of having table manners beaten into me with a stick," Livia said, swallowing, "and your food always turns me into a wolf."

"It is the finest compliment," the Lady said, and nothing more needed to be said after that.

"It was hard to tell," Abrax continued. "But it seemed to me that someone had found caves with running water, and brought very young animals to rear them there— and more than three. Far more than three."

Some of the good mood at the table vanished.

"You didn't tell us that." Quintus frowned.

"I had to gather my thoughts. I found several chambers, full of bones of various kinds. It seems like a number of them were brought in and left to fight each other for food."

"That used to be how we bred fighting dogs," Taurio said darkly. "The ones who survived were *vicious*."

The Lord and Lady said nothing, but Aemilius felt like they were watching everyone at once.

"We also found something like a camp," Abrax continued. "But nothing permanent."

"Breed and release," Livia said. "The village on the plains would have been about the right size for the winner."

They sat in silence for a moment. Then the Lady stood up, looking serious. "Is everyone done?"

"Unless they're planning to eat the platter, my love, I'd say yes."

She made a playful face at the Lord, grabbed the plate and disappeared behind the caravan.

Aemilius leaned over to Rivkah. "What's behind the caravan?" he whispered.

A 'ssh' and a wave of the hand were all he got for his trouble.

"To other matters," the Lord said. "I made this." He held out his hands, which were empty—and a moment later, a sparkling thing had appeared in the palm of his right hand. "What do you think?" He put it down on the table, slowly, so everyone could see. It was a spiral, wrought in silver, broadening in the middle and tapering off to needle-sharp points at the ends. He let it go—and it spun, and spun, and stars spun within it, and time spun up and down it, and none of them could take their eyes off it. "It's not quite finished."

"How?" Aemilius exclaimed, all manners instantly forgotten. "How is that not a perfect object?"

The Lord smiled graciously. "Because, Sardinian—I haven't handed it over to anyone. A made thing is nothing until it is given to the world." Gently, he reached out and stopped the spiral with a pinch of his fingers. "Here," he said, offering it to Aemilius. "I wish you to have this gift."

Aemilius felt heat rise in his cheeks as he became very conscious of everyone looking at him. *Say something*, his brain screamed at him. "Uh… thank you?"

The Lord nodded in acknowledgement.

"But why?"

"Because I have figured out where I know you from," he replied gnomically.

Frowns and suspicious looks around the table gave way to expectation as the Lady came around the corner again, carrying a pot that looked like it could easily fit all of Hanno in it. Aemilius's eye was drawn to the little man, who was positively bouncing in his seat, looking like a nearly middle-aged version of an over-excited child.

"The soup! The soup! It's the soup! The soup!" he jabbered in between little bursts of giggling.

The Lord swooped in with bowls that seemed to appear out of nowhere, and the Lady dished up bread rolls from her apron and ladled a thick, bright red soup that radiated warmth even from a distance, Aemilius dared to take another look at the spiral in his hand. It looked incredibly fragile, as thin as a hair, but it was firm to the touch and did not yield as silver would. The light caught on it, and as he held it up to look through it he thought he caught a glimpse of something in the middle, but it was gone again in an instant.

"Did you ask the young man?" the Lady said, as the Lord placed a bowl of soup in front of him.

"Didn't have to," the Lord said proudly. "Figured it out myself."

"Oh, did you?"

He stepped close to her and whispered something in her ear. She paused in her tracks, turned and gave Aemilius a speculative look.

"I see," she said out loud. "Interesting."

Aemilius tried to assemble the information he was receiving and form it into questions, but that was a battle he had no chance of winning the moment the smell from the bowl hit his nostrils. His half-formed thoughts were immediately elbowed out of the way by the immediate and all-consuming need to get the soup into his face right now.

And so he did. Slow-roasted tomatoes, herbs, heat and sunshine, sweetness and joy and a hint of lemon exploded in his mouth, and he felt happy and safe and warm. There was no notion that could fit into his soul other than to immediately have another spoonful, and another.

A hand landed gently on his arm, and he looked up, into the eyes of Taurio.

"Give it time," the Gaul whispered. "Breathe. Enjoy everything. You will not get food like this anywhere else." The hold wasn't firm, but Aemilius didn't even try to move his arm until Taurio had released it.

Around the table, the food had yet again changed and lifted their mood. At the far end, Abrax was finishing a joke about a Vestal Virgin, a carrot and an unfortunate donkey that had Quintus howling and Livia feigning disgust.

Rivkah, to one side, had fallen quiet. She met his gaze, and he thought that he had never seen anyone so alone and sad before. *Food is family.* Without thinking, he broke half of his bread roll and handed it to her.

She hesitated for a moment, but accepted the bread and turned quietly to the soup.

Moments later, the Lady returned. "How is it?"

"Oh, it is the morning wave, the air in the brook, the foam in the waterfall," Hanno burbled.

"He means he likes it," Quintus added.

"I know," the Lady said, kindly. "I too appreciate the flow of things."

Hanno looked up from his soup, beamed at her, then returned to caressing his spoon across the liquid, picking it up and watching the drops, then gently placing it on his lips and loudly slurping it.

"You eat like an old, toothless dog," said Rivkah with a scowl.

"You are right, daughter of Abraham," Hanno said. "With great appreciation, and thankfulness that I am still alive. But no dog, toothless or otherwise, has ever had soup this good."

"Do dogs like soup?" Taurio looked momentarily puzzled.

"Well, pigs clearly do," Prasta said, motioning towards his empty bowl. "If I hadn't seen it going in, I'd say you hadn't got any."

"Maybe I didn't?" Taurio gazed with eyes of hope and innocence at the Lady, who smiled.

"You did, my lovely bear. And you will not get any more, for I wouldn't want to spoil your appetite."

"Is there more? More food?"

"There always is, Sardinian," the Lord replied. "There is always more food."

"I am never leaving," Taurio said. "I quit this stupid Legion. I belong to them now. I'll mend the cart. I'll give the horse my clothes and pull the cart, if I have to."

Smiles around the table.

"You said that last time, and the time before that," the Lady said as she disappeared yet again around the caravan.

"And I meant it!" Taurio called after her.

"What news of home?" Livia asked.

"What news, what news...?" the Lord mused. "The Cornelii hate the Claudii. The Tulii hate the Servilii and everyone hates the Valerii. Same as it ever was. We haven't been home for years, mind, so we are maybe not the most reliable. We depend on Felix and his ilk for updates. He sounded quite busy when we met him," he added thoughtfully.

"He often says he is, and I never believe him."

"Spoken like a true Primus Pilus," the Lord said with a smile. "Never trust anything that doesn't neigh."

"Sounds reasonable to me," Prasta added.

"Could you come and help me for a moment?" the Lady's voice rang out from behind the caravan.

The Lord was on his feet in a flash. "Coming," he called, suddenly producing an amphora and taking the long way around the table, filling up glasses as he went and leaning it up against the caravan as he too disappeared out of sight.

"What's *behind* there?"

"Sixteen staff and a full kitchen?" Taurio said. "*No.*" The weight of his words pushed Aemilius back down into his seat. "You are *not* allowed to go back there and look. Nobody is. It is maybe not magic, what they do— but it is also magic, and if you break it I will personally rip, tear and smash you into pieces that will fit up a sparrow's arse."

"I'd probably say something like 'I apologise' or 'I understand,' if you want to keep your skull in roughly the same shape," Rivkah said with a smile. "You're learning things, boy, and I'll teach you something now. When you hear someone speak like *that*, someone else is very nearly dead."

"I'm... sorry," Aemilius stammered, and something in Taurio's shoulders and the set of his jaw was there, and then it wasn't, and suddenly he was again affable and smiling. "Good! Part of the joy of the world is to accept that which you cannot understand. Key to this job, funnily enough." He gestured at the Legion and got appreciative nods in return. "Not to say that you can't ask questions, of course—but it does help to just accept things from time to time."

The conversation was interrupted again by the Lord coming back into view. It was hard to tell how old he was; Aemilius had guessed him older than his father, but he moved and spoke like a far younger man—but even the Lord struggled under his load. In his arms he carried a plate that would have protected most of a grown man's torso, upon which was piled what looked like the meat from an entire spit-roasted lamb, fat still fizzing and crackling. Straining just a little, he placed the plank upon the table with an audible thump, only to spin away and head back behind the caravan. Just as he disappeared from sight, the Lady appeared, balancing plates heaped with green leaves, red vegetables and a jug the size of a man's head. Distributing them deftly, she smiled at them, and Taurio in particular. "I told you," she said. "I didn't want you spoiling your appetite."

He looked up at her like a worshipper. "In my land you would be queen," he said.

"And who says I'm not?" she twinkled back at him, taking her seat at the table.

The Lord rounded the corner, holding a vat full of roasted root vegetables which he placed on the table next to the mountain of lamb.

"Feed," the Lady commanded.

The Hidden Legion immediately set to doing their part to obey her order. Plates flew around the table and were soon loaded with meat and placed in front of the seated guests.

Aemilius could not help but stare. He had been better fed than most, in his life, but the best and most intricate of his father's feasts could not compare to this.

Lamb, so tender and succulent it would leap off the plate and back into nature if he didn't hurry up. Roasted peppers and tomatoes that he could taste when he saw them. Leaves woven into patterns by the finest artists. Roots and tubers coated in oil and herbs, crusted on the corners.

And finally, the Lady walked around the table and poured a golden-brown gravy over their dishes from the big jug.

"Ooooof." The noise from Abrax featured no recognisable words, but the meaning was crystal clear. Around the table, a chorus of rhapsodic delight arose, and soon the Legion was enthusing about flavour, profusely thanking the cook and trading stories about the happiest moments of their lives, none of which came close to this meal, in this place, at this time.

Aemilius took another bite and gently shut his eyes, feeling every inch of the warmth spreading through his body. Feeling his shoulders relax, he found the images of the past days fading somewhat, their edges growing dull. *So maybe there are monsters in the world,* he thought. *Maybe there are things I don't understand. But if there*

is also this, then there is hope—and then maybe there is
a reason to continue.

"Help me," Livia groaned.

"What?" Quintus mumbled, with his mouth full.

"Take my plate. Take it. And tie my hands behind my back. Because I am so full that if I have another bite of anything I *will* die. And I have *no* chance of stopping myself."

"Weak," Hanno said.

"For not being able to stop?" Livia said, a look of surprise on her face.

"For needing to stop," the little man grinned, heaping his fourth helping onto the plate. "The lake never asks the rain to hold up a little bit. It takes all it can get, and saves it for a dry day."

"You astound me, toad," Rivkah said. "You eat twice as much as the old fart. Where does it all go?"

"Into the flow," Hanno said happily, tucking into a thick piece of meat.

Abrax pushed his plate away, looking sated. "This... Your finest yet, I dare say. It would make the Emperor's cooks cry and quit."

The Lady smiled. "You are too kind."

"This beautiful animal did not die in vain," Prasta said.

"It did not," Taurio echoed. "It has given happiness and joy, and a memory that will last."

"All our sweetest hours fly fastest." The words were out of Aemilius's mouth before he could stop them, and he felt the familiar heat in his cheeks when they all looked at him.

Quintus had an unfamiliar look of approval. "He knows his Virgil."

"Who?" Rivkah shot back.

"Savage," Quintus huffed, not noticing the smirk on the girl's face.

The Lord and Lady both bowed solemnly. "A lovely boy, Virgil," the Lord said.

"Liked his chicken well-roasted," the Lady added.

"But now we must drink," the Lord said, standing up suddenly, fresh bottle in hand. "It will not do to leave travellers parched." He flitted between goblets again.

But after a while the Lady spoke again. "We have something else to tell you." Clouds drew together in the sky to match the darkness in her tone.

The Legion exchanged glances.

"It's never good for long, is it," Rivkah said drily.

"Much like Prasta's tunes," Taurio added.

"Where is it?"

"Oh, Livia." The Lord looked almost a little sad. "I wish we could just entertain you with food and drink and dancing bears, but in this age, it is not to be."

"There is a darkness," observed Hanno.

"There is, my short friend." The Lord nodded at the little man. "And in this case, there seems to be something brewing on a small island called Formentera. Do you know of it?"

Aemilius tried his best to remember his geography lessons, but all he could recall was the feel of the desk against his cheek and the sting of the rod as he was woken up again.

"Vaguely," Abrax said. "Baleares? South?"

"Correct," the Lady said. "We have been hearing that no traders or fisherfolk have come from there in half a year. Neighbouring isles have sent people, who have not returned. There are whispers of something evil."

Quintus sighed. "For once, I would like it if someone

told us vaguely what we are going up against before we got there."

"That would be helpful," Prasta added.

"But would it be as fun?" Taurio added, grinning, and only barely dodging a thrown pepper from Rivkah, which Prasta caught and ate in one motion.

"I fear she rather suggested you should go see," the Lord said.

Nobody replied, but around the table there were shrugs and grim faces. *This is what they do*, Aemilius thought. *And after we*—they—*killed the hydras, they all knew the next one was coming.* Nobody complained. Nobody tried to negotiate. They had no idea what they were going into—but they were all going to go.

And then he realised the Lady had disappeared behind the caravan again. He didn't have a lot of time to wonder, though—she reappeared almost instantly with a wooden tray, on which rose a small, neat pile of cubes.

"Oh…" Unusually, Rivkah did not have a swearword to hand. Instead, she stared at the stack with the heat of a furnace.

The Lady saw her look and smiled. "Yes, my dear. I did think of you especially."

The young girl's jaw worked so hard that she could have bitten through a horseshoe. *She's trying not to cry.* Anyone fighting for their life at thirteen summers probably hadn't had that much in the way of family, or love, or someone thinking of them. He briefly thought of reaching out to her, comforting her, putting a hand on her shoulder.

It did not take him long to decide that that would probably be a bad idea.

He did the next best thing he could think of—

distraction. "What are those?" he said, rather more loudly than he'd intended.

"Plakous," Taurio said with reverence. "One of four things the Romans *have* actually done for us."

Abrax's raised hand stopped Quintus before he could start correcting the Gaul.

Aemilius stared at the thing before him. He'd seen plakous before—his mother always called them 'poor man's jewels'—but none of them had looked anything like this. They'd been flat, splodgy lumps of sugar and honey. These looked like something you'd find at an emperor's artificers. Cut crisply into identical squares, glistening with syrup, with razor-sharp layers of honeyed gold, pistachio green, ruby red, and pastry that looked like captured sunshine, they practically screamed out to be taken and eaten.

In the time he'd taken to just look at the pile and gather his thoughts, seven of them were already gone.

"A good hunter never waits." Prasta offered a rare smile. He watched her bite into her square—and then her eyes shut and the ghost of a tremble passed over her lips. "Brigid's arse, but that is good," she said huskily. "Taurio..."

"Nope," the cheerful Gaul said. "I will not restrain you in any way, shape or form. Everyone must do their own battle with this devil."

The scene around the table looked like something out of a fresco. Every single one of them was lost in their own bliss. *If you wanted to murder this lot, now would be the time,* Aemilius thought, then felt guilty for suspecting the Lord and Lady. But on the other hand—harpies and hydras had not been enough to incapacitate the Hidden Legion, but honey-cakes seemed to be working.

Well—if I die, it'll be a good way to go.

He reached out for a cake of his own. It was gently sticky to the touch, and slightly warm. Bringing it to his lips, he felt oddly nervous—like he imagined going in for the first kiss.

And then he took a bite, and immediately stopped thinking about kisses. They couldn't *possibly* be as good as this. The warmth of the sugar, the caress of the honey, the crunch of the pastry—it was perfect.

And the next bite was different. And the same. And equally incredible.

All the thought he had room for was that he must have had some sort of cake before—but this felt like the first time. A wave of sadness washed over him. *Nothing will ever compare to this,* he thought. He finished it, and managed to snatch another. This time he decided to take it slow, and really try to taste everything—but it only took another two bites for his head to start swimming. The emotions stirred up by the flavours were simply too strong.

Aemilius glanced up at the Lord and Lady, and got a sudden chill. Who—no, *what*—were they? Their genial hosts had not even tasted the food. They leaned back like proud parents watching children who had just learned to feed without making a mess.

Lightning-quick, Prasta snatched the last one an eyeblink before Taurio got there. "See—the longer you stare, the less will be there."

For a moment, the big man looked crestfallen.

Gritting her teeth, Prasta produced a small knife—and cut the cake in two, putting half on Taurio's plate.

He stared at her with genuine surprise.

"One word out of you, boar, and I'll take it back."

Taurio beamed and picked up the cake with far more care than one would a newborn. Ever so gently, he placed it on his tongue and closed his eyes. To his side, Prasta did the same. There was a moment of contented silence, and then—

"We must leave."

Aemilius felt like his heart was being ripped out of him. Their hosts had risen, gracefully. The humble wooden table had become a battlefield of food, upon which a heroic victory had been won. Looking around, he saw that the sentiment was shared by the Legion. He was reminded of his nursemaid, who had at a young age taught him about food-love—the devotion you feel towards the one who feeds you.

At that moment, if anyone had so much as looked at the Lord and Lady with less than absolute respect, the Legion would have ripped them to pieces and turned them to dust.

Abrax spoke. "As ever, our meetings teach us one thing above others—that good things come to an end."

"But the sea is rain, and the rain is sea," added Hanno.

"Indeed, friend," the Lord said. "And our paths will cross again."

"When?" Aemilius blurted out, turning red instantly and expecting furious glares from his fellow travellers. Instead, all he got was sympathy. *They've all had the first parting.*

"We don't know," the Lady said, as she collected the dishes and bore them away. "But hopefully soon. You are good company." There was a clatter behind the caravan, the slam of wood on wood, and she reappeared. "Right, old man. Shall we?"

"We certainly shall," the Lord said, bowing to the

assembled Legion. "Would you mind…?" Aemilius was unceremoniously yanked from his seat on the bench by strong hands, and watched in stupor as the Legion set to work. The table was lifted up, disassembled into its component parts and slotted onto the side of the caravan, and the benches followed suit. "Thank you," the Lord said, vaulting into the driver's seat with ease. "Safe journeys." He snapped the reins gently, and the horses effortlessly pulled the caravan into an easy walk. It seemed to glide across the rocky surface, leaving… nothing.

Aemilius stared, dumbfounded.

He'd expected three cook-fires, a clay oven and at least two servants, but there was no evidence that a full meal for eight people—no, eight nobles of the finest families— had been served swiftly.

"Nobody knows," Taurio said fondly. "I lost a week of sleep the first time."

"Do… do they cook it in the caravan?"

"Maybe. Nobody knows. It's a mystery."

"A delicious mystery," Abrax added.

"Some say they are demi-gods." Livia smiled. "That they threw a party for Apollo himself, in disguise, and that he was so taken with them that he offered them eternal life and the caravan in return for their service."

"I've never had any sort of time for your pansy gods, but when I see Apollo I will thank him with a ballad," vowed Prasta.

"Oh, please don't," Taurio pleaded. "He'll take it all back and make us eat Celtic food as a punishment."

Moving quite slowly and deliberately towards their horses, Quintus grinned. "Our gods have parties and do fun stuff, twiglet. Yours look like they live in hedges and wipe their arses on porcupines."

"They do not!" Prasta bridled. "Alator will *smite*—"

"They all use the same porcupine," Rivkah chipped in. "He is caked in the stuff."

"And really annoyed," Livia added.

"I hate you," the Celt huffed. "Hate you all. Savages."

"I reckon she is in discomfort from too much food," Abrax said.

"Maybe we need to find her a porcupine?" said Hanno with a chuckle.

"*Hanno!*"

Soon after, they were all mounted and riding southeast at a leisurely pace. As he looked over his shoulder for the last time, Aemilius noticed that even the tracks of the caravan were gone.

VI

FORMENTERA

"TELL YOU ONE thing about the saddle. My first long journey really made absolute mincemeat out of my arse. Couldn't stand, sit or shit for days."

Not for the first time, Aemilius wondered how it would look when he stood up in the saddle, leapt athletically across to Taurio's horse, wrapped his arms around the Gaul's thick neck and strangled him. As with every other time Taurio had offered words of wisdom, in the three days since they left the Lord and Lady, he figured that since every single fibre of his legs felt like it was on fire, he would most likely lose his balance and fall six feet to the ground, to land flat on his face.

Maybe, if he landed neck-first, he could end the misery—

"And there we are," Quintus said. "Told you it was a shortcut."

"Yes," Livia replied wearily. "About seven times."

As they crested the hill, Aemilius saw what the old horseman was pointing to. He'd been aware of the sea for a while—the cawing of the birds in the distance, the soft whisper of the waves—but there had been nothing to see. Now, suddenly, the world opened up before them, and all of it was blue. The sea filled his eyes with it, sparkled with sunlight and offered the promise of a decent wash, something he was starting to feel like he had never had before.

The hill sloped down to what could charitably be called a village—a double handful of houses and huts, huddling around an inlet. Boats littered the beach, and to the north someone had bothered to build what even from a distance looked like a ramshackle pier. The sun, which had seemed to be right above them moments ago, was now sliding down behind them. Their shadows extended to the huts, dragging them along, inviting them to catch up.

Nudging his horse, Quintus took the lead. One by one, the Legion fell in behind him, picking their way single file down the path. Aemilius eased himself back into the saddle and tried to ignore his thighs, which felt like they'd been cut out of oak... using a hammer. *Save the energy*. After they'd left the Lord and Lady, the seven had just seemed to lean back into the travel. Conversation gradually died, replaced by occasional grunts, nods and two-sentence exchanges. Camp was made quickly, sleep was taken efficiently, watches seemed to be second nature. He had no choice but to fit in.

And each day it had been easier.

The morning before, he had found himself saddled and ready before he was properly awake—and now he was second from the back, holding the reins like someone who looked like he might know what he was doing.

I wonder what Father would think.

He thought about his father. He thought about the man, and the consul, Marcus Livius Sculla. Aemilius tried to remember what his father had looked like—and he couldn't. All that was left in his head was a vague idea of a face like the ones you might see on a coin, eyes trained on the distance. *A hawk.* He tried to remember how many times he had seen his father in the last year, and found himself wondering whether the old man missed him.

"Whatever's on your mind, you need to wipe it off your face. You look like a beaten stepchild." For a wild moment it seemed as though his father was speaking, but then he registered Rivkah, half-turned in her saddle. "Do you need me to slap you?" she added helpfully.

"No," Aemilius muttered. "I'm fine."

"You look like a donkey that ate a hedgehog."

He was reminded of his mother talking to a young woman of the household, instructing her in how to deliver the maximum damage in the fewest words. He thought of a blade in the night, gut-burning berries in the drink, a shove on a ledge, looked Rivkah in the eyes—and said, "Thank you."

She shrugged. "Just trying to help."

He bit down hard before the words *help less, you sour-faced bitch* escaped. He was annoyed and tired, but riding hadn't actually made him stupid. Not yet.

Slowly, they closed the distance to the fishing village. They could make out the silhouettes of fishermen mending nets and seeing to their tools, along with the occasional scrawny, scampering child or languishing mutt, hopeful that food would eventually materialise.

Unlike their previous stop, though, nobody paid them any mind.

They were well within calling distance before the first fisherman gave them even a shred of attention. A short lump of a man, he had leg-thick forearms and stubby fingers that skittered across an oft-mended net without looking. "We have nowt to steal," he rumbled. "And today's—hell, this whole week's—catch has been shite, so we have little to share. No young women, and definitely no horses the likes o' yours. And now that that's settled—what are you here for?"

"We need help," Abrax said.

The fisherman chewed the inside of his cheek. "Can't see what me and mine could help you lot with," he finally muttered, glancing down at the net.

"We need passage."

A sniff. "Where?"

"Formentera."

A glance. "Not my waters."

"We could make it worth your while."

"Aye, you probably could," the fisherman said. "But there is a problem."

"Which is?" Abrax said.

"I don't want to." And with that, he turned back to his net, fingers dipping and weaving, as if they didn't exist.

The Legion shared glances. There was some muttering, but Abrax shook his head and nodded at the next man over.

"Going the other way tomorrow."

"Hole in my boat."

"Hurt my knee."

"My wife is pregnant."

"My goat is pregnant."

At the last one, Aemilius looked around and was about to point out to the scrawny, leathery twig of a man who'd spoken that there was absolutely no hint or sign of any goat anywhere near the village, when Abrax smiled and nodded.

"Thank you. We will set up camp a ways away from the village, and we will be on our way by midday tomorrow." And with that, he turned the horse around and headed off, with intent and purpose.

They were clear of the cluster of houses in no time, riding silently back up the hill. Within moments, Quintus had pointed wordlessly at a spot, and following a nod from Abrax they stopped. Setting up camp was a quick affair, but Aemilius noted that somehow, following the big magus's silent lead, there was more care taken. Horses were tethered, tents brought up and laid out. Before the sun had properly sunk behind the mountains, the Legion had taken their rest in what looked like a very small version of a proper Roman camp. They were near enough to see movement in the fishing village, but far enough that details were hard to make out.

Aemilius waited patiently, but no-one spoke.

Rivkah rhythmically polished knives that seemed to appear from and disappear into her tunic at the same, eyeblink speed. He assumed there must be knife-belts of some sort in there, but he wouldn't have been surprised to find that she jabbed daggers in between her ribs for later use.

Prasta had produced ribbons of some sort of leather from somewhere and was busy working it, scraping the underside and occasionally throwing strips of meat into the fire, where they burned with a hiss and a stench. If the others minded, they did not show it.

Abrax seemed to have slipped into some kind of sitting half-sleep.

They aren't even jawing at each other. They are just... here. Just... waiting.

Quintus snored gently underneath his helmet.

Aemilius tried to make his mind wander, but it didn't want to go far. It kept throwing words back at him. *Hydra. Hidden Legion. Death.* His mouth remembered the taste of the meal at the table in the middle of nowhere, and he felt a small wave of sadness, which was immediately swiped away by the memory of a harpy claw shredding his cousin's arm. A moment before he lost himself in his own thoughts—

"Here we go." Livia's voice was gentle but firm.

Without any movement, the Legion came to life around Aemilius.

Abrax's eyes popped open.

Hanno cast one look over his shoulder, nodded, then went back to stirring his cup with his finger. "This one is for us," he said to no-one in particular.

The snoring from beneath Quintus's helmet came to a stop.

Aemilius peered into the dusk. Squinting hard, he could make out a figure walking away from the village, heading in the opposite direction.

"Why didn't he wait for nightfall?" Taurio sighed. "Would have saved him a ton of bother."

"Maybe he needed the exercise." Another strip of meat on the fire. Prasta had not taken her eyes off the task, but somehow seemed to know exactly what was happening.

What are you all talking about? Aemilius wanted to scream. The few insights that had been shared at the start of this miserable nightmare had now dwindled down to nothing, told by nobody. Mostly to push back the frustration, he looked away from his fellow travellers and tried again to find the walking man.

Who had disappeared.

"It'll be a while yet," Taurio said. "Have you seen many fishing villages around here?"

"No," Aemilius muttered. He vaguely remembered being dragged to see miserable peasants in hovels here and there. None of them had been near the sea.

"This is how they work, in these and most other parts. Fishing huts on the beach, houses up the hill. Keeps them sheltered when the winds come in. Our man has left his work for the day. He is getting his horse now, sneaking away from his mates. We'll be getting an offer of passage."

Aemilius stared at the faces, lit by flickering firelight. None of them reacted to Taurio's words. "How do you know?"

"It's like this in some places," Rivkah said. "If you come to the village, you are a Roman. And nobody wants to help the Romans."

"Or be seen to, at any rate," Livia added.

"But they have to eat." Another flick of the knife, another hiss.

"I wish you'd stop with the tanning. I'd like to eat something at some point, and the stink of that thing is turning even my stomach," Taurio sulked.

"You know full well, brute, that the longer I leave it, the worse it smells."

In the flickering light, Taurio grinned. "I always thought that was your mare."

"Hilarious."

"Both of you," Abrax admonished. "Stop it."

"Hey!" Taurio shouted in almost real outrage, batting at something near his face.

"Please forgive me," Prasta replied, with no sincerity whatsoever. "I meant to throw that on the fire. I can only imagine that will smell for a while."

"*Pack it in.*" Abrax's voice sounded like a stone door slamming shut in a vast chamber. "Rest. We might need to move swiftly."

It's like watching Father's dogs. All around him, the legionnaires had lapsed into waiting—resting, sitting back, conserving energy but still alert. A hare hopping past right now would not have great chances of survival.

Time passed, and shadows lengthened.

"There he is." Livia's voice was almost whisper-soft.

Aemilius stared into the settling darkness, but there was nothing to be seen. The fire crackled and snapped, but in between the sounds he could almost catch something— there!

The faint rumble of a rider in the distance.

Quintus sat up, quietly. "One. Careful, but not slow."

Aemilius listened harder. The hoofbeats had grown slightly louder, but he still had to work hard to pick them out. How on earth had Livia heard? He tried to casually angle his head so that he could take a better look. *An odd one.* She looked at times like every noblewoman he had seen at his parents' dinner parties—but sometimes there was a difference. An edge. There was more of the goddess Diana than of the patrician daughter about her— something mysterious, like she allowed you to see exactly what she wanted you to see and nothing more. *She might not look as dangerous as the others at first sight, but...*

The hoofbeats were now close enough to hear, and slowing down. "Ave Caesar," a voice rang out in the dark.

"Welcome, stranger," Abrax said, voice like flowing honey. "Join us. We have bread and cheese to share."

"Thank you." The hoofbeats stopped, followed by the sounds of someone dismounting and landing lightly. A figure emerged into the orb of light surrounding the fire, walking slowly and keeping both hands visible. A man; medium height, wiry build. Medium-length dark hair, olive skin. He had the sea in his gait, a roll in his walk like he had a couple of pebbles in his shoes. "I am Donato. I heard of your request."

"Well met, Donato." Abrax seemed to create his own field of attraction. There could be no question who was the leader of this group. *Just as there was no question Quintus was in charge at the village*, Aemilius thought. Keeping track of how the group shifted to match the occasion made his head spin. He leaned back, made himself small and resolved to watch and listen.

"You need to get to Formentera." Donato's Latin was rudimentary and accented, but understandable, with a heavy Hispanian accent.

"Yes," Abrax said.

"My brother and I have a boat. It will fit you, but not the horses." Aemilius glanced at Quintus, who showed no reaction. If it wasn't for the fact that his eyes moved, he could have been dead.

"We are not staying long on the island," Abrax said.

"My uncle will look after the horses."

"And we will pay him for his trouble."

The exchange was quick, as was the haggling over price and departure time. The group watched him leave. As soon as he was out of earshot—

"You can go without me."

"Oh, now, Quintus. We will store the—"

"No. I don't like the sound of it. This is wrong. Everything about it is wrong."

Abrax went to interrupt the horseman, but Livia's gentle hand on his arm stopped the magus.

"We don't know where we're going," Quintus continued. "Or why. And we are entirely reliant on some runty Spaniard to sail us there—at night?"

"Come on, old man," Rivkah said gently. "We *never* know what we are getting into. And besides, we've got the frog."

"Ribbit," Hanno added helpfully.

"Furibunda will be fine. She'll outlive us all."

"Heck, she'll eat our remains," Taurio added cheerfully. "Besides, the moon is out. Practically daylight, anyway. No shadows at sea."

Quintus scowled at all of them and fell silent.

The stars twinkled above them as they made their way to the beach where the Spaniard had told them to meet. Aemilius still struggled to place his accent. *Maybe he was from the north-west.* A vague memory of traders in the marketplace at the village, barking at each other. All sorts of variants of Latin, mangled almost beyond recognition. *Maybe the west coast…?* The sound of changing hoofbeats roused him. The dry crunch of gravel and the drumming of hard ground turned to a soft hiss as the horses reached the sand. The gentle lapping of waves in the distance had turned to a soft but persistent whisper. He looked up to see the silver of moon on the sea, and something stirred in him: a mixture of excitement and fear.

Adventure.

They dismounted before two men standing by a good-sized fishing boat, broad-beamed with a small mast, complete with a light boom. The Spaniard was in front of them, the leader of the crew. "Welcome. This is the *Luna*." He gestured to the boat.

"She knows the sea. Knows it and loves it." There was a tone to Hanno's voice that Aemilius hadn't heard before. Assessing. Knowledgeable. Crisp.

Whatever it was, it was enough for Abrax. "We are ready."

Quintus walked over to them with the reins to the horses. The Roman paused and assessed all three strangers silently, taking a good long time to look into the face of each one. By his shoulder, Furibunda whinnied and gently nudged his head. He muttered something, and the horse snorted as if in reply.

The eldest man took the reins, nodded seriously at the Roman and led the horses off. Quintus stood frozen in his tracks, watching the mounts as they walked away.

To Aemilius's surprise, it was Rivkah who stepped up to him and gently touched his elbow, guiding him to follow the rest of them as they pushed the boat out and hopped onboard. The gentle hiss of the sea laid a blanket of quiet down over the boat. Donato and the other man, who had not said a word since they arrived, had nudged them into their places and gone about their tasks with crisp efficiency. The tiller was manned. There was a heave, and a splash, and they were free of the beach. The sail—a small thing, but good enough to snap to when it caught what little wind there was—stretched gently, and Aemilius felt the smooth glide as the boat picked up pace. Muttered words between Donato and the boatsman, and glances at the gunwale.

"She sits low," Taurio muttered, sneaking a look at the sail. "Best if we don't get too much wind."

"Or what?" Aemilius said, hating the note of panic he could hear in his voice.

"We'll get wet," came the Gaul's short reply.

There was little to say after that. Aemilius looked back at the black line on the horizon. Land. Safety. There had been a few little pinpricks of light—torches, maybe, or campfires—but they had winked out of existence quickly. Now there was only the moon, shining down on them like a malicious silver eye.

Slowly, the hiss of the sea and the gentle rocking of the boat pressed down on Aemilius's eyelids. He started awake, blinking in the dark. His fellow travellers were arrayed about him, still and quiet. The shimmering sea was cut neatly by the black horizon, fading up to a soft grey in a halo around the moon.

Aemilius breathed in deeply. The sea air was intoxicating; there was a freshness to it, a reinvigorating taste of salt. And something else…

A stray beam of moonlight caught on some sort of metal ball, tucked away at the foot of the mast.

He blinked.

His head felt heavy. Not sleepy—*heavy*. Something was… not right. He tried to speak, but his throat felt dry. He swallowed once more, and felt his head drooping, felt his neck go soft. He tried to move, but his arms felt like lead.

Donato.

Aemilius tried to look for the Spaniard, but it was too late. He couldn't lift his head. The last thing he saw was his hands in his lap, useless and immovable.

And then everything turned black.

A GUST OF wind jolted him awake and he fell over, saving his life in the process, as the mast swung past at head-height.

"*Tiller!*" Taurio shouted.

Abrax swore in a guttural language and clambered over Rivkah and Livia, both slumped over.

Wind.

Panic finished the job of the wind, and Aemilius was awake. *Taurio said wind was bad.* And this wind certainly was. It howled like a caged beast, whipping up a broad line of foam on the waves around them. The boat rose and fell, throwing its cargo around like badly filled sacks. Quintus was busy with ropes, pulling this way and that, feet braced and arms taut.

"*Hanno!*" Abrax shouted, then noticed Aemilius looking around. "Wake him up. *Now!*" Rushing to his feet, Aemilius kicked over the metal ball at the base of the mast. It popped open with a click—a brazier of some sort?—and powder spilled out. "*Hanno!*" Abrax shouted again, over the wind.

Leaning over, Aemilius nudged the small man, but got no response. "*Hanno!*" Aemilius shouted, pushing harder—and Hanno toppled over, face smacking into the gunwale, body crumpling in a heap at the bottom of the boat.

Staring down at the fallen form of Hanno the Wise, Aemilius saw the bruise.

Someone had clouted him good.

"Hanno is out!" he shouted back at Abrax, turning just in time to hear the snap of the wind and see the sail swing towards his face.

The blow knocked the air out of him, and Aemilius felt separated from himself as he tumbled backwards, flailing for what felt like forever, falling, falling, falling until there was a sharp pain and then...

...again...

...black.

* * *

WATER AND SAND.

Water and sand.

On the third attempt, Aemilius managed to change the contents of his mouth from water and sand into air. He sputtered, spat and breathed in, hacking and coughing all the while.

Very good. Now, he thought to himself with the cold calm of someone who knows that they are dead, or about to be, *I have time to consider how broken my skull is.* The thumping, slashing headache that followed the thought squeezed tears from his eyes.

He felt the cold on his skin.

I am either dead and in the Underworld…

He opened his eyes, and stared up into the night sky, tasting the salt on his lips.

…or I am alive and on a beach somewhere.

For a good few moments he wasn't sure which option he'd prefer. Did the dead get headaches? If not, he'd probably have to seriously think about it if someone offered to kill him right now. He summoned all of his courage, searched with the palms of his hands and found wet sand. *Beach it is, then.* Pushing very carefully, he rose to a sitting position and was rewarded with a fresh wave of pain. Blinking away the stars, he willed himself to *open* his eyes and *look*.

Skies. Calm skies.

A brief flash of the panic on the boat came back to him. He wished it away. The beach stretched out in both directions, cut short by jutting rocks maybe half a mile away on either side.

On the rocks to his left he could see what was left of their boat.

Moving his head very slowly to the other side, he saw movement.

Heart thumping, he pushed himself up and ran as fast as his feet could carry him—

Which was exactly nowhere.

His legs folded like a newborn foal taking its first, tentative steps, burying his face in more sand and water.

Well, I'm dead now, he thought, and decided to stay there until the islanders came upon him and speared him where he'd fallen. Or a monster bit his head off. Or—

And then Taurio hauled him to his feet—"No time to snooze!"—and with not a single word of solace set off. Aemilius tried to rub his stinging eyes, but succeeded mostly in rubbing in more sand and brine. His vision was agonisingly slow in returning, but as he stumbled after Taurio's marching shadow, he learned more about this new place.

The beach was sandy, smooth and untouched. The sound of breaking surf suggested reefs further out, which may have been what did for the boat. On the beach, he could see shapes huddled together, dark against the moonlit sand.

Aemilius was surprised to find that even in the near-dark he could tell instantly who they were. *Four days together and I know them better than...* He didn't finish the thought, feet picking up speed as his brain made sense of the picture.

Livia, Prasta and—Quintus, perhaps?—were kneeling by a prone figure. Who was it? He felt suddenly sick, and lurched to the side. *No!* Gritting his teeth, he regained balance and hurried to see.

It was Hanno.

"Bastards," Rivkah muttered, standing slightly back from the group.

"What, uh, happened?" Aemilius stammered.

"The bastard Spaniard and his friend must have clobbered Hanno just before they dived overboard."

He had never seen anyone this angry, and instinctively took a half-step back: Rivkah looked set to disembowel those responsible, and in their absence anyone else would do.

"He's alive," she added curtly. "Just."

"But how could we all have fallen asleep?" Taurio wailed.

"Some kind of dust." Aemilius's words were followed by immense regret and more headache.

"What?" Abrax's head snapped round and he fixed him with a stone-cold stare. "Speak."

Aemilius's knees nearly gave way a second time. "I—was falling asleep, and I couldn't move, and I saw a metal ball of some sort; and then, when I woke up and they had gone, I knocked it over and some dust spilled out. And I don't remember seeing it before we set off."

A dangerous silence spread around him, like ripples in a pond. Prasta remained crouched by Hanno, but around them the members of the Hidden Legion fell in, forming a wide circle, looking out.

"We hunt," Rivkah snarled. "We are *not* prey."

"We are the Legion," Taurio added.

"We strike in the shadows and vanish like the dark."

"Abrax…" Prasta's voice was urgent.

"Is he waking up?"

"Turn around. All of you."

They did, to see that Prasta had risen from Hanno's side.

"What?" Abrax snapped.

Prasta pointed to Hanno's head, which lay nestled in a hollow in the sand. Next to it was another hollow, slightly smaller.

And another, and another.

And another, all lined up in a neat row.

Extending from the top of Hanno's head was a colossal footprint.

VII

FORMENTERA

"Giant." Abrax spat the word.

"What—*what?*" Aemilius sputtered. No-one replied.

"I told you. This is all wrong. All wrong." Quintus's voice was a low growl.

The silence that followed was tense—but nothing happened. No monster came charging at them. No demon howled, in the distance or otherwise. Above the hills the sky had softly changed colour, from a pitch-black to a fading grey.

A thought scratched and clawed at Aemilius's head and wouldn't stop.

"Why Hanno, though?" he said, wincing inwardly at just how loud and squeaky his voice sounded in the early morning stillness.

Taurio did not turn to look at him. "Because with him on board, we'd never have been wrecked." Nobody explained it further.

"Anyone care to come up with a plan?" Like the others, Livia sounded quietly furious.

"Hanno stays here," Prasta said with authority.

"I reckon even the old man can track the footsteps of this particular beast," Taurio said, grinning. "I stay with the wailing stick."

Prasta groaned.

"It is settled." The big magus stalked off, heading up the hill and leaving the others to scramble after him.

Stumbling on the beach, Aemilius could neither find his feet nor his words. "What—wait—we're—?"

"Yes," Livia said. "To all your questions. We are going off in the dark on an unknown island to hunt giants. While you were napping—"

"I wasn't *napping!*"

"—we took stock. We are armed. And whoever sent us here has made a couple of decisions for us, so it's time we started making some of our own."

Aemilius took time to think before speaking again. "Have you, uh, hunted giants before?"

Livia nodded towards Abrax. Quintus had caught up with the magus and was setting a punishing pace up the hill. "They have. A while ago."

"Ten years?" Rivkah said.

"Something like that."

Underfoot, pure sand had given way to tufts of grass. They clambered up a bank, and were standing on soft, green land.

"Not sure you could call that one a giant," Quintus said over his shoulder as they set off again. "Moecia—"

"Dacia," Abrax interrupted.

"Yes! That's right. He was in Dacia. Big guy, but not... He was just..."

"It was quick."

"And are you thinking this one might be the same?"

"No." The big magus's voice was final. "That footprint was nothing like—" He sucked in his breath and his step faltered.

"Abrax!"

A big hand, outstretched. "I'm fine," the big man said, sounding pained. "Just a… headache."

"Cave." Rivkah's warning stopped everyone in their tracks. "Up ahead, to the left."

Aemilius's heart thumped in his chest. On the hillside, no longer an indeterminate black mass but a sloping slab of dark grey in the twilight, the ground rose on both sides of a cave mouth twice the size of a barn door. *Why did it have to be a cave?* And then he tried to think of other, much better places to meet a giant, and didn't really come up with anything.

"You can *smell* it." Livia sounded like she wanted to spit.

"Could be worse. Could be the Gaul," Rivkah said. No-one replied.

Hoping against hope that the promise of dawn in the east would stop them, or at least slow them down and delay whatever horrors came next, Aemilius watched as the legionnaires wordlessly abandoned the light of the morning for the gloom of the cave. He watched as Livia moved forward, alongside Abrax. A gentle hand on the arm, a concerned look. Some whispered words.

The big magus shook his head but did not meet her eye.

Then he stepped forward, and Aemilius found himself falling in line without thinking.

The ground underfoot was hard-packed. "Footsteps," Quintus said in a low voice, holding up his hand. No-one needed to be told. Silence from now on.

Rivkah glided to the side, like a breath of wind. There was nothing in her hands—and then the glint of blades.

With every step towards the cave mouth, Aemilius's heart beat faster. There was a... *wrongness* about this, somehow. Like the hill had been ripped apart by something. A giant claw, descending from the sky and gouging a wound in the living earth.

The opening was about the width of three horse carts and the height of five grown men. A few feet in, the ground started sloping down and he found he had to mind his footing.

Quintus nudged Abrax, who flicked his wrist. A small globe of light appeared just above them, painting a flickering circle around the group. Rivkah flitted on the edge of it like a shadow, ready to disappear at the first hint of trouble. They moved slowly, cautiously, down the slope. The walls were there, just out of sight, but Aemilius could feel the oppressive weight of the rock above him. This felt less like a cave and more like a tunnel. He glanced back at the cave mouth. The sky was still there, and from here it looked positively inviting. *We can always go back.* The thought was reassuring, and he turned back to the darkness.

And looked down.

Just in time to see the soft glow of the globe glitter on a silky thread, strung across the cave at ankle-height, as it caught on Quintus's foot.

The last thing he could hear, before everything went black—again—was a soft hiss that sounded like sand in an hourglass.

Ow. Ow, ow, ow, ow, ow.

The headache felt like someone had unleashed a cat in his skull. The stabbing, throbbing pain felt almost familiar.

Before. Had this before.

The image of the metal orb on the boat rose in Aemilius's mind.

The taste in the mouth was the same.

Well, shit.

But there had been no boat, no Spaniard. Just the cave, and… a tripwire. He cursed himself for not having shouted a warning.

He realised he'd been hearing a voice, humming a simple, three-note melody over and over again.

It was like nothing Aemilius had ever heard. It bounced off the walls, like a bull trapped in a barrel. He eased his eyes open—just a crack—and almost smacked himself in the mouth trying to stifle the cries that wanted to burst out of him.

No, his brain said. *No, no, no, thank you. No.*

He could feel the bodies of the others, up against him. They had been thrown into a crude but solid wooden cage, in the middle of a vast, cathedral space. Thick, sputtering torches shed pools of orange light from flames that swayed gently, suggesting a draft.

And they were not alone.

The… thing walking around the cave was unlike anything he'd ever seen.

It was shaped like a human, and a powerful one, at that.

And it was the height of *three* humans.

And this was easy to ascertain, because in one hand it was holding two goats. They hung like ill-shapen sacks, like kittens taken by the scruff of their broken necks in its gigantic paw. In the other hand it held a torch the length and thickness of a man's leg. It was wearing human-shaped clothes—trousers and tunic—which for some reason made it even more uncomfortable to look at.

How big is that shirt? He briefly thought about how he would look in the creature's clothes, but he had to stop.

It was the *head* that sent Aemilius spinning. Apart from the broad jaw, thick lip and protruding fangs, it looked like a human head, but with no broad brow; and in place of two eyes, it had only one. Unaware that it was being observed, the creature looked... calm. And it was singing.

In Latin.

"Food, food, food." The voice was so deep that Aemilius struggled to make out the words. "Food, food, food. Master said there would be guests, and now they get some food." The giant jammed the torch into a crack in the wall about ten feet up, dropped the goats onto the floor and sat with its back to the cage. There was a sickening ripping sound, and half a goat pelt was flung over its shoulder. "Trim and cook, feel and look," the creature hummed. "Guests, guests, guests. Nice and polite, try as you might."

A movement at his shoulder made Aemilius stiffen. "Stay still," he whispered to his stirring companion. "Keep silent." He immediately held his breath, heart thundering in his chest—but the giant showed no sign of having heard them, still singing to the wall and the dead goats. Aemilius sighed with agonised relief—and the groan that followed from Abrax was thunderous. He squeezed his eyes shut, willing the sound to have never come—and listened to the silence.

The *absolute* silence.

Broken by a deep grunt, shuffling footsteps and muttering.

Then by a deafening crash, as something bashed into the cage. Aemilius's eyes opened in shock, and he found himself looking into the eye of the cyclops, crouching down a few yards away and staring at them.

"Awake!" the monster exclaimed, slapping his slab-like hands together. "You are awake! Welcome!"

Something stirred behind Aemilius, and Livia retched.

The cyclops frowned. "That's not words. Bleurgh. Talk!" The monster lurched, and a club half the size of a man rose into view.

Aemilius shrieked and turned away.

"No squealing!" the cyclops bellowed. "Hurts my ears!"

"Shut your rancid mouth, you arse-ugly, boil-faced monstrosity," Rivkah barked. "You look like a blind child ate modelling clay and took a shit."

The cyclops bellowed. "No! Rude! This is not right and good! Master said you were great warriors and that I should challenge your best one!" He pulled himself up to his full height and crossed his arms. "In the name of honour, I demand that you send forth a champion."

"Eat rotten rat and die."

The club flew, and the cage rattled. "*Quiet!*" the cyclops screamed. "You cannot just come into my cave and insult me! I was told that you were great warriors, and—"

"Who told you?" Decades of command gave Quintus's voice a whip-crack authority.

"Master," the cyclops replied huffily. "Master knows everything."

"And who is the mas—"

"*Champion! Now!*" he bellowed. The words boomed and echoed around the cave.

"And if we refuse?" Livia had dragged herself to her feet. Even after puking out what little she had left in her, she still somehow managed to look and sound like a noblewoman suffering a mild inconvenience.

The cyclops looked at her, twisting his features into a sly expression. "Then I take the stick"—he reached down and picked up a wrist-thick, wickedly sharp javelin—"and jab it through the bars a couple times."

Behind him, Aemilius heard Rivkah curse in her language.

"That's not a nice thing to say, small child," the cyclops replied. Then he growled something back at Rivkah that Aemilius did not understand, but seemed to hit a mark.

"Bastard," she muttered, furiously.

"Send me your champion," the giant demanded petulantly.

There was movement among the bodies trapped in the cage, and Aemilius was pushed to the side. "I am Quintus Aurelius, Primus Pilus of the Fourth, champion of the Hidden Legion, and when you let me out of this cage I will kick your scrawny arse back into the hole you crawled out of."

"Quintus—no," Livia whispered hoarsely. "Wait. Let's—"

Quintus muttered to her almost imperceptibly: "He has the strength to drive a spike through all five of us, and there is nothing that says he won't use it. Time is not one of our assets, Your Grace. So I am going to buy you some. Mind that you use it." He straightened up and bashed a cage bar with his fist. "Well, one-eye—are you going to let me out? Or are you *scared?*"

The cyclops laughed, an unpleasant sound, deep and raspy. "Not scared of you. On a horse, with a hundred of your friends? Maybe. But not you.

"But Zeno is not stupid. If I open the door now, you scatter like chickens and then I have to catch you all, and some of you might get to your nasty little toothy blades and Master said I wasn't to let you go. Hands out.

Now." Aemilius dared a glance back. Livia looked sick, but Abrax looked near death. The fire in Rivkah's eyes would have put a blacksmith's forge to shame. Quintus avoided their gaze, staring straight forward, profile fit to grace a coin. None of them volunteered to put their hands anywhere near the giant. "Hands out now—or I start poking. If you bleed too much it might attract the rats. They're nasty, them. Found one the size of my toe the other day. Crunched and popped in my mouth. *Arms!* Out, to the elbows!" The giant held a coil of rope that looked like a round of twine in one of his enormous hands, and the javelin in the other.

Livia was the first to move. Her arms looked slender and eminently breakable, sticking out from the cage. Slowly—tortuously—Abrax followed suit. Not knowing whether he was doing the right thing, Aemilius copied them, and was joined by Rivkah.

Zeno stepped close to them, and they all wished he hadn't. He smelled like a full tavern on a wet day, boiled animal hide mixed with dirt and sweat. Aemilius felt Abrax's convulsions next to him and tried to lean in to support the big magus, wondering what on earth he thought he was doing. *Something. I'm doing something.*

And an idea occurred to him, and it had to be pushed out quickly, before the rest of his brain caught up.

"Mighty Zeno," he said, fighting hard to keep the panic out of his voice and not listening to the screams in his head. "O King of Cyclopes—have you—" Pain exploded in his shoulders as the giant quickly wrapped a rope around his arms and pulled tight, yanking a couple of times for good measure.

"No talk," the cyclops rumbled. "Or I turn your little arm-sticks into my mid-day snack."

Aemilius clamped his teeth together so hard he thought they'd snap, squeezing his eyes shut, pushing back the scream. His arms felt like they were about to fall out of their sockets, and he only barely noticed as the door to the cage swung open. It slammed shut again, rattling his teeth, and he opened his eyes as much as he could without letting the tears out.

Quintus Aurelius was a solid figure of a man, even in his old age. He had taken good care of his body, relied on it to earn his keep his whole life, trusted it to preserve him from death on countless occasions. His legs were hardened from steering warhorses; his arms and back honed by fighting an unholy variety of creatures hell-bent on killing him; fear was no more than a faint memory. And all of his experience, and all of his calm, and all of his deadly knowledge amounted to nothing next to Zeno.

Next to Zeno, he looked like a child.

"Your champion is puny!" The cyclops's face twisted in a grotesque smile.

"Hand me my sword and we'll see."

"No, no, no. Zeno is honourable. We fight like we were made." The javelin fell to the ground with a thud and the sly grin came back. "No blades."

Breathe.

Quintus was silent for a moment. Then the old man cricked his neck. "Very well," he said quietly, calmly, rolling his shoulders. "A fair fight it is, then."

"Exactly!" Zeno sounded delighted. "Fair fight."

A swipe, and a side-step.

Aemilius felt the gust from the slab-like hands on his face.

Breathe!

Almost pulling the air in, he forced himself to breathe. Ignoring the flaming pain in his shoulders, he shouted, "Zeno!"

"Shush!" the cyclops shouted back, annoyed. "Busy! Fighting to the death. Talk later!"

Quintus was moving slowly, dipping to his right, inviting the giant to make the first move—but Zeno was not falling for it.

"Tricksy," he said approvingly. "Old."

"At least I'm not ugly."

"Oh! Zeno is a very pretty boy."

"Says who?"

"Master says I am big and strong and handsome." The cyclops beamed with pride.

"Two out of three is not bad. But your face looks like a pig shat on an eyeball."

"Rude!" Another swipe, another side-step—this time, followed by a quick step forward and a vicious elbow to the giant's forearm. "Ow! That's not very nice," the cyclops sulked. "You should stay still."

"Give me my blade and I'll do all manner of things," Quintus said, sidestepping another swipe.

"No!" Slowly, the cyclops changed stance, looking less like a boxer and more like a wrestler. Aemilius watched with horror as the massive figure crouched, spreading his arms out wide, and inched towards Quintus, forcing the old horseman back towards the wall. *Do something!*

"*Zeno!*" he shouted again.

The cyclops bellowed in fury and lurched towards the legionnaire. Quintus moved quickly, ducking under an outstretched arm—but he was not fast enough. The giant kicked out and caught the Roman's outstretched leg with a loud snap.

"*Zeno!*"

Too late. Quintus screamed in pain as the cyclops grabbed him by the knee, roared with effort and flung him, like a child's toy, into the wall. There was a horrifying crunch as the old man's body hit the stone and bounced off, landing with a single thud.

Quintus Aurelius, Primus Pilate of the Fourth and veteran of more wars and skirmishes than he could remember, lay motionless.

For exactly one heartbeat.

And then Rivkah screamed.

The sound ripped through the cavern and threatened to shred Aemilius's eardrums. She thrashed and yanked at her ropes next to him, hurling terrible threats, screaming, crying.

"*Hah!*" Zeno roared. "*Puny* horse man! *Zeno* is the winner!" He turned to the cage with a grotesque grin, coloured with rotting animal remains. "Master said Zeno could beat the champion! This was fun!" Surveying them with his one eye, the monster looked suddenly and horrifically happy. "Again! *Again!* Next champion!"

Aemilius could feel Rivkah draw breath, and much to his surprise his own reaction was not to sit back and listen to a stream of curse words and threats that would shave the scales off a cobra.

Instead, he twisted and kneed her in the gut, knocking the wind out of her.

I just did that.

Better get on with it, then.

"You are indeed mighty, Zeno!" he said, as loud as he dared, ignoring Livia staring daggers at the side of his head. Above him, the giant frowned as if wondering where the noise was coming from, and Aemilius got the very clear sense that he had not been considered a threat. *Well…* "And I think another fight would be a splendid idea!"

"Yes!" The giant lit up, like a dumb baby. "Another fight! *Who is the next—?*"

"—*but first*—" Aemilius shouted, louder than he'd ever shouted before. "But first I want to ask you for your advice!" In different—very different—circumstances, he would have had to laugh. The confusion in the hideous face was utterly earnest. "Because you are also very wise."

The giant's brain caught up. "*Yes!*" he shouted. "Master says I am very wise."

"And only a very wise being—nearly god-like, I would say—would get to wear anything as magnificent as that!" Aemilius said, dimly aware that Rivkah was breathing again and was somehow being restrained by Livia. A distant part of his mind suggested that if she weren't, she would be breaking his neck with her feet right about now.

Zeno bent down to their height, keeping clear of their tied hands. It was not quite enough to save them from the stench, and beside them Abrax moaned feebly. "You mean the Good Word?" He pulled on a crude leather strap around his neck, and from the folds of his shirt a medallion rose.

It was a thing of darkness.

Pitch-black, it almost seemed to draw in the light. It radiated menace, and on it could be discerned the faintest trace of purple lines. It was hard to judge the size of it next to the cyclops's slab hands and ox-neck, but it looked to be the width and breadth of Aemilius's hand. "Yes," he said, fighting to keep his tone jovial. "It is glorious. Tell me more! Such a precious thing."

"Master said it was all mine." Zeno beamed. "I was

the best, and I should be allowed to have this because it is very pretty. He also said it would help me."

"How so?" But he realised, with a cold terror, that he didn't need to ask. *Abrax.*

Zeno had sat by the cage, the murder of Quintus forgotten. "I don't know," he said thoughtfully. "I think Master was worried that I would burn myself? He said it protected against fire. But Zeno knows his torches." An idea occurred to him. "If you still don't want to fight, maybe I could stick a torch in? Meat smells nice when it's burning."

Again, Rivkah twitched next to him with unmistakeably murderous intent, but Aemilius caught Livia hissing something. *Time. She's giving me time.* Another thought occurred: *Or else she is happy for me to die next.*

Either way… here we go.

"I've got something to show you."

Aemilius was sure his ribs would crack with the thrashing of his heart as the cyclops's massive head sank to his level and one baleful eye stared at him.

"What?" the monster rumbled. "I took all the blades and the things."

"Not all the things. I have a surprise." *And maybe my surprise will be that he will reach out and rip my arms out of their sockets, and there won't be a single thing I can do about it.*

A slice of forever—and then Zeno's face lit up. "A surprise! For *me!*" With terrifying speed, the massive hands shot forward and deftly loosened Aemilius's ropes. "Show me!" His clapping hands slapped together like oxen colliding. "Now!" The door to the cage creaked open, and Aemilius stepped out, all too aware of the utter silence of the others.

This was now his adventure, and his alone.

I have one chance.

That was the last thought he had, before he looked up and his mind went blank.

Seeing Zeno from what now felt like the safety of the cage had been bad enough. But standing in front of a... creature who could not be much less than fifteen feet tall was something his brain wasn't prepared for. *Breathe.* Aemilius struggled to remember who he was, forced what he was pretty certain would be his last ever smile... and bowed. "I am honoured to be in your presence. Master was wise to choose you."

"Yes. Yes, yes, yes," the giant rumbled. "Now where's my surprise?"

Cold metal bashed into his chest, and Aemilius found himself idly wondering whether something as thick as a man's forearm still qualified as a javelin.

One chance.

He smiled. "It's right here!" Reaching slowly, carefully up to his neck, he unhooked the leather strap and fished out the silver spiral given to him by the Lord. Even in the feeble light of the torches, it sparkled.

"Hand it over." Zeno's voice was cold. "I know what you're planning."

The surprise in Aemilius's voice was authentic. "Do you?" *Because I don't.*

"Oh, yes. We talk about it all the time, me and my brothers. Because we just have the one beautiful eye, you squishies will try to get in good and close and then jab"—the javelin twitched, and Aemilius was driven back—"right in, good and proper. It's not very nice," the giant concluded darkly. "Not very polite."

You have a point. That would have been a good idea.

"Oh, but I would never," Aemilius said. "Couldn't reach, for one thing. The other? You'd skewer me like a piglet!" He pointed to the javelin.

Zeno looked at him, and a chuckle like rocks tumbling down a hill rattled out. "Hurr, hurr, hurr. Piglet on a skewer. Yum." A massive hand stretched out. "I think I might let you live."

"And will you, in your magnificent grace, let us out?"

The giant looked confused for a moment, then he shook his head. "No. Not them. *You*. I'll let *you* live. And you can stay here with me and listen to my stories. I have many stories. Now, show me my surprise!" An impatient twitch of the palm, another near-skewering.

Well, Aemilius thought. *It was worth a shot. But I guess we all die now.* He looped the leather cord over his head, slowly—all too conscious of the metal spike levelled at his chest—and dropped the spiral into Zeno's palm.

The cyclops rumbled appreciatively. "Pretty." He brought it slowly up towards his eye, to get a better look—and the silver luminescence bloomed, spreading from his hand. "Very pretty. Ooh! Hurr hurr—and it tickles!"

...tickles?

The javelin fell to the floor with a clang, as Zeno tried to slap the spiral out of his hand... but it was too late. Spinning and twisting, it bent and stretched—longer and higher—and up—until it touched the medallion. Like a viper, the silver thread struck, wrapping itself around the black slate, crackling where it crossed the purple lines. Zeno's face, lit up from below, was panic and fury. "Get it off! Foul, wicked magic!" He turned to Aemilius, almost pitiful. "Help me!"

But another voice—two voices—rose to drown him out. "*Abrax!*"

Livia, and Rivkah.

Aemilius spun on his heel, just in time to save his life.

The greying shell that had cowered in the cage since they awoke was gone, replaced by an angry god. Abrax stood tall, hands blazing white-hot, smoke billowing from the bars in front of him. Rivkah had twisted herself free of her ropes and was pushing herself as far from the heat as she could. Livia—was not. Face contorted in pain, she forced her hand closer and closer to the big magus's shoulder.

"Abrax—no!"

Just as she touched him, a sphere of fire the width of a man's torso exploded out of nowhere, incinerated the bars of the cage and roared through the gloom, smashing Zeno in the chest and throwing him across the cave floor. A wave of heat followed it. The fire washed over the cyclops and drowned his screams. Slowly, like a falling oak, the massive figure collapsed: first, to his knees; then onto his elbows, flames licking at him like hellhound tongues, stripping skin and cooking flesh with their touch. Slowly, ever so slowly, he crumbled to his side, and still the flames feasted on him, hungrier with every flicker.

"*Abrax!*" The scream ripped Aemilius's attention away from the horrifying spectacle, to what was happening in the cage. The big magus was transfixed in fury, staring at the corpse of the cyclops, mouth moving silently in incantations that flowed with the patterns woven by his hands.

Livia's hand landed on his shoulder.

Slowly—all too slowly—his face changed, twitched, returned to humanity.

And then the noblewoman collapsed, sending Rivkah scurrying back towards the heat. Standing frozen in place ten yards away, staring at them, Aemilius could feel his skin tighten and redden.

Abrax hollered wordlessly and staggered away from the two women, huddled at the base of the cave. The bars crumbled as he pushed through them. "Stay away!" he croaked. Then, "Livia! *Livia!*"

In a daze, Aemilius bent down. The giant's javelin weighed as much as a cart's axle, but he forgot to wonder whether he could lift it. Straining, he hefted the great spear and walked towards Zeno, prone on the ground. Even through charred flesh and blood-red blisters, there was still strength in the frame, a monstrous endurance.

Lifting, twisting and balancing, he aimed the tip of the spear at the giant's throat—and plunged it in.

A final, heavy shudder, and Zeno lay still.

He stared at the spear. The way it joined the charred flesh on a throat the size of his leg. The way the blood welled up around the shaft, steaming as it met the cold air of the cavern.

Because it has just been boiled.

Considering how far he had travelled and how little he had eaten in the three days since the feast with the Lord and Lady, Aemilius Sculla, son of Marcus Livius Sculla, descendant of the Aemilii and the focus of a mysterious prophecy, managed to throw up a spectacular amount. The contents of his stomach landed on Zeno's steaming corpse with a dull hiss, followed by a watery, yellowish bile that he forced himself to spit out, seemingly endless amounts of it, and every time he breathed in the smell hit him again, the smell of roasted meat, and he felt the saliva in his mouth and he gagged and threw up again. He pushed himself away from the spear, but his legs failed him, dropping him on his backside.

Which was when he realised that someone behind him was shouting.

"Keep your eyes open, you bastard! If you so much as *think* about closing them, I will rip your tongue out and make you eat it!"

His eyes widened. He had heard Rivkah swear—more than he had heard her talk, come to think of it—but he had never heard Livia raise her voice. And it had an immediate effect. It felt like someone had attached strings to his hips and pulled, hard. He was on his feet and heading towards her, ready to obey her every wish, before he even realised he was moving. As he stumbled, one quaking leg in front of the other, he blinked and tried to comprehend the scene before him.

There was a hole in the cage, big enough for three men to walk abreast.

Where the door had once stood there was now a pile of soot.

Abrax knelt, head bowed, looking like he'd stumbled out of the cage.

Livia crouched next to him, holding his head in her slender hands, tugging at him, speaking loudly. "Stay here!" She spoke words in a smooth, flowing language Aemilius didn't know, frowning with frustration. "Come back!" *Too much. This is too much. Too strange.* Over Livia's shoulder, Aemilius could see Rivkah lying in the far corner of the cage. He rushed to help, stumbling like a calf learning to walk as he swerved past the two bent figures. When he got back into the cage, checking reflexively that a phantom door wasn't going to slam closed on him, the girl was struggling to her feet, hissing with the effort.

"Don't," she said between gritted teeth. When Aemilius didn't back off immediately, she added, "Sore."

He blinked, staring at her.

Rivkah's hands and forearms were bright red.

Completely and utterly overwhelmed, Aemilius staggered backwards, turned—

—and saw Abrax, saw his face—

—and fainted.

"How BAD is it?" the big magus rumbled.

"Not good. Not a… disaster… but not good."

"I lost control. Quintus—" His great fists clenched at his side.

"I know." Livia laid a hand gently on Abrax's forearm. "I know. Just… I can't lose both of you at once. I need at least one grumpy old fart in my life." A tired smile was her reward.

"Wake up." Next to them, Rivkah prodded the unconscious Aemilius with a toe. "We need to get going." Mumbling incoherently, Aemilius tossed as he tried to get away from the interruption and back to sleep. "Wake *up*."

"*Ow!*" he clutched his side and sat up. "What are your toes even made of?" Then recent events came back, all at once. "Abrax!"

"I am here."

Aemilius twisted around, and wished he hadn't. "What, uh—I—uh—?"

"Eloquent as always," the magus rumbled.

It was a while before Aemilius realised that he was staring, and that they were letting him. Where there had been smooth skin before, there were now wrinkles. His cheeks had changed shape—hollowed out—and his mouth was thinner.

"Magic is force. You can control how much of it you use, to an extent. Whatever Zeno was wearing blocked my access to the force, but when you tricked him I found it again… and I did not hold back." The magus looked at the burnt corpse, and for a moment Aemilius thought he was going to unleash another wave of deadly heat.

"It cost him years of his life," Livia added reproachfully.

"Sorry I fainted."

"You weren't to know. Now, let's get out of here. Do you have any last words?" Rivkah nodded over to the far wall.

Quintus.

Aemilius's heart sank. There had been too much happening at once. The body of the old soldier lay still— too still—where Zeno had thrown him. *No. Don't want to. Don't want to.*

But I am going to.

He forced himself to walk, to take step after step, towards the body of the old man. Forced himself to take it all in. The stillness. The smell. Sweat, blood and shit. The impact had snapped the horseman's neck and almost knocked the top off his skull. His hair was matted with blood, and his eyes were frozen, staring into the distance. Aemilius thought back to the voice, the half-murmured instructions, the relief as he had learned to ride a horse.

"Quintus Aurelius," he whispered. "Please forgive me."

NOTHING HAD EVER smelled sweeter than the air outside Zeno's cave. The sun was halfway to its zenith, and the sea sparkled like a basket of sapphires. It had been hard to watch the grimace on Abrax's face as he unleashed a spark that flickered towards Quintus, latched onto the old soldier's body and started turning it to ash.

No such kindness had been extended to Zeno. The rats would feast on his remains.

Aemilius pretended to find the device he knew full well they'd tripped over on the way into the mountain. Abrax looked at it and scowled, but offered no thoughts. Now they walked in silence down the hill they'd snuck up the night before—it could have been weeks ago. Rivkah moved gingerly, refusing all help. Livia watched Abrax, wincing at his every step—and Aemilius followed, fighting to stay afloat in a sea of emotions.

The smell of Zeno's burned corpse sat in his nose.

The sight of Quintus, lifeless at the base of the wall, played upon his mind.

The searing heat of the fireball—

"There." Rivkah pointed. Down at the foot of the hill, the familiar figure of Prasta, waving.

"They're alive." Livia's voice was close to breaking.

A surge of relief was followed by a wave of shame. *But we are not. Not all of us.* Aemilius bit down, hard. To keep the tears out of his eyes, he stared at the angular shape of Prasta.

He saw the moment when she realised that there were only four of them.

Saw her approach slow, then stop.

Saw her shoulders drop, her head bowed.

Aemilius bit down harder still, feeling his teeth creak.

"Where are the others?" Livia called, as soon as they were within range.

"Beach. We got the boat."

"Hanno?"

"Awake. Sore." Her face fell, momentarily, as she saw

Abrax. Then, her eyes fell on Rivkah. Without a word, she strode to the girl and snaked an arm around her shoulder, taking the weight.

They continued picking their way down the hill.

Some legion we are, Aemilius thought. *Limping and wheezing.*

Before long the grass thinned out, turned to scattered tufts, and then they were on the beach. When they saw Taurio, he waved to them, then went still, arm falling to his side.

The sand made every step feel heavy, like it was mocking him. His face felt flushed, and he kept his head bowed, looking down, praying that no-one would ask him how he felt.

They came to where the small magus sat, looking a bit the worse for wear, a grapefruit-sized bump on his temple.

"The water flows," he said solemnly. "And our friend, he flows with it."

"He does."

Hanno looked up at the big magus. A brief silence, then—"I trust that whoever sent him to the great sea suffered, and horribly."

"He did."

On his skin Aemilius felt again the scorching heat of the fireball, and smelled Zeno's fate.

There was a moment of silence.

"Somewhere, someone planned this." Livia's voice was perfectly calm, perfectly rational and utterly terrifying.

Abrax nodded. "Someone is hunting us. Hunting us and testing us."

"Great!" Taurio said. "Cracking skulls was starting to feel a little boring. This I am going to really *enjoy*." He extended a hand to Hanno and helped him up gently. "Shall we take the boat?"

"The waves are making beautiful music," the small man nodded. "It is time to go join their song."

As one, the Hidden Legion moved towards the boat that Taurio and Prasta had dragged ashore, and only Aemilius seemed to notice or worry about the fact that there was a gaping, child-sized hole in the middle of it.

VIII

THE SEA

DEATH HAD COME yet again to Aemilius, and it stared him in the face, and for some reason he couldn't fathom, that was all it did. He stared back and searched for words that took a long time to come, and when they came they did not feel anywhere near serious enough for the occasion.

"Why…" he began. A while later he continued. "Are we not, uh…" His brain eventually allowed him to finish the sentence. "…sinking?" Nobody paid him much mind. Abrax stood in the prow, unmoveable, like the boat had grown out of the roots of the tree he'd been carved from. Livia sat by his side, grim-faced. Taurio sat at the stern, manning the tiller. Rivkah sat next to him, sharpening a knife. Prasta sat on Taurio's other side, beady eyes trained on the answer to Aemilius's question.

Hanno the Wise sat, calm and serene, with his back to the mast, smiling dreamily.

"We are not sinking because we do not want to sink," he intoned.

"I don't know if anyone who sank ever *wanted* to sink." Aemilius could hear the hysteria creeping in at the edge of his voice. This was magic—but it wasn't the kind that came suddenly, exploded and then disappeared. The water, infinite and deep and cruel, was there and it wouldn't leave, and for some reason it was not flooding through the hole in the boat, the hole big enough for him to jump into, and he couldn't take his eyes off it.

"You are, of course, correct," Hanno said, nodding slowly. "But few of them thought to ask the water."

The young Roman's shoulders slumped. "Yes. Of course. Please, water, can you not drown me?"

Hanno smiled. "That is indeed the way. You have to ask it nicely."

All of a sudden there was a *plop* and a fist-sized burst of sea water popped up through the hole. Aemilius squealed instinctively.

"The water likes you," Hanno said, smirking. "It likes the noises you make."

Heart thumping, Aemilius bit back his first three replies. Looking around, he could see the odd twitchy smile and twinkling eye. *I am so glad I amuse you*, he thought bitterly—and then guilt washed over him again, and he fell quiet.

It seemed like none of them had figured it out. None of them seemed to realise that Quintus's death was all his fault. They could throw him overboard at a moment's notice—and maybe they should.

"That's why they smacked the frog on the head." Rivkah had looked up from her knives. "They must have known that there was no way we'd have been wrecked if he was awake."

"Correct." There was an edge to Hanno's voice, as if being part of a shipwreck was a personal insult.

"Makes you wonder what else they know about us." Taurio looked completely at home helming the skiff, but his expression was a mix of anger and worry.

"We have to get to land and get a message to her," Abrax said without looking back. "Anything else will wait."

"Not for long, baldy."

"He will not be forgotten." Livia stared ahead, still and unmoving.

"Oh, don't you give me that high-class unflappable Roman elite horseshit, Your *Majesty*. He was our friend. What are you going to do? Commission a monument? Use some of your allowance to pay for some *extra* nice mourners?" Rivkah spat something in Hebrew.

Livia turned, slowly, controlled. "If you don't shut your little whore mouth right now, I will happily slice you three new ones."

"Oh, will you."

"Yes."

Rivkah was on her feet. "Please. *Please.* Go on. Stand up, you shrivelled old harpy. Show me how exactly you're going to do that."

Livia rose, just like a noblewoman from a comfortable chair. A knife had appeared in her hand from out of nowhere. There was no tension in her, no aggression— just the look of... Aemilius searched for the words.

A butcher.

Someone who had held a knife all day, every day, for a long time.

There was no anger in the noblewoman's frame. Where Rivkah was fire, Livia was ice.

And, Aemilius calculated, they were going to have a knife-fight just about exactly where he was sitting.

"Uhm... maybe... we could... talk?" With his eyes he pleaded for Taurio to step in, but the big Gaul looked very much like someone who had survived to his advanced age by knowing exactly when not to come between angry women with knives. "Abrax?" But the big magus seemed utterly unmoved by the brewing duel. "Anyone?"

"Shut up," Rivkah snapped. "Or you're next. I'm just going to slice up this old—Hanno!" Rivkah kicked furiously at the water lapping at her feet. "We're sinking!"

All eyes turned to the little man at the mast. The water had risen to his knees, soaking him, but he seemed not to notice. His eyes were closed, and tears streamed down his face. "The sea shares your pain, daughter of Abraham," he said gently. "It cries for you."

"If you don't fix this, you'll be sharing some pain as well," Rivkah growled, advancing on the African.

"Stand back, bitch," Livia snapped, moving to within swiping range from the other side.

Breathe.

Looking around in a panic, Aemilius could not see land anywhere. He was stuck on a sinking boat with murderous maniacs, and he was going to die.

Again.

He stood and raised his hands, exposing his stomach and chest. "Stab me."

Rivkah shot him a look that would have stopped five brawlers in their tracks. "Told you to sit down, you little—"

"*Me*. Stab *me*," Aemilius shouted. "Quintus's death is *my* fault, and if I wasn't here he would be, and therefore if anyone should die on this boat it should be me." He stared Rivkah straight in the eyes. "Go on. Stab me," he commanded. He could feel the tears flowing, but he didn't care. "Come on, then!" His mind spun and flailed, and he could taste the blood bubbling up from his punctured lungs. "*Stab me!* It's what you do, isn't it? Slice me! Carve me up!"

And for the first time since he had had the misfortune of meeting her, he saw Rivkah falter. "I, uh—"

He turned to Livia. "Fine. You, then, secret-keeper. Kill me."

Livia didn't shy away from his gaze. "I will not," she said.

Fully mad, Aemilius turned away from them, and looked towards the eternal horizon. "If none of you will do it—" Stepping quickly, he placed one foot on the gunwale and made to leap off the boat, to sink into the cold embrace of the sea—

And the boat *bucked* under him, shifted and caught him as he fell, scooping him up and depositing him back onto the thwart he'd been sitting on.

Few minds, however lost, will not be cured by a sharp whack on the backside, and Aemilius was no exception. The words that had filled his mind were immediately shunted away by the pain.

When he realised that he had failed to jump off the boat, his mind caught up to a few other things as well.

The water that had flooded the boat seemed to somehow be disappearing back down the hole.

Nobody was dead.

And everybody was staring at him.

After what seemed like an eternity, Livia spoke. "Tell us. Why do you think Quintus's death is your fault?"

"I, uh, saw the tripwire. Just a moment before it caught. But I was too slow to warn you. And then I thought I could maybe distract Zeno with the spiral, but I couldn't get him to listen. If I'd just been louder, or quicker—" Too scared to look at anything but his feet he winced, realising what he had just said. Now it would come, surely. If they knew that he'd had the idea before the fight, how could they do otherwise? Quintus's death was his fault. He might as well have held a knife, a knife like the one that was sure to open up the soft skin of his neck and slice open his arteries—

They're taking their time about it.

Aemilius realised slowly that he was not, in actual fact, being executed.

He dared to look up—and something had changed.

For one, Rivkah and Livia were no longer armed. They stood within arm's length of each other with no hint of their former violence. From the back, Taurio calmly regarded them all. Prasta was busy rooting in a sack—and even Abrax had seated himself.

"Here. Eat this." The Celt's bony hand shot out, holding something fist-sized and yellow.

Aemilius accepted hesitantly. "What is it?"

"An apple?" Prasta looked a little confused. "You've seen them, right?"

He crunched down and sweetness spread in his mouth. Around him, the faces of the Legion had changed. Gone were the hard mouths, tight eyes and rock-set jaws. Instead, there were six kinds of sadness. There was the same silence, but different. There was no tension, no threat. It was not a companionable silence, or a tired one. It was the silence of loss.

He watched as Prasta glanced at the space that should have been occupied by an old, grumpy horseman, and he saw the pain in her face.

He saw Rivkah shut down something inside herself, something that housed a lot of hurt.

He saw the momentary softness in Abrax's eyes, as he remembered.

Taurio spoke. "It's hard to find the right words. We've done this before—a lot—and still, those two probably would have carved each other to ribbons if you hadn't lost your mind."

"But think about it," Livia continued. "We were there with you. If we'd thought for a *moment* that you had done anything on purpose to bring about the death of Quintus Aurelius—"

"—do you think we'd have let you come on the boat?" Rivkah intruded, eyebrows crawling upwards. "Do you think we'd have let you *live?*" A smile broke through like a ray of sun through the clouds. "Well, actually. I would have."

"Long enough to watch as we removed the muscles from your legs, one by one," Livia said, matching Rivkah's grin and receiving a nod of approval from the younger woman.

"Yes. And I will absolutely tell you that Prasta would have kept you alive way longer than you'd think possible, while you went through suffering more exquisite than any of the Lord's and Lady's courses," Taurio added proudly.

Abrax leaned forward. "Don't listen to them," he said gently. "I mean to say—they are honest to a fault, and they would absolutely have done what they say. But don't listen to them."

Aemilius found himself drawn in, entranced by the open face.

"What you need to do," the magus continued, "is forgive yourself."

"W—what?"

"Baldy's right," Rivkah said. "You did everything you could, and your stupid spiral did help us out of a tight spot."

"The very tightest," Livia agreed.

"We all loved the old bastard, even though he smelled of horse crotch—"

"Have you sniffed a lot of horse crotches?" Taurio grinned.

"Don't need to. Camping with you is roughly the same," Rivkah shot back. "But the point is—we were set up, and led into a trap. We were *meant* to die."

"And that we didn't, is largely thanks to you." Livia caught his eye, and Aemilius found his chest swelling.

"I—uh—" Emotions thrashed and rolled within him like fish in a net. "Uhm."

"That's what studying Virgil gets you," Prasta said. "True poetry."

"Leave him alone, twiglet. Virgil is one of the good ones."

"Oh, so you wouldn't smack him too hard on the head like all the other Romans?"

"Didn't say that," Taurio replied. "However, because I *didn't* get to him to smack 'im on the head, he did write some decent poetry."

Relief washed through Aemilius. *Not getting stabbed and thrown overboard will do that to you.* He decided to be brave. "Can I ask a question?"

"You can," Abrax rumbled, back at his place at the prow.

"Where are we headed?"

"Shore," Livia said. "We need to summon Felix."

"S-s-summon?"

"Yep. It's not easy," Taurio said, voice heavy. "The biggest problem is the virgin sacrifice. Prasta—have you ever sown a Roman boy's balls back on?"

"Yes," Prasta said thoughtfully. "He screamed a lot, though. 'No, no, it hurts, why the forehead, they keep slapping me in the eyes…'"

"Look at his face!" Rivkah squealed, snort-laughing. "Calm down, O noble Roman conqueror. We're not going to chop your balls off."

"Not today," Livia added sweetly.

"Aw," Hanno said, without opening his eyes. "You promised."

To general laughter, Aemilius relaxed back into his seat. Birds cawed overhead, and the wind snapped in the sails. He was alive, and while he wasn't quite ready to take on board what Livia had said, some of the waves inside his chest had calmed down somewhat.

Summon a ghost.

He shrugged.

Why not?

ONE LAST PUSH and the boat slid effortlessly onto the soft sands, landing perfectly and wedging itself down. He knew it couldn't be true, but it almost seemed like the wave that bore them in waved goodbye as it returned. Aemilius looked at Hanno, who exhaled, eyes still closed.

"Goodbye for now," the short man whispered.

Around him, the Legion was already moving. Prasta had scooped up two sacks full of whatever they'd managed to salvage after the shipwreck. Rivkah was on dry land, assessing their environment. The sun had disappeared behind the horizon a while ago as land rose before them, but the night had not yet stretched out overhead. He looked back from where they came, and the enormity of the sea made him shudder. It was so impossibly big. Suddenly Aemilius felt crushingly small, insignificant and pointless. He thought back on Zeno, how he'd towered over them and flung Quintus to his death like a child with a puppet.

What was the point of it all? Why should they even—?

"It is beautiful, like a knife."

Aemilius did a small jump and stifled a yelp. The water-magus was all of a sudden very close to him, staring contemplatively out to sea.

"And big, like an angry mother. But you mustn't fear it," he added, laying a gentle hand on Aemilius's arm. "The sea is life. It will only swallow you if you let it."

The silence that followed seemed to fill the beach and the sea, and was only interrupted by the sound of air bursting into flame, immediately followed by Rivkah's gentle voice.

"Right, you two snail-arses. If you stay sitting there for another blink I'll tell the old man to burn the boat for warmth with you in it."

"Old man?" Abrax said, incredulous.

"Face facts," Rivkah said. "Now Quintus has gone and got his head smashed in, and you've spent however many years of your life grilling that cyclops, you are now the old man of the group."

"Oh, no," Abrax said. "I am not willing to accept that. I am not old."

"Tell your face," Rivkah said gleefully.

"Leave him alone," Livia said scornfully. A heartbeat's pause, then, "The youth of today just don't know how to respect their elders."

Out of sight somewhere, Prasta and Taurio hooted with laughter.

"You are hilarious, all of you," Abrax grumbled. "I'll try to remember that when you need your lives saving, if I can in my dotage."

Aemilius turned towards the sound of sizzling sand, and watched with fascination as a dancing flame moved over the ground like a trained dog at the command of the fire-magus. Before his eyes, the dark line that followed the flame turned into a circle, lines twining and twisting, expanding outwards then turning in on itself, jumping and skipping—and then, just as quickly as it appeared, it had disappeared with a pop.

"That should do it," Taurio nodded.

Looking at the complex pattern on the ground, Aemilius found his mouth had gone dry. There was something... uncomfortable about it. Like this was a thing he wasn't supposed to see. Something nobody should know about. This sense of unease was a pressure in his chest, and the Legion wasn't helping. There was something unnerving in how *relaxed* they all were. *This is magic!* He wanted to scream at them. Five days ago he hadn't known that this world existed—and now he was amongst them, walking in a children's tale of giants and hydras and harpies and monsters and—

And a summoning symbol on a beach in twilight that suddenly thrummed with energy. A faint, corpse-green light crept in from nowhere and snaked around the black lines.

He felt something in his chest pull tighter, squeezing in, and a memory came to him of his cousins wrestling with him, pushing him to the ground and sitting on him until he couldn't breathe, and he almost smiled and almost cried and he could taste the lightning in the air and—

Zzzzsh—

Felix Scipio, Centurion of the Third Legion, was drawn to them out of thin air. He looked around with a scowl. "*What*," he snapped, "do *you* want?"

"We were led into a trap," Abrax growled back. "Quintus is dead. And someone knows a lot about us."

"Inconceivable. I gave you the message myself. Straight from her."

Already almost overwhelmed, Aemilius managed to notice that Livia had somehow appeared close enough to Rivkah to catch her as she erupted.

"He's *dead!* Did you not hear us, you scorpion's arsehole?" She made to charge the ghost, but was held back surprisingly effortlessly by the older woman.

"Keep your bitch on a leash," Felix said. "If Quintus Aurelius is indeed dead, I am sure his ancestors will welcome him. He was a noble Roman." He seemed to notice the fury and confusion in Rivkah's face. "Misguided and stupid for spending his time with you, obviously—but he made the best of it."

"That is probably the closest you'll get to saying the right thing," Abrax said. "The fact remains that we were set up, trapped and shipwrecked on an island with a cyclops, trapped again and robbed of the means to a fair fight. We were all meant to die."

"And yet you didn't."

"When I die," Taurio said. "I wish to die with a ghost club, and I will hunt you down, you absolute goatfucker, and I will smash your ghost skull to pieces over and over again."

Felix smirked. "I am *petrified*. Much like your ancestors."

Taurio's growl turned the smirk into a grin.

"Please forgive me. I forget that barbarians get angry at logic and humour."

"There is no *time* for this, Felix!" Abrax snapped. "Who is hunting us? Why? Is this happening in other places as well? We need *answers*."

"You people and your pathetic life spans. Quintus is lucky to be rid of you. I think you'd all be happier if—"

Somehow, Abrax seemed to grow taller. He snarled a phrase in a language that brought with it shadows of ancient stone temples, a stinging wind and the rays of a deadly sun.

"All right, all right. I'll go! But I would like it noted that I do not appreciate—"

Abrax shouted three words, clapped his hands and Felix disappeared with a loud bang.

"And yer ma as well!" Prasta shouted after him.

Livia was already half-way to Abrax. "Breathe," she said, soothing. "Breathe. Remember. Breathe."

In the cooling night air, there was a shimmer of heat around the fire-magus. "Bastard," he snarled.

"In my village we'd set that man to punching his own face repeatedly to save us the work," Taurio said.

"Are we sure it was a barbarian who stove in his head?" Aemilius added. "Seems to me a centurion like that would be quite at risk from his own men."

This raised a chuckle from the group.

"He is an absolute arse," Prasta added. "But sadly, we need him."

"We need him to do a job," Abrax said. "And if he doesn't do it, we need to... help him."

I hope Abrax never helps me, Aemilius thought. "What happens now, then?"

"Now," Abrax held the silence for a moment. "We wait."

RIVKAH AND TAURIO found them a campsite quickly, and the Legion settled down for the night. There was a quick conversation that involved some pointing, but Aemilius didn't catch what it was about. Prasta issued a quick inventory of their possessions, revealed that while the four of them had been trapped in the cave, she'd found a sack with their belongings that the sailors seemed to have thrown overboard in haste.

"Weak," Taurio muttered. "Weak and stupid."

"Or confident," Abrax said.

"Still. Waste of a good sack."

"And you'd know, Gaul, carrying a sack on your front at all times."

"Quiet, twiglet. You wouldn't know a healthy man if you saw one."

"Considering I'm travelling with a hog, a frog, a runt and an ageing torch, you're not wrong."

The inventory done, they found themselves partially armed but low on anything else. Aemilius noted that they seemed almost entirely unworried about this. Prasta disappeared into the gloom and emerged very soon after with two rabbits, which Taurio skinned with a borrowed knife and threw to Abrax. Moments later, the sound of sizzling meat sent Aemilius's heart leaping and his mouth watering.

"No food like camp food," Rivkah said, smirking as she hacked off a slice of half-burned, half-raw rabbit.

One by one they fell silent as they nibbled and gnawed on roasted meat.

"I miss him."

"We all do, Princess."

"Remember that time in Lavici?"

"Ooh!" Taurio practically bubbled with glee. "The bet!"

"Funniest shit I ever saw." In the flickering light of a small fire-orb, Rivkah's eyes sparkled. "Tell the runt."

Not a runt, Aemilius sniffed inwardly.

"So we were called to investigate a wolf-thing—size of a horse, human head, fangs, that kind of thing—"

"All bullshit, of course."

"That's Etruscans for you. Always exaggerating. But anyway—we happen upon this troop of thugs. All horsed, ten—"

"Eight."

"Fine. Eight of them. Well-armed, well-trained young thugs. Supposed to be Fifth Legion, but Quintus was having none of it."

"They asked us where we were going. He took the lead and did *not* show them the respect they felt they deserved," Taurio added with delight.

"The leader—cocky young thing he was, too, all chest-puffed and feather-ruffled—told him to shut up," Prasta said.

"Spotted that he was carrying a military-issue sword but as he was clearly not in a legion anymore, he should surrender it," Rivkah added.

Aemilius drew an involuntary breath.

"And"—Abrax paused for effect—"he called him an old man."

"Oooh."

"Which, to be fair, he was," Livia replied. "But like many before them, they did not know the simplest of rules."

There was a silence, and Aemilius sensed that they were all looking at him. "Which is?"

"Beware an old man in a young man's game," Taurio said, voice thick with mischief.

"So Quintus said—"

"'Make a soldier happy.'" Rivkah's gravelly impression was spot on. "'Sorry. *Former* soldier. Show me how good a rider you are.'"

"'I'll throw down my sword.'" Livia mimed the motion. "'Can you pick it up without slowing down?'"

"And he throws his gladius to the ground, like that—*thwack*," Rivkah said, grinning, "and it stands up in the dirt."

"And just like the first drop of rain on a still and peaceful lake, the challenge spreads." Hanno was a shadow in the dark, a pair of eyes in the gloom. "This young man's friends are now goading him. Challenged by a has-been! What excellent fun."

"It bears mentioning that it's so far away from him that you could have ridden four horses through the gap." Abrax smirks. "There is no way any one of us could get to it. Obviously."

"The boy doesn't back down. Of course he doesn't. Stupid Romans never do, deserters or not. Yanks the reins, charges off and turns his horse on a coin."

"Impressive turn, too."

"Absolutely. With fire in his eyes and the hooting and hollering of all his friends ringing in his ears, and he spurs the horse—and charges." Taurio glanced over at the slim Celtic woman lounging next to him. "Twiglet?"

Prasta smiled the lazy smile of a fond recollection. "As the rider starts off, our old man shoots me this... look.

And because at that point we'd been riding together for years, I know what he wants."

"And we watch the leader of this band of thugs, posing as legionnaires, thundering towards us." Abrax smiled as well.

"Somewhere within him he might have wondered why none of us seemed even slightly worried about this," Rivkah added.

"And at the very moment the cocky little bastard's gaze drops from us to the sword, as he leans over in the saddle with *perfect* control, Quintus's eyebrow rises, ever so gently. And I throw him my staff, and Furibunda just *hops* sideways—still don't know how the hell he made her do that—and he swings it—*beautifully*—"

"The sound." Taurio sighed with the memory of it. "The pure, beautiful *crunch* of that boy's kneecap smashing into bits."

"I liked the scream." Rivkah smiled.

"And because I've had to deal with shitheads like that my whole life, I liked when he fell off his horse, and the nasty landing."

"The moment he connected, Quintus was standing in the saddle," Livia continued. "He jumped, and then he was on the ground, kneeling next to the screaming boy's head. In his time he must have been a marvel to watch."

"Still was, up until the end." There was no questioning the respect and love in Rivkah's voice.

"I swear," Prasta added, "Furibunda squared up to the other seven horses and stared them down."

"The other noble deserters were paralysed," Livia said. "They hadn't imagined that a rag-tag band of travellers would even hesitate to hand over their goods."

"They did *not* know who they were picking on." Taurio smiled. Around the campfire, there were nods and smirks.

And then, no-one spoke.

Aemilius looked around at them, but they all seemed gently lost in their own thoughts. "And then what? What happened?" he blurted out.

Livia looked at him as if she'd just remembered that he was there. "Oh, we killed them all."

"He picked up his gladius and ran it through the little shit's throat," Rivkah said. "Didn't hesitate. I don't think he ever thought about it. Like squashing a bug."

"He was as cold as anything, when he wanted to be."

"They trained them right, in the old days," Livia said. "I think the thing that tipped him over the edge that day was that those boys were pretending to be legionnaires."

"Pretty much the one Roman I never thought to knock some sense into." In the darkness, Taurio sniffed once and cleared his throat.

"And then there was the time—"

"Sssh." Abrax's raised hand stopped Livia in her tracks. They all rose to their feet. Even Aemilius could feel it—the thickening of the air. He looked at his forearm, touched the raised bumps of skin, the hair standing up on end.

This time it didn't surprise him. He saw it happen—the shimmering dot in the air that stretched and elongated into a line, the line that warped to form a crack, and the way one part of reality gently separated from the other as their world ripped apart and Felix stepped out of the gap. He was still green and Aemilius could still see through him, and his head hurt when he tried to look through the gap in the world and see where Felix had come from, but something about the sight was less uncomfortable this time around. *I am getting used to this.*

"She sends her sorrow." The centurion seemed somewhat less than his haughty self, and out of the corner of his eye Aemilius thought he saw Prasta and Taurio share a glance. He still looked down on them, but from a somewhat lesser height. "And I, in turn, offer my condolences." Behind him, the rift into the underworld faded out of sight.

Abrax offered no pleasantries. "What did she say?"

"She took the matter seriously," Felix said curtly. "Didn't like it one bit. She seems to"—the word seemed unfamiliar and distasteful to him—"*care* for you."

"More than a ghoulish messenger boy, at any rate."

"Shut it, street rat," Felix snapped, but there was significantly less imperious conviction in his voice. "She says that you must recover."

"So we're going back?"

"I am afraid not, Livia Augusta." Felix bowed his head. "You are going to Hispalis."

There was a moment of silence.

"…Why?" Rivkah snapped.

"I know you dislike civilisation, scorpion-sucker," Felix said with glee, "but your elders have to do some work. The concept might be unfamiliar to you."

"Can I stab him?"

"Won't work," Taurio said sadly.

"I wanna try. I'd start with—"

"Hispalis," Felix interrupted.

"Why?" Abrax snapped.

"I don't know," Felix snapped back. "After all, I am just a ghoulish messenger boy. They will send a replacement for Quintus. Look for the Red Woman." A familiar, shimmering shape formed behind him, granting him passage back to the underworld. He took one last look at the legionnaires. "And be careful. Flaxus looked terrified."

"He always looks terrified!" Taurio protested.

Felix fixed him with a glance. "Be careful, Gaul. It's cold down here."

And with that he disappeared.

The silence was palpable.

"I hate him so much," Rivkah muttered.

"My only solace is that it sounds like she properly ripped into him," Prasta offered.

"I agree." Abrax's voice was heavy. "And that worries me."

"He was winding us up!"

"I smelled no lies on him." Hanno ignored Rivkah's scoffing.

"I don't like this," Taurio muttered. "I don't like this one bit."

And none of them mentioned the one thing Aemilius wanted to know. "What did he mean by a 'replacement'?"

"There should be eight," Livia said, wearily. "That's a conturbium. We were sent to fetch you. You were our eighth man. Quintus is gone, which means there are now seven. So they will send a replacement."

"What—someone *else?*"

"He's just so sharp," Rivkah said, busying herself with her bedroll. "A real thinker."

Around him, the legionnaires went to bed, and the question went unanswered.

Someone else?

A replacement?

It took Aemilius a long time to fall asleep.

* * *

A HEAVY HAND on his shoulder woke him way too soon.

"Whu…?" he mumbled.

"Rise and shine, son of the Empire," Taurio rumbled.

Aemilius blinked, squinted and realised very slowly that he couldn't actually see the Gaul. "Sorry—but—it's not morning. Is it?" he added belatedly.

"Please. Can I slice him open? I'll make it neat," Rivkah muttered somewhere else in the darkness.

Over in the east he could just about make out a patch of sky that might be slightly less black, but Aemilius found that he did not need an answer to his question. It was definitely not far past midnight. "Uh, what are we doing? Why are we awake?"

"Got one job to do before we set off," Taurio said.

He couldn't see the big Gaul's face in the darkness, but something about the tone of his voice made Aemilius squash the follow-up questions before they escaped. *Now is a good time to follow quietly*, a sensible part of his brain whispered.

IT TOOK A while before his eyes got accustomed to the dark, but eventually he managed to make out Taurio's broad shoulders, Abrax's tall silhouette and Prasta's hair. Rivkah, Livia and Hanno must be somewhere, but they were a lot harder to spot. No-one spoke, but there was a clear sense of direction to their travel. This was not some leisurely scouting mission—it was a march. He contented himself with putting one foot in front of the other and allowing his thoughts to drift.

Quintus's last moments played on his mind.

The way the old man's strong, solid body had flown through the air, flung by the giant's colossal hand. The way it had lain still.

How quickly it had cooled.

In the darkness, Aemilius cried hot tears as the shock of it overwhelmed him like the sea, wave after wave of it, flooding his soul. He saw his own life in Quintus's, he saw his father and his father's father before him, and he saw that death came to them all. The picture bled into another, and he tasted again the salty fear in his mouth when the hydra had burst out of the cave, all writhing necks and snapping jaws. The thunder in his chest as he'd run into danger to fetch Rivkah out. A small snort escaped him at the ridiculous idea that he'd ever be able to save Rivkah from anything, and he found himself smiling through the tears.

What *was* this?

Was he a prisoner? Or had they realised that he'd secretly wanted to escape the villa and the shadow of his father? Was he any safer with this lot than he would be on his own? Would they—?

The elbow in the ribs took him by surprise.

"Stop, you arse," Rivkah hissed. "We've told you three times. We're here."

Working hard not to wince, Aemilius belatedly remembered that no-one could see his face in the dark. "And where is…? Ah."

He heard the gentle lapping of waves on sand.

He saw the familiar curve of the hills, sloping down to the beach, a black shape in the darkness.

And in the distance he saw the fishing huts.

They were back at the village.

A shove in the small of his back, and he noticed the legionnaires had gathered around him in a tight formation, moving forward.

"IT IS A simple question," Taurio said amicably, in passable Hispanian. "You tell us, and we do not kill your entire family."

The man on the ground coughed. His mouth moved, but no words came. In the flickering light from the fire orb, his face was a picture of terror.

"Your knee," Prasta noted.

"Ah. Sorry. She does keep me right." The big Gaul shifted so only most of his weight was resting on the man's sternum. "Let's try again. Donato. Medium height, dark features. Had an eight-seater with a single sail. Where is he?"

The man was crying now, eyeing the club in Taurio's free hand. "I don't know," he wheezed. "I don't know..."

"He says he doesn't know."

"He does at that, bard," said Taurio mildly. "Should we torture him?"

"We could," Prasta said calmly, kneeling and gently but firmly grasping the man's chin. Turning his head to face her, she looked him straight in the eyes. "I once kept a man alive for seven days. He wept blood for five of them."

"And that's without her playing the whistle," Taurio added. "Let's try one more time. Do you remember seeing three men that you didn't know?"

"Yes! Yes," the man blurted out. "Strangers. Came half a day before you showed up. Brought a boat, but didn't make any move for our fish."

Aemilius wondered what it might have been like to be dragged out of bed sleeping, through a very fresh, smouldering hole in the wall of your fishing hut, then pinned to the ground and surrounded by a shadowy group of killers lit by the work of a fire magus. He thought for the first time since before he met the Hidden Legion that maybe his fate could have been worse. *At least they were* rescuing *me*.

"Talk," Rivkah appeared at the man's other side, looking like a demon in the light. "Did they come back? Where did they go?"

"Spit it out." Livia sounded calm, but there was a warning in her voice.

The man's eyes darted between the numerous and equally credible threats. "H-H-Hispalis," he stuttered. "Heard them talking. Drop-off, then Hispalis."

"Thank you, friend," Taurio said. Standing with a grunt, he reached down and easily jerked the man up to a standing position. "Now stay still while we talk to your friends." For emphasis, he wrapped a beefy arm around the man's shoulders. Aemilius was uncomfortably reminded how fragile a human neck is.

Approaching them cautiously, torchlight glinting on nicked and worn knives, stakes and hand-axes, was a group of maybe thirty people—fishermen and their wives, young and old, all looking wary but ready for whatever might happen. *Death has come to them,* Aemilius realised, *And it is us.*

As often before, his feet moved before the rest of him caught up.

He stepped into the gap between the two groups, hands outstretched. "We were ambushed by a man that said he was from this village," he said in desperate Hispanian.

"We know now that they were strangers, and just like they did, we will disappear once we've got what we came for."

"And what is that, runt?" snapped the foremost of the fishermen, a square-built specimen of a man who Aemilius estimated would rip him to unrecognisable shreds in two blinks of an eye.

"Information, which we have, and horses and a cart, which we left here." *It would be really handy if the horses could just show up and we didn't need to go through you to get them.* But sadly, the leader of the locals had done some thinking of his own.

The fisherman grinned. "There's thirty of us. There are"—he eyed Aemilius and smirked—"seven of you. I don't care how handy your friends are, *boy.* You're not walking out of here alive." Somewhere in the distance, loud enough to be heard, there was a crash, like someone had gone mad with a sledgehammer on some wood. Behind the leader, glances were exchanged, but no-one moved.

And here we are.

A memory came to him then. His uncle's deep voice, gently murmuring instructions in his ear as he played his father at latrones, the white pieces moving seemingly at random until a suggestion, a plan...

He smiled as lazily as he could.

"I hoped we could avoid this," he sighed, working to sound as bored as possible. "But there are *six* of *them.* I'm not actually part of this unit. I've just been sent to do a write-up on them."

"A what?" The fisherman spat.

"A write-up." Remembering his history lessons, he brought forward the most dismissive look he could muster, meant to communicate that he was clearly talking to an idiot. *Feels good to be on the right side of that one, for a change.* "A list of their various crimes, misdemeanours and horrors. They are, to a man, excessively cruel. The big one likes to bite the heads off live animals. There have been complaints." Aemilius's heart was beating so hard that the ground must be trembling with it. Why had he done this? What on earth had convinced him that this would be a good idea?

Confused and angry, the big fisherman brandished the forearm-long knife. "Enough talk, runt. I'm going to gut you first."

As casually as wandering into a market square, Rivkah strolled up to Aemilius's side. "I regret to disappoint you," she said, in a voice that suggested she didn't care at all. "I have *long* since reserved the right and the pleasure to gut this shrimp when the time comes. And sadly—for you, and for me—that time isn't now." She rolled her shoulders, and there was something about the motion that made at least four of the fishermen take a very slight step back. "Now. We were saying something about—"

"*Horses!*"

And eight horses came thundering out of the darkness.

The effect was instant. Everyone had been so intently focused on the encounter between Aemilius and the leader, and had then moved their focus so completely onto Rivkah, that nobody had noticed the hoofbeats. Shouted voices followed fishermen jumping back to save their lives as the big animals charged through the throng, heading straight for Aemilius and Rivkah.

This is it. This is how I go. Trampled by—

He didn't get to finish the thought.

The lead animal reared up on its hind legs, a chiselled form in the darkness, a steed of kings—and screamed.

Aemilius was dimly aware that at least half of the sailors had run away into the darkness, away from the hell-beast. Behind it, the other horses ground to a halt, and still the horse screamed, once, twice—a third time—and he thought if it screamed again the skies would tear apart and the world would end... and then, finally, it came back down to the ground, tossing its head and groaning.

Time stood still, and then the beast looked up and straight at Aemilius, and he knew.

"I'm so sorry," he whispered. "I'm so, so sorry, girl. I'm sad too."

Furibunda whinnied and moved closer to him, sniffing the air.

Out of the corner of his eye he could see Taurio walking their prisoner over to his few friends that hadn't fled, smiling as he handed the man over, but the horse's head insistently eclipsed the view. She nickered once, then rubbed her head against his chest. Hesitantly, he reached out and touched her neck. The heat of her radiated against his hand in the cold night air, and time did not matter at all—until she nudged him again, impatiently this time, and snorted.

"Come on," Rivkah muttered behind him. "We're going."

Aemilius came back to the night and the village. The fishermen had gone, vanished back into their huts, glad to have been spared death on this night. He was surrounded by legionnaires, each holding a horse by the reins. From somewhere, Hanno's donkey had appeared. Not quite believing what was happening, he reached for the reins of Quintus Aurelius's horse and let her lead him towards the stables and the cart.

A little while later, and without another word being spoken, the Hidden Legion rode into the dark, heading south.

IX

THE SOUTH AND HISPALIS

THE TUFTS OF long, dry grass whispered gently as the horses trotted through. In the distance blue-green hills turned to reddish-yellow hills, and back to blue-green. The occasional torn strand of soft cotton stretched across the sky, and Aemilius couldn't care less.

"So tell me about Hispalis."

Rivkah twisted in the saddle. "Shout it out, scumbags. Who had 'before noon'?"

Behind them, Taurio cursed. "Why did you have to open your mouth, you Roman tadpole?"

"I did," Prasta said with glee. "The Gaul trusts too easily. He said tomorrow. Abrax thought he'd break before camp last night."

Aemilius blinked in confusion. "What do you mean?"

"When it rains in the desert, the water disappears," Hanno added helpfully. "The ground cannot get enough of the water. It always asks and asks and asks for more."

Rivkah answered his glance with a smirk. "We've been betting on when you'd start yapping."

The rising sun at their backs did little to help with Aemilius's annoyance. He was about to snap back at the girl when Furibunda snorted and tossed her head gently, as if to say *leave it*. Without thinking, he leaned forward and patted her on the neck, receiving another soft snort for his troubles.

"Still can't believe last night," Rivkah said.

"You are lucky to be alive," Abrax rumbled from the front.

"I, uh," Aemilius stuttered. "I didn't mean to—I, uhm, just thought—"

"I thought it was hilarious," Taurio said. "There have been complaints!" He hooted in appreciation. "Complaints! And Prasta hasn't even touched her flute!"

"To be fair, that was funny." Livia swayed gently in the saddle. "And we knew what you were trying to do, and it was, well…"

"A piss-poor effort," Rivkah finished.

"Be nice," Livia admonished. "It wasn't *piss*-poor. Just… not quite polished."

"In the same way my horse just dropped something that wasn't quite polished," Prasta added.

"Fine," Aemilius said, convincing himself that the warmth about his ears was sunburn. "So what should I have done differently, then?"

Livia smiled. "Feel free to contribute, all of you. I know you will."

"Hey—if *you're* going to teach the kid to be brazen, none of us will utter so much as a tiny, provincial peep." Prasta somehow managed to lean back in the saddle, sitting as comfortably as an empress on a throne of cushions.

"Thank you, my dear." Livia nodded her respects.

"Just listen up, chicken," Taurio interjected. "In every craft there are artists, and there are masters, and there are gods—and then there is her."

"Saw her sweet-talk a *bear* once," Abrax added. "Calmed it right down. Stepped up to it and opened up its throat before she walked away. The poor thing was more than half dead before it realised."

Aemilius swayed alongside the others, hills stretching alongside them, the valley before them. After a morning's canter, they were going easy on the horses as the temperature rose. *How much of this is true?* He glanced at Livia, tried to imagine her killing a bear in cold blood, and decided he didn't really want the answer to that question. Instead, he smiled and bowed his head once. He was ready to listen.

"What do you think you did wrong?"

His composure vanished in an instant, and he was back in the classroom with his history tutor and his history tutor's thumb-thick stick. All the words he had ever learned marched out of his head instantly. "Uh—uhm… I don't know?" he squeaked.

"Good answer." Seeing his face, she said kindly, "Always admit when you don't know. Saves time and sharpens the lesson." She paused for a moment in thought, before continuing. "So. You are standing in front of a man. He is… a Greek, and he wants something. You want something different. Completely different. You want to keep your stomach, intestines and lungs *inside* your body, and he has made clear he wants them *outside* your body. He has also suggested that your cock would be better placed in your mouth, along with your balls. He is a big guy, and he has his weapon—a gladius, let's say—and it looks nicked and stained. It's definitely not for show, and you are absolutely, categorically sure that you will not be able to take him. What is the right question to ask?" Before his eyes, Livia seemed to grow bigger; squaring and hunching her shoulders, she shot her neck forward and scowled.

Aware of all eyes on him and not quite free of imagining the mutilations, Aemilius sweated more than he should. "Uh... would you like money?"

"No. I'll take it when you're dead."

"Let me go? Please?"

"No—you stole my sister's honour"—hoots from all directions—"stole my sister's honour, and I will only be satisfied with blood and death."

"Run away?"

"Your back is to the wall."

"Well—then I'm done for," Aemilius said, irritated. *What a stupid game.* "You win. I'm dead."

The angry Greek disappeared in a blink, and Livia was back. "That would be rather inconvenient, don't you think?" She was still smiling. No threats had been made and no insults had been thrown, but Aemilius felt somehow more reduced than he remembered from any of his various tutors.

"Yeah. Yes. It would be."

"So what is the right question?"

He thought for a moment. "Taurio?"

"Yes?"

"How would Livia get out of a situation like this?"

The big Gaul chuckled. "See? I told you. He is not as stupid as he looks."

"Which is lucky," Rivkah added. "Because he *looks* like he might forget to breathe one day."

"Only because of the way you smell."

She made a face at him, but did not fire back. Aemilius held back his smile.

"Doubt," said the big Gaul.

Livia nodded almost imperceptibly.

"That's the first thing I can think of," he continued. "She always starts with doubt."

"So how would I make this mad Greek doubt... his sister?"

Taurio looked back at him, eyebrows raised. Aemilius thought for a moment, then turned to Livia.

"Oh—is this about your sister?"

"Yes!" The Greek was back. Livia pulled a face of mock fury. "Beautiful, innocent, sweet, uh—"

"Cassandra," Abrax rumbled from the front.

"Cassandra!" Livia shouted. "My darling Cassandra! Who said you'd had her three times over behind the stables—"

"Forgive me—did you say 'Cassandra'?"

"Yes," Livia snapped. "Three times! Behind the—"

"Red hair, plaited? Bit of a small, pouty mouth?"

Livia blinked. "What? No. She's about—"

"Yay high?" Aemilius put his hand up to his chest.

Livia, playing the angry Greek, frowned. "No. She's taller than that."

"Oh—*oh!*" Aemilius beamed, then frowned in confusion. "Blonde? Absolutely massive—" He was about to mime an expansive chest when Livia interrupted.

"No! My sister—"

"And you are absolutely sure this was behind the stables?"

"Yes!"

Aemilius scratched his head. "Then... I'm not sure I know what you are talking about, I'm afraid."

"Oh, but you do! She is only half a head smaller than you, a great deal stronger by the looks of it, and she described you in detail!"

"Did she? What did she say?"

"Runty-looking Roman."

"And what did she say I did?"

Livia feigned outrage and heartbreak with a face that seriously challenged Aemilius's ability to not burst out laughing. "She described some *things*—filthy Roman *things*—"

"It's so strange," Aemilius said. "Because I do remember a girl like the one you described... but I only saw her in the distance, running off with a tall, olive-skinned man with dark hair."

"*What?*" Livia hissed. "What did he look like?"

Open the palm...

"They were a bit of a distance away, and they were running quite fast, but I thought..."

"Did he have a bit of a limp?"

"Yyyes. I think he may have." *...and roll the dice.* "Maybe on the left, but I can't be sure."

"Stavros," Livia hissed, glaring away into the middle distance. When she looked back, all hints of the furious Greek had disappeared and the Roman noblewoman had returned. She looked him up and down with renewed interest. "Not bad, young man. Not altogether bad."

Aemilius felt his cheeks redden and fought to keep control of his voice. Going for the safe option, he decided to silently radiate total confidence in himself. His scalp tingled.

"See?" Taurio said to Prasta, behind him. "The boy is promising."

"Perhaps."

He turned back at Livia, and found her still studying him.

"And thus concludes lesson one. Doubt is a weapon."

"How many lessons are there?"

But Livia had already turned away and was rocking gently in the saddle. Hoping for answers, he glanced over at Rivkah.

"Don't look at me," she shrugged. "But based on how smart Princess there thinks she is, I'd guess there's loads."

Beneath him, Furibunda snorted in agreement, and around them absolutely nothing changed.

ONE—TWO.

One—two.

Clip—clop.

Clip—clop.

The sun had risen, and peaked over their heads, and was now sinking towards the horizon. They had long since lapsed into a comfortable silence that had slowly changed into a sort of trance. Aemilius was there, he was rocking back and forth, he felt a dull ache in his legs that was far more manageable than the liquid fire of the first days, and his brain was numb. It took him a moment to realise that Prasta and Rivkah had separated from the group, and another to realise that the riders approaching were a familiar shape.

"Camp," Taurio grunted. "Runt. Come here."

It took Aemilius a moment to realise that he was being spoken to, but once he stepped back into the world it was an easy task to guide Furibunda with his knees to pull up next to the Gaul.

"It's time you earn your keep."

"What keep?" Aemilius scoffed. "Are you paying me?"

"Do you want to live?" the Gaul said calmly.

"Uh—yes?"

"Good. We're keeping you alive. That's the keep."

Aemilius shrugged. "Fine. What do you want me to do?"

"Fire," Taurio grunted. "You—"

"Small and light, triangle first, layer it so that the fire can breathe and collapse in on itself. Biggest sticks on the outside. How long do you want it burning for?"

Taurio blinked.

Aemilius glanced to the horizon. "Sundown, sunset or nightfall?"

"Uh... nightfall."

"Right." Swinging by the cart to pick up a bundle of firewood, Aemilius nudged Furibunda towards where Prasta and Rivkah were headed, and caught up with them just as they had dismounted and started brushing the horses. He jumped off with ease, tossed the bundle to the ground and stroked Furibunda's jaw. "Would you let Rivkah rub you down, girl?" he muttered. "She stinks like a fox's arse and her temper is worse, but she'll treat you good. I need to start a fire."

The mare snorted and nuzzled him once, then turned and started walking towards where Rivkah was rubbing her horse with firm, easy strokes.

"I have been rejected in favour of your gentle hand," he called over to her.

"Too right," Rivkah called back. "Your horse is smarter than you are."

"My horse is smarter than you are, too."

Rivkah shrugged. "Not an insult. C'mere, girl. You are going to wait for just a moment, and then I'll get to you." She clicked and Furibunda snorted once, standing politely and waiting her turn.

Working swiftly, Aemilius assembled his tinder bundle. Since the first time Taurio had showed him, he'd made a habit of noticing when others had done it and thinking through the movements. "Build the nest where the fire is born," he muttered to himself. "Then build it a house to live in and destroy." He was vaguely aware of the rumble of the cart to his side, and the movement of horses around him, people dismounting and low conversations, but none of it came close to distracting him. The wood felt nicely light and dry in his hands, and the sticks behaved themselves. A pyramid of wood grew before him, and he assessed his work. Enough? No—not quite. He added the last of the sticks gently and stepped back to look at his work. "That'll do," he thought to himself. "That'll do." Realising belatedly that he didn't actually have anything to light the bundle with, he looked for Taurio—

With a soft *whoosh*, a spark popped into life in the middle of the nest and spread rapidly, crackling and burning through the kindling.

Aemilius looked over his shoulder. Out of earshot but close enough that he could see their faces, Abrax and Livia stood side by side. They were both looking at him, and neither of them looked away when he caught their eyes. Their expressions were hard to read. Had he done something wrong? Livia's lips moved—a short sentence. Abrax nodded once. They turned and moved towards the horses.

"Well done," Taurio said, behind him. "I reckon that's us done. Except, of course, if you want to eat anything ever."

He got to his feet and shuffled over to the cart, where the big Gaul was already rummaging.

"SLOW DOWN." A sigh. "Please." The water was in the pot, and he'd managed to pick out the right bundle of herbs, and the vegetables had been easy to chop—but no matter how often he stared, Aemilius could not follow Taurio's hands when the big man had a rabbit to skin. "Could you show me that again?"

The Gaul sighed again. "Always with the questions. You lay it on the back, like so."

Aemilius muttered a confirmation.

"Slice open here—and here—" Taurio drew his short skinning knife almost like a painter's brush around the rabbit's legs. "Hold here—and pull like this." With a long ripping noise, the hide came off the body, slowly, like watching someone take off a jacket. "Work your fingers under—like this—and then work it down towards the head."

He watched as the Gaul's thick, strong fingers worked delicately to pull the hide over the head. When the neck was exposed, Taurio snapped it with a quick twist, worked the knife into the break and sliced through in a swift motion.

"And there you are."

Aemilius reached for the third and last rabbit. Without ever looking like she was expending much effort, Prasta had produced three of the animals—skinny-looking things, but then there wasn't much to live on around here—and Taurio had thanked her profusely and possibly somewhat ironically for the bounty of the hunt. They were about to go into the stew, and a while later the meat would fall off the bones and into their bowls. Taking care and feeling very much aware of how slow he was, Aemilius worked his own knife around the rabbit's legs, cutting the lines like he'd seen the Gaul do.

"Not bad," the big man rumbled. "Now pull." He gripped the hide and made to drag. "Gently. A giant like you could rip that poor thing in half."

Aemilius chose to take the advice but ignore the smirk in his mentor's voice and eased the hide down. To his surprise, it looked much like what he'd seen Taurio do, if twice as slow. Eventually, the rabbit was skinned and ready to go.

"Not bad, runt. Not bad. Obviously, if you were in charge of the pots we'd all die of starvation, but there'd maybe be a decent meal once every three days or so."

"Thank you. I was taught how to do it by an old man—"

"Hey!"

"Near death, he was. His knees sounded like a forest floor in autumn—squeaking and squishing in equal measure."

"See, Prasta? I put my life at risk and give all my knowledge selflessly, and what do I get? Arrogance and cheek."

"No more than you deserve." Prasta was laid out on the ground, all knees and elbows, looking almost asleep. "How long till food?"

"About the length of three of your interminable ballads."

Prasta rolled over. "Hungry," she groaned. "When we get to Hispalis I am going to pay someone to put a lamb on a plate for me and get out of the way. When I am queen of everything, we'll build all cities within a day's ride of each other and anything past that can belong to the monsters, as far as I care."

"The Empire—" Taurio began.

"'—are the real monsters. They ate my horse and rode away on my village,'" Rivkah mimicked. "Stuff it up your arse, old bear."

"I can't," Hanno replied in his best Taurio impression, without moving a single muscle. "The Empire stuffed it up my arse long ago."

"I'm not old!"

"Old enough to keep moaning about the same things, over and over. It gets boring."

"While we wait for the stew, we have things to do," Abrax said, in a voice that invited no-one else to speak after him.

"And what's that, baldy?" jibed Rivkah.

The magus was un-moved. "We have time. In Hispalis, we might not." He fixed his intense eyes on Aemilius. "We need to look to your training."

Rivkah let out a short, sharp laugh. "Hah! Good luck. I'll start training this, uh"—she reached for a fist-sized rock—"rock here. I'll call him, uh, Marius. Let's see who gets them to do tricks first."

Abrax ignored her. "You have seen us wield powers that you did not know existed."

Aemilius nodded.

"And you have not asked many questions."

"About magic?"

The magus nodded. "Almost all people live in ignorance. They do not know, not for sure, that there are powers above and beyond their own. They tell the stories—maybe they even believe. But they don't know, and they certainly do not understand."

"No-one understands," Hanno added.

Abrax smiled. "Especially not if you explain."

"Where does the power come from?" Aemilius's mind was racing. The questions that had crowded his mind since he saw the harpies burning came rolling to the fore. "Can you learn to do it? Or are you born with it?" His mouth opened and closed like a fish.

"Shouldn't have told him he could ask questions," Rivkah said, rolling the rock over and around her hand in a smooth movement, then down her forearm, popping her elbow and catching it in mid-air. "We'll be here all week. See? Marius can do this already."

"The power..." Hanno hesitated, searching for words. "The power comes from the drip of the drop, the crashing of the wave, the relentless fall of the rain. It comes from the flood and the flow, the kiss of the brook, the pull of the deep that fills you with water and makes you the water."

"There is power in everything," Abrax continued. "Sometimes it is bound—"

"—and sometimes it is not."

"True. Fire comes from the sun, and it gives heat that lives on in everything, everywhere. I can draw on that heat, form it and shape it. But if I do not control it..." Abrax thought. "Have you ever run down a hill?"

"Yes."

"The hill pulls you down. So you lean back, and you watch your tread. And if you stumble..."

"You fall." Aemilius imagined the hill, and imagined the fall, and remembered the heat on his skin and the smell of Zeno's skin burning, the fat cooking, the meat roasting. His mouth watered, and he felt sick. "And if you fall, it's hard to stop falling."

Abrax nodded slowly. "Indeed."

"Is that what you learn? To not... fall?"

"In a way." Hanno rose up onto his elbows. "You start small, and you learn your powers, and you don't overreach. Because like most all things, the power costs."

"It costs life."

Abrax looked at Livia and nodded. "It does. A morning here, half a day there."

"And in the cave...?"

"Years." Abrax's voice was hard. "Seven. Maybe eight. I was weak, and I lost control, and I hit him far harder than I had to." He flinched as Livia placed her hand gently on his arm. "It could have gone quite badly."

"But it didn't," she said.

"Thanks to you," he said, placing his hand over hers. "Like always."

"Look away," Rivkah said. "Mummy and Daddy are about to give each other a special—hey!" She flinched and dropped the rock, shaking her fingers and blowing on them, and glaring at Abrax.

"I will tolerate much of your yapping, when it is directed at me," the magus said darkly. "But you will *occasionally* show some respect."

"Oh, please forgive me," she shot back, voice dripping with irony. "It was a fucking joke. Do they have them in your particular corner of the sandbox?"

"They do," Abrax replied. "Your face, for example. Pretty funny just then."

"One of these days I'll murder you in your sleep," Rivkah muttered.

"That'll be the only chance you get," Livia added, smiling. "Now get back to training your rock. I reckon he'll be on your level in a day or so."

Rivkah made a face that suggested she was ready with some suggestions as to what Marius the rock could get up to next, but did not speak.

"I have never asked," Abrax said. "Hanno, my friend. How—when…?"

"I was five." A strange smile played on the water-mage's face. "I was five, and I was running along a riverbank. My grandmother was with me, and she shouted at me to slow down, and then she watched me lose my footing and fall into the water. Five feet down, it was, and hurt like a bastard when I landed. I heard her screaming, because she knew that there'd been a couple of sightings of crocodiles in the past week, and I think she thought that was me done for. But I must have been afraid, because the water parted."

"What? Like—What?" Aemilius stuttered.

"I was sitting in its cradle, and it had closed over my head and flowed into my nose and eyes and ears and I asked it to leave and it did," Hanno said calmly. "I didn't know that you couldn't talk to the water. I reckon it was glad of the chat. Must be boring to never be asked to do anyone a favour."

Aemilius glanced at the others, who were all looking at Hanno. *Did none of them know this?*

"The water wasn't deep, but there was enough to drown a small boy. A space formed around me, and I could get to my feet and walk out of the river. Pissed off the crocodile to no end," the little man chuckled. "He was there, snapping at me like a dog at a butcher's shop door. Obviously, the moment I got out, my grandma yanked me up, by the ears, and slapped me around the face until I cried and asked to go back to the crocodile. Shortly after that she took me to an old man who lived in a hut on an island, and told him about me, and I stayed with him for a while after that. The first day I stayed there, the river threw him a fish." The small man smiled at the memory. "Like that—*pthwoiie!* And I remember thinking, small as I was, that I wasn't quite sure what was happening, but that it might be a good time to pay attention. And I did. For ten years."

"So you do have to be born with it," Aemilius said. He couldn't quite mask his disappointment. Stories of magi had fascinated him, and he remembered being devastated when his cousin told him they weren't real. For a moment he wished he could rub his face in it, but then he remembered that his cousin's face had been opened up by a harpy.

"I believe there is a spark of magic in everyone," Abrax said. "But not everyone finds it, and not everyone wants to use it."

"Some stories say that it's given by the gods," Aemilius said, looking at Abrax. "Do—did—they...?"

"Not to me," Abrax said curtly. "And I didn't have an old man on an island. I had parents, and a farm, and then I made a mistake and I had to go. It took a long time and a lot of care to learn, but I realised I had to work to control it, or..."

The words hung in the air, drifting towards the fire.

"So... every time you use magic you get... older?" Aemilius ventured.

"If it doesn't kill you, yes," Hanno replied. "Think of it like a horse. The horse will take you where you want to go, but you have to feed it. In our case, we feed it with our life."

"But how then can you get good enough to not die? If every time you do it you get older, and everything costs, you must not be able to control it until you're old, and then you have no time and therefore no magic left." The words tumbled out of him, and his good sense followed a while later. He looked up at Abrax, horrified that he had said things he shouldn't, but the big magus did not look angry at all.

"It's simple… but also maybe a little more complicated than that," he mused. "You know how you feel after you've had a good sleep?"

"More of a memory than a feeling, these days."

"Fine. The feeling after a good meal—say, the one with the Lord and Lady. How you feel…"

"Rejuvenated," Livia added.

"Thank you. Some things drain you, some things feed you."

"I am one for sleep," said Hanno.

"Food," Taurio said.

"Food is also good."

"No—now. Food. It's ready. If you want it, come and get it."

Conversation ceased immediately as the legionnaires produced bowls and spoons, lining up like obedient children at the Gaul's pot. Soon after, all that could be heard was contented slurping as the stew was demolished.

Rivkah was the first to finish hers, and the first to speak again.

"Who do you think they'll be sending?"

"My guess is as good as yours," Prasta said. "We could do with a bit of muscle—"

"But we are also going into a proper city," Taurio noted, "rather than a nowhere town. They'll probably send some stick figure of a noble—no offence intended."

"None taken," Livia said, with a smile. "I rarely know what she's thinking, but I do know who I'd rather not have. Graxus."

There was a brief pause.

"Oh. Oh, no," Rivkah said, sounding horrified. "Oh, please, no."

"I hadn't even thought of that," Taurio added. "That is absolutely the worst of all possible choices."

"And yet," Prasta said, holding out her hands to quieten the voices of protest. "And yet it probably makes the most sense."

"From a purely practical angle... maybe," Abrax said.

"If she wants to find out what's actually going on, magic-wise," Prasta continued, "he is the expert."

"He is a toad," Hanno spat. "A contemptible, shitting little toad."

"Wow," Rivkah said. "I thought I disliked him the most. Did he piss in your river or something?"

"Everything reeks around him." Hanno twisted his lips in distaste. "He stinks of anger and bitterness and death."

"He may be an arse," Prasta said, "but he is our arse."

"What's with you, twiglet?" Taurio rumbled. "Why are you standing up for him?"

"No reason. He gives me the creeps just like you. I just wanted to prepare you for him."

"Can I ask for my training to not just include the history of magic," asked Aemilius, "but maybe also a hint of who this Graxus is?"

Looks were traded, but no-one volunteered.

"Why don't you do the honours, twig," rumbled Taurio, "seeing as you love him so much?"

"Shut up, boar. Right. Graxus."

"Full name—Graxus Septimus Valerius," Livia added.

"When Abrax said there was magic in everyone... not everyone finds it, not everyone wants it, but some people that want it and find it should not have it. Graxus knew of magic from an early age, and he *hunted* it. Only child, rich family, father dead early—his mother paid to gather everything ever written about magic. He built a library unlike anything in the known world. He gathered a host of tutors, trainers and sages. Most of them were absolute chancers, of course—but some of them knew some things, and all of them gave everything to Graxus. His uncle was in the Seventeenth," Prasta continued.

"Sadly," Rivkah added.

"So is he the most powerful magus in the world, then?"

Abrax winced. "I... wouldn't say that."

Hanno spat.

Prasta hesitated. "No. Not really. Maybe. But he is definitely the most knowledgeable."

"He cannot do with fire and water what they can," Livia said, indicating Hanno and Abrax. "And he doesn't care about what he calls 'small magic'—but he knows. He knows and understands a lot about it."

"He is an insufferable prick, is what they're trying to say," Rivkah said. "A smarmy little git who thinks he is a scary magus."

"Are you going to say that to his face, though?" Taurio said.

Rivkah scowled and muttered something that wasn't quite a threat.

"Anyway," said Prasta. "As you can hear from the reception of our lovely fellow travellers, having Graxus added to our happy troupe is such an awful possibility that it is just about inevitable. I suggest we get some sleep. Like Abrax said, we might not get a lot of rest once we get to Hispalis."

IT HAPPENED GRADUALLY. The hills sloped down to a verdant valley, and the valley opened up to become so broad that the hills were hard to see on either side. Farmers and field-workers paid them little heed, and slowly the roads became more pronounced, more formal. They passed travellers on foot and the occasional cart became the occasional pair of carts, then a short train. At midday they were part of a loose caravan of sauntering horses, walking farmers and loaded carts and carriages. When the first line of blue appeared on the horizon, a while after midday, it had been a long time since they had been alone on the road.

Aemilius leaned over towards Rivkah. "Are they all heading there as well?"

"Oh no," Rivkah replied. "They are just out on a stroll. It's their grandmother's birthday, you see, and they wanted to surprise her. All the farmers with their produce, and the craftspeople with their sacks of stuff, and the workers and the children and the whores. Just off to see their grandmother."

"She must have put it about a bit, then, because this is a *lot* of grandchildren."

Rivkah turned away, but not quite fast enough to hide her smile.

Around him, the crowds grew with the setting sun. A flow of people, heading in both directions. On the horizon he could now see a row of grey lines against the blue sky—smoke from fires of various kinds. He tried to remember Rome, but it was too long ago. His family had left in haste and not spent a lot of time talking about it. He had a vague impression of impossibly big buildings and lots of people, but he struggled to pin down what was real and what was invented in the Governor's villa as a bored child.

He was suddenly struck by the pure adventure of it all. About a week ago he had been a youth, with other youths, racing horses and wasting time. Now he was a sellsword in some kind of secret army. Granted, he didn't actually have a sword or feel confident about using one, but he was around people who could. And they were riding into a city to seek out and destroy an unknown enemy, without alerting anything or anyone. He flexed his thighs and arse muscles, enjoying the soreness. That was another thing—it seemed like he knew how to ride a horse now.

Almost as if she could read his thoughts, Furibunda snorted.

"Not long now, girl," he muttered, laying his hand gently on her neck. "And when we do get stabled, I promise you we will find you the best oats."

She snorted again, tossing her head gently in agreement, and carried him into the evening.

The sun had nearly set by the time they saw the gates. Decisions had been made by Abrax and Livia, but they hadn't quite carried down the line to him. About half a mile before reaching the crowded bridge they turned off the paved road and down a broad, well-trodden path. He looked at Rivkah and made to ask her what was happening, but her utter lack of interest in their direction stopped him. This was happening, and that was that.

They rode down the path, alongside the walls of Hispalis. Seeing as no-one was telling him anything, he busied himself looking at the fortifications. He vaguely remembered his tutor telling him something about tribes and wars in this part of the country, but it had clearly not made a lasting impression. The river they had been following, which had at the start of the day been a tinkling, easily crossable stream, had now broadened and deepened enough to happily swallow any horse and rider. A sturdy bridge traversed it, but one that would be easy to torch if need be. A ramshackle collection of carts, covered wagons and hastily-built shacks covered the open ground before the city walls. It was hard to make out details in the fading light, but he concluded that Hispalis looked, above anything, safe. Safer than anything he'd ever seen.

The press of people crowding to get across the bridge seemed to agree with his evaluation.

So where's the monster?

His thoughts were interrupted by Furibunda deciding to stop, mostly because that was what Hanno's donkey was doing. He realised that they had reached a large building—two floors and what looked like a stables behind it. On the outside was a large sign with a picture of a woman, wrapped in red.

Livia had dismounted and was leading the way, with Abrax following. They disappeared through the stone doorway, the big magus ducking slightly to avoid smacking his head. They reappeared very quickly, motioning to go around to the back. The legionnaires did as they were told, and came to a stables where a broad-shouldered youth waited for them to dismount and took their horses without question or comment. A small side door opened, spilling out the sounds of loud conversation, the strains of music and the occasional curse. He followed

Taurio and the others into the inn. After three days in the saddle, the walls felt like they would crush him, and he tried to block out the noise. Before he knew it, he was squeezed into a corner between the big Gaul and Rivkah. As if by magic, big stone glasses filled with cold, pale yellow wine appeared.

"Oh, thank the Gods," Taurio sighed, taking a long and appreciative sip.

Suddenly dazed and exhausted, Aemilius felt like he was watching from above and behind himself. Plates of food—roast pig, with fist-sized chunks of turnip and a thick sauce that tasted of apples and burnt sugar—appeared, and he shovelled his food into his face, washing it down with the wine. The rhythm of the inn was settling, the movement of shadows and the flow of conversation. A warm feeling grew in him, and he wanted nothing more than to crash into a bed. A bed! Imagine. The sounds of his fellow travellers talking and joking were comfortable, and the noises of the other guests had turned into a soothing burble. When the youth approached their table, he was surprised. They'd already had their wine and their food. Had someone else ordered something? If so—why would the innkeeper let this unfortunate kid wait on their table? He looked sickly, weak and above all annoyed to the point of open contempt—and he was approaching their table empty-handed, to boot.

"Took you long enough," he sneered.

Aemilius blinked in shock and was about to tell the kid to go get shat on by a pony, when Abrax spoke.

"Well met, Graxus."

X

HISPALIS

Aemilius tried his hardest not to stare, and failed.

Graxus, the strongest and wisest magus of the Hidden Legion, appeared to be no more than two or three years his senior, and completely lacking in deference to match. He was reedy to the point of collapse, and his straw-blond hair looked greasy and unkempt. He wouldn't look out of place working in an inn, but you'd feel sorry for the innkeeper for having fathered such a runt.

"Is this him?" the boy asked, with the barest hint of a nod in Aemilius's direction.

Aemilius started to notice things. The raised eyebrow, the aquiline nose, the thin-lipped sneer. He was reminded of an older cousin, a boy who'd visited them with ill grace some summers back and been outraged at the few things he hadn't been disgusted by.

"What are you smirking at?" Graxus was now staring at him, and there was an edge to his voice.

"Nothing," Aemilius replied. "You just remind me of someone I knew." *Someone who, after the first two days of a visit to a cousin, got very ill from eating finely grated pig shit.*

Graxus gave a sniff of contempt, pulled up a chair and sat down at the head of the table. He turned back to Abrax. "I expected more."

"So did we." Livia's voice was silk and honey, and it was very clear that she was not talking about Aemilius.

Graxus glared at her. "I am going to give you what you deserve, Livia Claudia, which is nothing. Your mother says hello, by the way."

Nobody moved and nobody spoke, and when he saw Livia's eyes, Aemilius knew with pure certainty that he had never seen anyone who was luckier to be alive at that moment than Graxus.

"So how did you kill the muck-shoveller, then?" the magus drawled. "Seems a bit careless."

"Stay calm," Abrax murmured. "We've seen this before." He turned to Graxus. "We lost a friend. He served the Legion and gave his life to save us, and it would cost you nothing to show kindness and understanding. This is no way to lead."

"You don't know the first, second or third thing about leading, magus," Graxus spat. "None of your lot do." He indicated the assembled legionnaires. "And if you want to *serve the Legion*, you find the nearest Roman and do as you're told."

"If you go by the Imperial standards of honour, dignity and bravery, you'd be following all of us." Livia rose, gathering to herself the grace of all her foremothers. Her withering glare could have destroyed a season of crops. "Your life's achievement to date is that you just happened to pop out of a posh—"

Several things happened.

Livia coughed once, then went still and silent, clawing at her throat.

Graxus, red-faced, flicked his wrist and drew his hand back to strike.

The table shook as Taurio sprang to his feet, club in hand.

A gust of wind came from nowhere, sending all candles and torches flickering and swaying towards the teenager.

And all the liquid in the cups and jugs on the table rose up like some sort of swaying, amorphous animal and split itself in two. Half of it attached, lightning-quick, to the flames forming around Abrax's hands, suffocating the fire with an audible hiss. More horrifically, the second half formed a shimmering shield over the mouth and nose of Graxus.

"I will say this simply, so you understand," said Hanno the Wise softly. "Release Livia, or I will drown you and look you in the eyes as your life fades away. Do you understand?" The African had not moved. Or barely; Aemilius watched, entranced, as the short man's fingers moved subtly, softly, like... *Like seaweed in a pond*.

Staring at the water-magus, wide-eyed, Graxus tried something that could have been a counter-spell and gawked in horror as the water in his mouth and nose seemed to expand, stretching his face painfully.

"No," Hanno said calmly. "A spell from *that* book will not save you."

Graxus flicked his wrist and Livia coughed again, sinking into her chair. Rivkah offered a hand of support, but the slender woman had already regained her composure. Aemilius watched a mask of calm descend over her face. She looked at Graxus, who was recovering from a coughing fit himself. "Graxus of the House of the Valerii, I spoke dishonourably and exhibited conduct unbecoming a Roman. I hereby retract my words, and offer you my apology."

Slumped in his chair, Graxus waved his hand dismissively. "I got angry. Shouldn't have."

"Every sea has a storm," Hanno offered, smiling. "It's rarely fun, but makes for good sailing afterwards."

Out of the corner of his eye, Aemilius noticed Prasta's hand on Taurio's arm, as she murmured and gently eased his grip off his skull-crushing club.

"Maybe so," Graxus said. "Maybe so." A thoughtful expression crept across his face. "That was... something," he continued. "It's surprisingly tricky to get anything out when you're full of water. I tried the Dissipo from—"

"—the *Libris Aqua*."

"Yes!" Graxus lit up, looking happy for the first time since he'd approached their table. "Have you read it?"

"I wrote it."

The smile stretched across Aemilius's face like a cat in the sunshine. He glanced over at Rivkah, who caught his eye and smirked in return. Over to his side, Taurio finally let go of his club and muttered something under his breath that was best kept that way.

"Oh," was all that Graxus could manage. "Good book. I'm not too strong on water. I'll read it again when I get back." He leaned in. "Now—I was sent here with all haste. There are signs."

"We know," Abrax said. "We've been fighting them."

Something niggled at Aemilius. The rhythm. The rhythm of the lights and the talk and the shadows. Something, somewhere, was not quite right. Like a branch of a tree, not quite moving with the wind. He felt *watched*. Something...

"Listen up!" Graxus snapped. "Even you. I hate repeating myself."

"Sorry." He heard his voice coming out, and hated it. It was, immediately, the simpering response to a scolding teacher. *All it takes is a Roman.* Aemilius looked down onto his plate and tried to push the sneer off his face.

"The augurs talked for a long time and disagreed on much, but not on this: that evil is rising, and that it is going to be in the west, and it is going to be among a lot of people."

"And this is the largest municipality this far west."

"Yes." Graxus regarded each of them in turn. "I got here two days ago and there has been nothing obvious… but there's a foul stench in the air. A foul stench." He fell silent, and for a moment Aemilius thought that young face looked afraid.

THE SUN BEAT down mercilessly, bouncing off the white walls and the packed cobbles.

"I just don't know how people can bear it," Taurio grumbled, wiping the sweat off his brow.

"And yet they do," Prasta replied, angling her way ahead of the big Gaul. "Keep up, old bull."

"You're from a forsaken and cursed rock in the middle of the ocean! Your home is even worse than mine for the weather. Why are you not suffering in this heat? And I'm not old," he muttered sulkily.

As if she'd finally found the spot she'd been searching for all day, Prasta stopped and leaned up against a whitewashed wall, in the shade. "See there?" she muttered.

Taurio nonchalantly glanced in the direction of her gaze and nodded.

"Let's go and have a listen," she said.

The narrow street opened up into a small plaza, a space maybe eight houses long on each side. A platform had been raised in the middle, but at present it stood empty. Two older men in identical tunics stood by it, looking bored in the way that only guards can—relaxed but ready, not moving and not wanting to move, eyes trained onto a point that only they knew. A young woman, face pinched in fear, was pleading with them, and they were ignoring her.

"Who will hear me, then?" she cried. "Who will help me?"

No response.

"Please! I beg you!"

There was a trickle of people passing in and out of the plaza, and a handful standing by a merchant's stall buying food, but if they heard the woman, they gave no sign. Skirting around the edge of the square to get to where they needed, it seemed as if her fellow citizens thought her grief and despair might be contagious.

Taurio glanced at Prasta. "She is being ignored."

"Not quite," the gangly bard muttered. "Look."

Almost hidden by the shadows of an alleyway to their side, another young woman followed the exchange intently.

"Where is he?" the woman in the square wailed. "Where is my son?"

"We don't know," the younger of the guards snapped. "Get away."

"We will ask," the older said, with a reproving look at his fellow. "We will ask."

The woman took one last look at them, and their absolute lack of movement, and burst into tears, rushing away from the guards. Like a ghost, the girl in the alleyway followed the grieving woman.

"Here we go, old bull." Prasta sauntered off, as if she'd suddenly remembered she had somewhere to be.

"Not old," Taurio muttered as he shuffled after her.

"SO WHAT EXACTLY does 'investigate' mean?" Aemilius shielded his eyes against the sun and tried to look as casual as Rivkah, which was surprisingly hard. For someone who relished moving so much, she could sit with her back up against a wall like she'd been born there. "Is there someone you can ask?"

She looked at him with the tired eyes of an older sister who had just found her baby brother with his hand trapped in a jar for the fifth time that week. "And which one of your genius questions would you bring out?" She scrunched up her face and mimicked him. "'Excuse me, sir—is there a giant hydra in your back garden? Are you a cyclops? Oh, no—that's just the shape of your face. So sorry. How about you, madam? Is that your hair or a nest of snakes? Snakes. I see. Yes.'"

"Fine," he snapped. "Yes, yes, yes. I know. Stop asking questions. Just one, though—do you want me to be useless and quiet, or useful and annoying?"

Rivkah sighed. "Is there a third choice? Could you be useful without being annoying?"

"I could—if you explain to me what we do and how I should do it."

She thought for a while, then shrugged. "I don't know. Hard to explain. You just go out and sort of... listen."

"For what?"

"You'll know." And with that Rivkah leaned back and let the sunshine wash over her, doing everything but telling him out loud to shut up and get on with it.

Aemilius tried to get comfortable, but it was hard. The ground was packed and sandy, baked hard by the relentless sun. All around him, the white walls were uncomfortably bright to look at, so he focused on the red clay tiles. They had found a spot where they could sit and observe a bustling main road, with stalls tucked in beside it and alleyways curling off in all directions. It reminded him of an ant's nest he'd kicked over when he was a boy—a mistake he made once, and once only. The bites had taken weeks to heal.

In order to distract himself, he looked over at the stalls. They all looked fairly similar—big, flat handcarts with two wheels and legs to stand on when they weren't being pushed. The merchants' main strategies to attract customers were colourful canopies mounted above their wares, and impressively loud shouting. Oranges— oranges for sale. Come get your oranges. Sausages from the valley. Straps and bags, leather for all. Best in the region. *Not the best spot for listening,* Aemilius thought drily. *What is there to see?*

But Hispalis had been equally confusing everywhere they'd looked. They'd walked around in the early morning, trying to get a feel for the place. The city was set on a gentle hill, bordered by the river to the south and west, and protected by the city walls to the north and east. The main bridge, to the south-west, led visitors along a broad, straight avenue to the main gates. The main square was situated a short way past that, a huge space lined on three sides with rows of big houses, with the Governor's villa dominating the north side of the square, a sprawling construction fronted by a colonnade. In its surroundings it looked oddly out of place, like a giant's fork stuck down to claim the territory. *For the Empire.* The sentence rung hollow in him, and seeing something that spoke so loudly of Rome—or an idea of it, at any rate—had felt strangely alien. He remembered little, but Rome had always been kept alive as an ideal in his father's house, something to aspire to. Here, it felt imposed, oppressive.

Just like us, he thought, *listening for nothing by a road that has everything.*

Except...

"Rivkah..." he said, cautiously.

"What."

"I've not really been to that many big towns, I have to confess. But..."

"Just get it out," she sighed.

Aemilius looked around. He checked the merchants, the side streets, the main road. He looked at the women buying food. He looked at the men. He saw the animals, the houses, the street, everything. Except...

"I'm just wondering... Where are the children?"

THE INN WAS quiet. A few old men scattered around the main room sat in solitude, nursing cups of wine. As instructed by Graxus and confirmed by Abrax, the legionnaires had all returned from their trips around town and were enjoying the respite from the baking sunshine.

"...and all their old women are swathed in black," Taurio continued. "I saw a grandmother that could not have been wearing fewer than six black carpets, just thumping along. I say that—she may have died years ago. Maybe the cloth was all that was holding her up."

Graxus arrived last, looking haughty. "Peasants," he spat. "Nobody wanted to tell me anything."

"Can't imagine why," Rivkah said quietly.

The young magus made a face at her. "What have we found?"

Prasta began. "We saw a woman begging guards in the square to help her look for her son. They did nothing— but another woman followed her. We saw them talk, cry and embrace—and they went off together."

"This is a big town, right?" Rivkah added to nods around the table. "Did anyone see *any* children about? You know—hitting, chasing, squealing, running rackets, murdering drunk travellers—doing kid stuff. Aemilius noticed it."

There was silence around the table for some moments.

"...Shit," Livia said slowly. "You're right. There was something *wrong* about today." She gave Aemilius an approving nod.

"I saw some children," Graxus said. "They looked well-mannered. Well-bred and well fed. In carriages."

"The word you're looking for is *rich*. I'm talking about proper kids. Not hobby dolls. Hanno—did you go down to the river?"

"The water told me there was a shadow in the night. A terrible thirst."

"Did it tell you any details?"

"No. Sometimes, water is not concerned with specifics."

Graxus scoffed. "What is that supposed to mean?"

"What?" Hanno smiled sweetly.

"All of it!"

"I can't tell you." His smile widened. "Because I don't know what you are asking. *I* am very much concerned with specifics."

Graxus bit his lip. "Fine. First—what was the shadow of? Second—when did the water see it? Third—which water? And fourth—why do you talk to the water?"

Aemilius just caught the flicker of a look passing between the legionnaires, followed by the ghost of a smirk, before Hanno spoke.

"The shadow was a shadow, but it was made without light. A dark figure of some sort. I could see it in the waves, but not clearly. Water has little use for time, and water rarely stays in the same place for long, so asking which water saw the shadow is not fruitful. As for your last question—" He paused and grinned, teeth flashing white in the gloom. "I talk to the water and ask it politely, which is why it sometimes does what I ask of it. You might remember."

A stifled snort from Rivkah did not quite escape Graxus's notice—but he did not rise to the challenge. "I see," he said calmly. "So what you're saying is that sometimes there are shadows in the night."

Hanno chuckled. "Yes. One of them is some kind of thirsty monster, but yes."

"Nobody knows what's going on exactly, but apparently there are enough grieving mothers around that the ones who still know where their children are, are keeping them at home. Just in case, as it were," Aemilius said.

"*Someone* must know something," Abrax said. He turned to Livia and raised an eyebrow. "We need a better... class of information."

The Roman noblewoman groaned. "If that is what must happen, then so be it. I'll need the usual things."

"And are we thinking, maybe… two?" Prasta asked.

Rivkah swore in Hebrew and Aemilius realised the rest of the group were looking at them.

"Yes," Livia said slowly. "We are definitely thinking two."

STARING AT HIMSELF in the mirror, Aemilius didn't know whether to laugh, cry, curse or all three. He felt sick to his stomach. Standing in front of him was the reflection of a skinny, knock-kneed Roman servant, complete with a perfectly ill-fitting tunic and sandals. *Where in Hades's name did they get all this from?* Prasta had gone out to the stables and returned with it instantly. He thought about the plan, such as it had been presented, and felt like he needed to void his bowels through any means, and then immediately do it again. Maybe if his eyeballs popped out from vomiting, he could…? No, there was no way out of this one. He had to be brave.

And then Rivkah emerged from her room, and Aemilius nearly died.

Gone were the simple travellers' trousers, tunic and belt that she wore like a second skin. Instead she was fitted in a tunic like his, which hung upon her like it didn't really want to, turning them into a matching pair of awkward teens.

"Don't. Say. A word," she growled. "I've been forced to do this once before—once—and I cursed so much before we arrived that Livia had to convince everyone that I was a mute."

Aemilius thought about a couple of things that it would be a really good idea to not say, and instead just nodded. "So—we dress up in this, and then what?"

"She swans into the Governor's villa, sprinkles a little bit of magic on it and gets people talking. We're just there to provide cover and respectability, and maybe ears. Apparently fancy Romans never travel without a bloody retinue."

"That sounds about right. Do we go down?"

"This is the worst part," Rivkah sulked. "I don't want to have to kill Taurio when he laughs at me."

"I'm sure he doesn't want to die either. Come on," he said with confidence that he didn't feel.

As it happened, Taurio was off somewhere else with Prasta and Hanno. Graxus gave them the once-over and seemed to see nothing to be scathing about, and Abrax met them outside by an expensive-looking horse and cart. For the second time in a short while he had to fight hard not to laugh, but this time it was from shock. The long, flowing robes of the magus were gone, replaced with the well-tailored and well-worn uniform of a gladiator, and Aemilius suddenly felt very, very small. Abrax looked like he had been chiselled out of flint. Arms bulged and strained against the sleeves, his powerful chest tapered down to a slim waist and the muscles visible below the tunic would not have looked out of place on a horse. The gladius hanging off his belt looked very much not for show. He was every inch the soldier-for-hire, ready to wearily do horrible things without a second thought. Glancing to his side, he saw Rivkah smirk.

"Apparently fancy Romans also rarely travel without someone who looks like they could do some damage."

"I see," was all Aemilius could squeak.

Rattling along at the back of the cart, he tried to remember everything he'd ever learned about servants.

What did they do? He searched his mind and found very little. Servants were just sort of... *there*. They were there, and then things happened if you needed them to. He was deep in thought as they approached the gate and only barely noticed when the guards waved them through without question. When she straightened her back, raised her chin and steeled her eye it was frighteningly easy to slip into Livia's wake. *This is what the mothers of Emperors look like.* He looked away and tried to train his eye on his surroundings.

The fading evening light was changing the town. The glaring brightness of the mid-day sun was gone, replaced with flickering torches mounted high on house walls. The people had changed, too. Day-workers had changed into night-revellers, and singing could be heard from dive bars in narrow alleys. A shout from somewhere, followed by a sharp argument. Something breaking. He closed his eyes and blocked everything out. It was better to let his mind rest and prepare for the coming challenge, when—

The coach stopped.

Rivkah nudged him. "Move," she hissed under her breath. "We're here."

In a half-daze he stumbled after her, to stand obsequiously as Livia descended from the carriage, supported by Abrax's hand. It was all he could do to not gawk as the giant Carthaginian played the fawning subordinate.

"They've been doing this for years," Rivkah muttered under her breath. "Should have told you. You're going to see some... different things tonight. Now stop staring and *think*, Roman." With that she moved, eyes downcast, and fell in line behind Livia, who walked, without hesitation, through the colonnades of the governor's mansion to a massive, steel-bound wooden door. The two soldiers at the front watched her approach, but said nothing.

Like a soldier in a battlefield charge, she didn't even slow as she approached them. "Livia Claudia, to see the Governor." Her voice rang with authority.

The soldiers swung the door open without question—and the Legion was in.

Immediately, Aemilius relaxed. This was not a hillside hydra, nor a cyclops's cave. No, this was a battleground he understood.

Beneath his feet, the mosaic flowed in pleasing, regular patterns. The vestibule was bigger than his father's, but there was something about the paintings; he couldn't quite put his finger on it, but the paintings on the wall felt less... refined... than those at home. He tried to keep half an eye on Livia, in order to better act his servant's part. *Think like a servant!* He glanced at Abrax and shuddered. Somewhere, someone the big Carthaginian's size was leathering someone Aemilius's size for fetching the wrong sort of grapes.

A nervous-looking stork of a man in well-tailored robes with hands that spoke of indoor work came flapping towards them. "Livia Claudia—we weren't told—I would have—"

A beatific smile and the slightest of nods stopped the majordomo in his tracks. "I should have sent a missive. The fault is all mine."

"Oh—oh, no—I would not suggest—"

Livia silenced him with a glance. "We shall speak no more of this," she purred. "Is the Governor receiving visitors? I would love to sit somewhere with clean water and no sand, if only for a moment."

The majordomo bent over almost double, then disappeared, robes swirling about him as he did his best not to run.

As he vanished through a doorway to the side, the corner of Livia's mouth crept up ever so slightly.

"Still got it," she whispered.

"Did you worry?" Abrax rumbled.

"No."

The silence did not last long. The stork-man returned, smiling. "Livia Claudia, the Governor will see you. Let me guide you to the tablinum." As he led Livia away by the arm, he looked over his shoulder at the other three. "Someone will come for you," he snapped, and that was that.

Aemilius felt his chest tighten. "He's just taken her off by herself. Should we worry?"

"No," Abrax said. "She is in a good mood, so I think she'll not hurt anyone too badly."

Rivkah stifled a chortle. "You should see your own face, little rabbit. What are you afraid of? Are these not your people?"

That's the problem. Worry changed to annoyance. "Well—they are... but I just haven't ever snuck into a villa under false pretences before. It feels a bit strange."

Rivkah was about to answer when a servant girl of about twelve materialised seemingly out of nowhere. "Come with me," she said quietly, then turned and headed off past a column obscuring the entrance to a corridor. Rivkah just ghosted to the front. It was not until he was actually in the passage, Abrax crowding the walls behind him, that Aemilius realised she'd gone first because she was best equipped to defend herself if it was a trap. He thought about what it would be like to always think that everything might be about to kill you, and then realised that was essentially his life now, and then they were through into a sparse room, just off the kitchen, with rough benches set in a horse-shoe around a table. Before they'd sat down, cups had appeared on the table. Almost instantly, the girl appeared with an amphora about half her size. The wine was poured and she darted off again.

Rivkah raised one approving eyebrow at Aemilius. "Not a bad house, this."

Remembering his role at the last minute, he shrugged and made a non-committal noise.

The girl appeared again, expertly balancing three wide bowls of stew that smelled considerably better than they looked.

"Thank you," Abrax said slowly.

She looked up at him with something between concern and fear, and muttered something that could have been 'you're welcome.'

Across the table, Aemilius noticed Rivkah looking at the girl with a frown.

"Have you eaten?" she said, doing a pretty good job of mimicking Livia's authority, and when the answer was too slow in coming, "Sit."

Wide-eyed, the girl obeyed as Rivkah pushed her bowl across the table.

"Eat." Then she looked up at them. "You need to go check on the horse."

"Yup." Abrax picked up his bowl, brought it to his lips and simply poured the contents in, swallowing as he went.

Biting his back teeth to neither laugh nor stare, Aemilius focused on shovelling as much stew in his face as he could before clambering to his feet and shuffling after Abrax. Out of the corner of his eye he saw Rivkah pour the remnants of his bowl into her own, in front of the servant-girl.

Ahead of him, the Carthaginian was striding confidently down another corridor, past the kitchen. The cookfires had burned down to embers and three stocky figures were shuffling around in the half-light, clearing up and preparing for the next meal. Nodding as he passed, the big man picked his way through the corridors and out into the inner courtyard, where he cut through towards the back.

Across the courtyard a welcoming fire burned up in the tablinum, a perfect vantage point where the Governor could sit at his desk and see through to the atrium. Even at that distance, Livia's silhouette was striking. She looked so delicate, like a statue carved out of porcelain, but Abrax did not seem to see or worry unduly.

He was about to ask where the big magus was going, but then remembered Rivkah sending him to check on the horse.

The now-familiar, soothing smell of the horses reached him just as they turned the corner. The stablehand, a stick-thin boy of about ten, started to see them, but settled again quickly.

"Just here for Livia Claudia's horse," Abrax said. "No need to fear us."

"Weren't afraid," the boy replied sullenly. "Not of you, anyway. Big lump."

"Watch your mouth," Aemilius snapped, echoing the words he'd heard so many times. "Elders and betters."

"No ye'r not," the boy shot back. "Elders, maybe, but no' betters. Bet you can't lay a hand on Balios."

"Bet you I can," Aemilius replied, completely on reflex, and regretted it immediately as the boy's face contorted in impish glee.

Balios, as it turned out, was a sixteen-hand liver chestnut stallion who seemed to have allowed himself to be stabled just once in his life—for this night only—in order to take a small break from killing and breaking absolutely everything. Even from behind, at a distance and half-hidden by the stalls, he radiated ill temper.

"Don't do it," Abrax muttered under his breath.

Correct! Listen to the big man! the voice in his head agreed, at considerable volume. *Say no! Tell the kid to go sleep in dung! Don't do it! Do not do it!*

"Easy," Aemilius said out loud, and wondered in panic why he had.

"G'on then," the boy goaded. "Le's see ya."

Heart thumping, Aemilius inched towards the big horse. A deep snort and a stamp suggested that this had been noticed and was very much not appreciated. He closed his eyes and conjured up the image of Furibunda in his head, murmuring as he went.

One step—then another—and another—

The crashing rattle of a kick against the gate shook him, but from somewhere, a strange calm was setting in. The murmured voice of Quintus thrummed somewhere in him, in his spine, and he opened his mouth and let the words escape. "I know," he half-whispered. "I know. I know you could. And you would, too, if you had the chance. And you will. You will. You know you will, and I know you will. The plains will be covered with the crushed skulls of your enemies, and you will rise and kick the sky, and you will rule them all, and be their lord, and they will run with you and keep running and you will run and run and run and the horizon will come to you and the world will be in your eyes and the speed and the speed and the speed will be you and the thunder will be in your hooves and you will be king of the world and"—the brush was in his hand, and he didn't know where it had come from, but it was there and it moved along over the terrifying strength of the beast—"once you get there you will simply turn and go the other way and conquer those lands again, because you are truly the king of kings and none is your equal. And one day, if you ever die, you will ride on the big plains in the underworld, and when you get there a leathery old bastard from the Fourth Legion might meet you, and when you do, thank him from me," Aemilius whispered.

A soft whinny, and a massive head nudged his shoulder. "I know, big lad. I know. I am going to head off now, but woe betide whoever steps in your way. Kick them twice from me." He put down the brush. The big horse snorted once. Turning around, he walked away from its stall and remembered, slowly, that he wasn't alone.

Abrax and the boy were fairly indistinguishable in their stunned surprise, and he remembered just in time that he had a role to play. "Nice horse," he said, off-hand—and then, suddenly, he realised why he'd done it. "Was that what you were scared of?"

"Naw." The boy looked at him, sizing him up. "'E's alright. Have to give him an apple sometimes to make him forget to kill me, but 'e's alright."

Aemilius made his voice soft, willing Abrax to slink into the background. "What is it, then?"

The boy made a face, as if to dislodge something from his teeth. "Nuffin'." He paused for a while. "Just been annoying, 's all."

"Mm." *Come on…*

"Can't go out," the boy continued. "Florian won't let me."

"Is that the—?" Aemilius waved his arms awkwardly, mimicking the stork-man.

The boy snickered. "Yup. Got a broom up 'is arse. Apparently, been a couple kids go missing in the Pileta."

"The…"

"Pileta," the boy repeated. "It's the south-west quarter of town. We call it the 'sink' because that's where the scum sinks to, just before the river takes them."

Charming. "So you've been stuck here?"

"Yeh," the boy said, kicking a pebble. "Still. 'S not so bad. There's food, and it's warm at night. So where have you been, then? Where are you coming from?"

He was about to start making up answers when Florian marched in, snapping his fingers, only registering mild surprise when he saw Aemilius and Abrax. "Oh. You're here. Good. Livia Claudia's horse and cart. Out front. Now!" Spinning on his heel, he stormed off again.

The stable boy pulled a gloriously annoyed face, silently mimicked the majordomo's order and set about getting their horse out of the stall. Working without thinking, Aemilius went over to where the cart stood, readying the harness. Moments later they were sitting in the front, leading the horse out at a gentle saunter. He waved to the stable boy, who waved back.

"That was good work in there," Abrax said quietly. "We know more about what's happening, and where to go next." He pulled deftly on the reins, guiding the horse to a standstill just as Livia Claudia exited the Governor's villa, smiling over her shoulder at a short, pot-bellied and richly dressed man in his mid-forties with stars in his eyes, followed by her lethal 'servant' Rivkah. Moments later they were on their way, moving far less quickly than any of them wanted to.

"We found—oof." Rivkah's elbow was astoundingly pointy, and Aemilius winced at the impact on his side.

"We are still servants," she hissed. "And people might be watching. *Don't* look. Just play your part, and wait. We'll share when we're clear of the bridge."

There was nothing to do but obey. He watched as people scurried along to be home before dark—merchants with their wares, tired workers hunched over. The town seemed busy, yes, but safe enough.

What's out there?

WHEN THEY GOT back to the inn, the others were already in place.

"Table. Sit," Livia snapped.

"Go fuck a hedgehog, princess," Rivkah snapped back. "Every moment I spend in this getup means someone is closer to dying."

"Go change, then. But be quick."

Abrax had already disappeared. Aemilius sprinted up the stairs after Rivkah. They met again outside the rooms a few moments later.

"I never thought it'd feel so nice to get back into these things," he said, tugging on his dusty tunic.

"A servant's clothes are nothing but a dog-collar." She sneered. "And I only do it because I have to, but they know I hate it and I will not allow them to forget." She turned and disappeared down the stairs, leaving Aemilius to scramble to follow. He was last to the table, where everyone else was seated. Taurio passed him a cup.

"We don't know exactly what we're facing," Prasta began. "But we know that it has caught four children in two nights."

"Bodies?" asked Livia.

"One. Drained."

"Shit," she muttered.

"We were told that they'd gone missing in the south-west corner of town, near the river," added Abrax, nodding to Aemilius.

"Any sightings?" Livia looked at the assembled group.

There was no reply.

"One of the children was taken from his room," Taurio said. "We found the crying woman from yesterday. She told us. The window was open."

"Why did the stupid peasant leave her window open?" asked Graxus.

"I'd guess she thought it would be safe, since she lives on the *third floor*."

"Shit," said Livia again.

"We'll have to go out tonight," Graxus said with finality. "Equipped and ready."

"Groups?"

"You, you and you"—the teen pointed at Rivkah, Aemilius and Taurio—"with Abrax. I'll go with you three." He nodded at Livia, Prasta and Hanno. "And we go on foot."

Aemilius looked around, but no-one seemed to protest. When it came down to it, the Hidden Legion seemed well-drilled in taking commands. *That's one way to stay alive, I suppose,* he thought as he followed Abrax out the door. *Especially when you have no idea what you're up against.*

XI

HISPALIS

Entering the city as mercenaries was significantly harder than swanning in as Roman aristocracy, Aemilius decided. He had drifted off for the blink of an eye, and suddenly his three fellow legionnaires had changed—morphed into slightly sloshed party-goers talking too loudly and singing rude songs. Granted, for Taurio that wasn't that big a leap, but it was all he could do to keep it together when Abrax started slurring his words and leaning on the big Gaul as they marched up the avenue towards the town gates. The gates themselves were closed and bolted, but a side door big enough for a horse and rider to pass through had been opened, manned by a watchman who looked fantastically annoyed to be there.

"Stand," he growled.

"If you'll stand for me, big boy," Rivkah purred with just enough edge on it to make it sound as much like a threat as a proposition.

The watchman pulled a disgusted face. "Where are you headed?"

"Where is one ever headed, in life?" Taurio began, sounding like a synthesis of every awful bard in every awful inn in the world. "The world is big, and the roads are many—"

"Shut up," the watchman snapped. "Keep it down, stick to the laws and don't cause trouble or I will be happy to crack your skulls myself."

"I'll crack your skull twice, stud," Rivkah said, and the group shuffled through the gate as the watchman tried to work out whether that was an invitation, a threat or both. They stumbled around the corner, at which point the drunken stumbling melted away and Aemilius found himself having to shift it to keep up.

Taurio glanced at Rivkah.

"What?"

"Crack your skull twice?"

She made a dismissive sound. "Worth it. Guys like that are confused by sandals. Or fruit with a peel."

"Fair enough."

With that, they fell quiet again. There was a purpose to their walk, a swing of the hip that would, Aemilius imagined, look to an observer like they belonged there. *Which is true, sort of.* He thought of the special skills around him, and not for the first time wondered what on earth he was supposed to contribute. More brawn than Taurio? More death than Rivkah? More absolute destruction than a *magus* that could command *fire?* Pushing the thoughts from his head, he clutched the dagger that Prasta had found for him and focused on looking.

As evening moved to night, Hispalis had changed again. The streets were quiet, and the only people about moved with an urgency and purpose much like the Legion's own. There was a feeling of fear in the air.

This was not a time to be about. In the empty square, the white buildings magnifying every sound, made whispers bounce around and set the darkness dancing in perfect step with the feeble light from the mounted torches.

And even in the silence, he only just heard the cry.

It was reedy and stifled, almost like that of a baby bird.

A child, shouting.

"Mother!"

It was followed by a full-throated wail of anguish, and they were running, sprinting towards the sound. Out of another alley a hundred yards further down, the other four legionnaires came running flat out. With a flurry of hand signals they broke off to the other side, circling a big block of apartments for the poor.

There! On the side of the house, painted in stark relief against the white: a shadow. A man, with something slung across his shoulder, climbing up a rope ladder to the roof. Aemilius managed a squawk and a desperate gesture—but that was all it took. He watched Rivkah leap up onto a barrel by the side of the house, flowing in a fluid motion onto a brick ledge too small for a finch to sit on, launch herself onto a windowsill and vault up to the first floor. She sprang from one perch to another, always rising, always risking her life. He felt sick to his stomach just watching her, the voice in his head screaming *Do something!*

"Door!" he shouted at Taurio. "Stairway!"

He had only heard his father talk about the insulae, the tenements in Rome where they housed the poor, but they were apparently all built with the same idea—little boxes stacked high, with stairs to get up and down. If they were kept well, they were decent places to live. If not... He shuddered.

Around them, the flats were coming to life. Half-dressed and tough-looking men emerged from doorways, holding cudgels, sickles—whatever was to hand. *Nobody has left their weapons out of reach*, Aemilius thought. *Someone is going to get caught tonight. Someone unfamiliar. A stranger running around...* The realisation hit him like a bucket of cold water. Whatever they were chasing might not be the most dangerous thing here. He pushed all thoughts aside and bellowed, in his best mimicry of a southern accent, "The bastard went down the road!"

A blink, a heartbeat—and then he saw a thick-armed man with a broken nose and a docker's hook echo the shout. Moments later, the mob were rushing down the road to follow the invisible enemy.

Abrax paused to let three strong men past, glancing at the doorway to the block the shadow had come from. Then the three of them ducked inside and sprinted to the stairs. They were treacherous, worn and slick from hundreds of sandals going to and from work every day, but fear and fury pumped in him and he found himself sprinting ahead of the two older men. He found the ladder up to the roof, charged up—and saw Rivkah, standing over a pool of blood and the corpse of a man displaying her handiwork.

"He skipped over the roof, kid on his back, out cold," she said calmly. "Left this one to slow me down. Handy fucker, too."

"Uh..." Aemilius pointed vaguely at the three-inch cut on her forearm.

Rivkah shrugged, almost apologetically. "As I said, he was handy. Let's go."

He gasped for breath. "Where... to?" and immediately regretted it as she headed off for the ledge at a sprint.

What happened next was a blur, and he threw himself into it, and chased her as fast as he could, and when his foot hit the ledge he pushed as hard as he could and then he looked down and death came to him again and he thought about how it would feel to smack into the wall and fall like a sack of potatoes down to the stones below. And then the impact of the next rooftop under his feet almost knocked the wind out of him, and he fell over and rolled and giggled hysterically. He clambered to his feet to spot Rivkah disappearing over the far edge of the roof.

The shouting made him rush over and peer down.

Rivkah was on her way down the rope, almost in free-fall.

Below her was a mess of bodies, flailing arms and pain. In the cramped alley, at least ten hooded shapes were jabbing, circling and gouging at three familiar outlines, standing over a fallen figure.

Panicking, Aemilius looked around in a frenzy. He could see Abrax running towards the edge. He could see the top of Taurio's head heading down the stairs again. And then his feet were moving, and his knees were bending, and the plant pot was rising and he screamed in frustration and wished for more muscle and staggered towards the edge and aimed and let go. A dull crunch, a loud crash and the pot was gone, along with at least one skull. A change in the tone of the fight below suggested that shortly after his missile arrived, so did Rivkah.

Abrax showed up at his side.

"Down," he snapped.

Arms still burning, Aemilius scrambled to grab the rope and started his descent. A faint *whoosh* of heat and the magus descended past him at a controlled pace, robes billowing in the air.

When he reached the ground, he met a group with grim faces standing in a pile of dead and dying men.

"They were waiting in the shadows." Livia seethed. "We walked straight into it. The first thing they did was throw bricks. I can't tell if they were aiming for him, but…"

Aemilius glanced down.

A man lay at his feet. He wore the same robes as Graxus had, but he was three times the youth's age. Before his eyes, the corpse seemed to shrink and age, faster and faster.

"It comes to us all," Hanno said quietly. "We are but guests."

"It felt like they knew."

Abrax stepped closer to Livia. It was not a big gesture, but it was enough to take some of the edge off her fury. "A trap," he said.

She nodded.

"I don't know about you," Prasta said, "but I am getting quite tired of this."

Grim nods around the group.

And that was when Taurio arrived, huffing and puffing. "I saw him," he wheezed. "Ran straight past me. Kid on his back. Strong bastard. Knocked me over."

A couple of eyebrows raised suggested to Aemilius that this was not a regular occurrence.

The big Gaul drew a breath. "It was the sailor. Heading to the west."

No-one asked anything else. As he started running, Abrax flicked his wrist, and at his feet the body of Graxus burst into flame. Two turns down an alley and past a square, and a shout drew their attention, followed by an uncomfortable cracking sound. Sprinting towards the disturbance, feet slapping on the cobbles, they came to a group of workers strewn about in a street. Some were bleeding from their noses, others lying at an uncomfortable angle. One of them, an ox of a man, saw them and weakly pointed down the alley.

They ran.

Shouts, sounds of pain, shadows in the night.

"This way!" Rivkah ducked down an alley.

Aemilius followed, as did Livia. The others thundered on down the road.

"We walked here yesterday," the girl added.

He tried to remember, but all he could think of was how close he'd been to just lobbing the plant pot over the edge and hoping for the best. They ducked past feeding troughs and barrels, stacked carpenters' boards and a shop front, and burst onto a broad street. In the distance they could hear some kind of bird cawing.

And then their quarry rounded the corner.

His hood had fallen off on the run, and Donato's face looked slick with sweat. He was carrying a child, maybe six or seven years old, over his shoulders. He ran on for another dozen yards or so before he saw Aemilius, Rivkah and Livia blocking his path. He looked at them almost quizzically, as if he'd invited them for tomorrow rather than today. In turn, they stared at him, blinking in confusion.

"We meet again." His voice was calm—annoyingly so.

Rivkah's daggers were in her hands in a blink. "You're dead," she growled.

Donato smiled an indulgent smile. "No," he said, almost sadly. "I am not."

Behind him, the others came around the corner. Abrax's hands immediately lit up, but he stopped short of setting the world on fire. "Who sent you?" the big man bellowed.

Turning so he could watch both groups at once, the man they knew as Donato smiled again. "My father sent me." The smile turned into a sneer. "He sent me to finish that which he started. The Empire"—he spat—"the Empire shall be brought to its knees."

"I *am* going to crack his skull, but he does have a point."

"Shut up, Gaul," Donato snapped. "You and your limp-wristed forefathers invited the Roman into your homes."

"You little—"

Donato's voice grew louder. "You took everything they gave you. The roads. The governors. The yoke. Slaves," he spat.

"Enough," Abrax said. "Put the child down, and you'll die a quick death."

Donato smiled again. *He is too confident. Why?* Aemilius's heart pounded.

"You did very well with the harpies," he purred. "That was too easy. But I knew it would be. The hydras..." He pouted melodramatically. "I liked them. I think the winner would have been a beautiful beast. But you killed them as well."

If he knows so much about us, why is he so sure of himself? He looked around, stared at every nook and cranny, searched for hidden enemies. But there was nothing.

"The cyclops... poor Zeno. He just wanted to be loved, really. That, and drink the spine-juice of the occasional human. But it cost you the rider. I rather enjoyed that."

Ambush? Trap? He saw the legionnaires slowly encircling the lone, hooded man, cutting off escape routes.

"And now you're here, and you are searching for something, and with typical Roman arrogance you think you've found it."

Frantic now, Aemilius checked again. He stared at the shadows behind everyone, willed the dark to move, checked the alleys—

"And in a way... you have." And he cried out, "They are all yours, my beloved!"

And finally, Aemilius looked up.

It took him a while to understand what he was looking at, though.

She looked like a woman. Hard to tell from that distance, but she seemed tall and slim. Her hair was dark, which contrasted with her shimmering white skin. She wore something that could have been a Vestal robe once, but now it just sort of floated around her *like a drowned girl's dress, like a corpse shroud*—panic tugged at him and he pushed the thoughts away.

How was she standing like that, though? There was nothing to suggest what she might be balancing on. He realised that he had started pointing and making noises, and the *whoomph* of a fireball wrenched his thoughts back into the square. He willed himself to watch this new enemy burn to a cinder—and recoiled when she waved the flame away like one would a pesky insect. Then the woman on the wall spread her arms wide and a blackness flowed from her cloak, spreading over the square. Prasta shouted something but Aemilius didn't hear it, because he'd just drawn a breath, and suddenly his stomach was tied up in knots and something was trying to escape out through his eyesockets. All he could do was to clutch his belly with one hand as he collapsed to the street. The others were similarly afflicted, although he couldn't see Prasta and Taurio. He breathed hard through his nose, fighting the wave of nausea that threatened to close his throat, as he rolled over...

...just in time to see Donato shoving the boy to the ground and dashing down a side street.

There was a brief sound like the flutter of crow's wings, and Aemilius dared to glance up just as the woman on the wall descended gently to the ground.

He got a better look at her face and wished he hadn't. It looked like a twisted sculptor's idea of a beautiful woman—high cheekbones, perfect alabaster skin, blood-red lips—but her eyes were entirely black, like someone had prised them out and replaced them with raven-stones.

Around him, the Hidden Legion was agonisingly slowly getting to its feet.

"You're dead, bitch," Rivkah slurred.

The woman noticed her. Silently she raised her hand, working her fingers as if teasing thread from a cloth. A single strangled cry was all Rivkah could manage, staring at her hands in horror as vines erupted from her forearms and twisted together, binding her tighter and tighter. Livia was by her side in an instant with a dagger aloft, face white as a sheet, cutting through the vines and swearing between clenched teeth as they grew back.

The woman landed next to the youth, settling gracefully and sinking to one knee. She reached for the boy's neck, tenderly, and lifted his head, exposing his throat. Aemilius watched in horror as her lips peeled back and bared fangs as long as his little finger, poised to sink into the unconscious boy's soft skin.

"No!" he shouted.

The stranger paused for a brief moment, then resumed her approach, sniffing the air around her prey like a fox.

"*No!*" Aemilius tried again, staggering to his feet and shuffling towards the boy and the woman. "You can't! The boy is poisoned! The man—uh, Donato—is trying to kill you!" He wasn't sure whether he'd created confusion or annoyance, but he'd settle for either.

The creature hissed at him, warning him to back off her meal.

He did not.

"Listen to me! Look!" Heart thumping, he bared his own neck, then made an exaggerated grimace. "Bad! The boy is bad!"

The woman-creature barked something at him in a harsh, guttural language.

Aemilius held out his hands in what he hoped was a timeless gesture of incomprehension and advanced. "You need to run! Run away while you still can!"

And then death came to Aemilius yet again.

It was in the tilt of the head, the slow rise, the unfurling spine. It was in the robes that billowed even though there was no gust of wind in the square, and in the metallic taste of magic in the air. And with it came a sound that was more like a feeling, like the deep rumble of shifting earth, and on top of that sound, like the buzzing of an unseen stinging fly, was the faint, tinny sound of a whistle played badly.

Prasta!

This time, Abrax didn't need to tell him to stand back.

The woman's head twitched and double lids blinked over the raven-black eyes, trying to dislodge the sounds, but it didn't work, Out of the shadows of an alley Prasta emerged, and now the bard was not moving like a collection of angry sticks. She swayed and glided and undulated, the tin whistle moving with her, layering and building discordant notes, long and short, into a tapestry of distraction. The creature walked towards her—a staggering step at first, then another, picking up pace as it passed by Aemilius, with a blast of cold air fierce enough to pucker the skin on his arms and set his hairs on end. As the monster's back was turned, he reached for his dagger and thought to plunge it in her back... until he caught a glimpse of Taurio, cautiously wheeling around to the monster's rear, cradling something small in his hands.

The creature let out a shriek that cut through to Aemilius's bones. It seemed it had come as close as Prasta would let it, and now it thrashed and flailed at the bard, just out of touching range. Beads of sweat formed on the tall woman's forehead, but the strains of the flute stayed strong. Behind the creature, Taurio raised some sort of small clay jar in his hands, set his shoulders, and sprinted towards the creature—only for it to extend an arm sharply, causing the big Gaul to stop as though struck and fall to his knees, clawing at his eyes.

Summoning all of his courage, Aemilius ran to his big friend, snatched the clay pot from his hand, sprinted into the cold embrace of the creature and smashed the pot on the back of its head.

Pain exploded in his hand.

He screamed—and screamed—and kept on screaming, his skin melting and liquid heat spreading up his arm. He stared at his hand, red and peeling—and then, beyond it, he saw the creature sinking to the ground, a horrifically expanding hole in the back of its head, the stench of burning flesh and hair assailing his nostrils as he threw up and collapsed.

He was dimly aware of bodies and faces as the world blurred around him. Heat was replaced with the most incredibly soothing cold balm, and he cried tears of pure relief. There was a wet, crunching sound somewhere close but out of sight, and the next thing he could make out was Prasta's annoyed face.

"That was not smart," she chided. "You really shouldn't get that stuff on your skin."

"I... know that... now," Aemilius wheezed through gritted teeth. "Thank... you."

"No, thank *you*," Taurio rumbled behind him. "You saved us when I choked."

Prasta made a dismissive sound. "Witches. Her lot are an absolute arse to deal with. You never know which ones have which tricks."

"Call that a witch?" Abrax joined as Aemilius was being hoisted back on his feet. "That was no witch. That looked to me to be a mormo."

A *child-snatcher*? Aemilius almost scoffed at the idea—but then he thought he'd seen enough in the past week to not immediately dismiss fairy tales. "Are you saying mormos actually exist?"

"Considering you broke one of my nice clay pots on the head of one, I'd say yes," Prasta said drily. "It's rotting over there, if you want to take a closer look."

Sharp, bright sounds were coming from the corpse. Taurio was kneeling over its head with a bag, a small hammer and a chisel. "Teeth might be good for something, I reckon," he said to no-one in particular.

"Bitch is down. Where'd the bastard go?" Rivkah snarled. The vines on her forearms had withered away the moment the apparition had been burned.

"That way," Aemilius pointed to where Donato had

disappeared—and suddenly he knew with absolute certainty where the man was headed. "Down to the docks."

THE CITY WAS a blur around them. The houses had long since become one mass of windows and white plaster, but once they knew they were heading for water they simply pushed Hanno to the front and followed his unerring sense. Aemilius could only focus on two things—the mixture of pain and relief in his hand, and the fury driving the Legion. They had gotten a good look at their enemy this time, and now it was time to go hunting. Left, right, right, left—Hanno's feel for water had them dashing this way and that, but suddenly a bend in an alleyway brought them to the river.

This late in the night, it was a magical forest of masts bobbing gently over a silver stream. A row of piers stretched to the west, disappearing into the shadow of the city wall. A dock to the east, then another, separated by a broad wharf.

"There!" Hanno pointed. Far in the distance, a small boat with two sails was about to disappear around the bend in the river.

Livia immediately started barking orders. "Prasta, Taurio, Rivkah—find us a boat."

Aemilius watched them disappear into the mess of vessels.

"Abrax?" she prompted.

The big magus stood on the docks, straining to see. "It's too far. I couldn't be sure to hit him. And it would be too big."

"Hanno?"

"I have asked the water, but there are forces at play. I cannot pull her in. Not at this distance. And he's going fast, too, with no wind."

"Shit. Where to, though?"

"Wherever he is going, we're going there too," Abrax said darkly. "We need to have a quiet word with our friend."

Silently, a broad-bellied one-master glided towards the pier, and Taurio bellowed to them. "Good evening, travellers! Would you like to come aboard? Me and my friends here were thinking of going fishing for bastards."

XII

THE SEA

Heart racing and blood pounding, Aemilius gave himself to the thrill of the chase. The moon was sheltering behind a bank of thick cloud, reducing the world to shades of ghostly grey, but if he squinted hard enough he could make out a splash of darker shadow up ahead, drifting into and out of sight as the river twisted and turned. Hispalis faded behind them without so much as a whisper. He could feel the force of Hanno's magic in the water driving the boat, and looked around to feast on the impending destruction of that bastard Donato, painted on the faces on the legionnaires.

Except it wasn't.

What little he could make out in the gloom was a mix of anger, annoyance and boredom.

"Why aren't we going faster?" Rivkah looked sullen.

"I can negotiate with the water, but the rocks are a different matter," Hanno said.

The water mage's voice sounded faint and distant. Almost... *diluted*. Aemilius tried to imagine what he must be doing—sending his consciousness into the water, moulding it to his will, holding it all together— and stopped immediately as he sensed the enormity of the headache coming on. Taurio sat at the tiller in the back, breathing heavily as he leaned this way and that. Next to him Prasta sat, muttering directions as and when they were needed. Abrax and Livia hauled on the sail.

Mostly to satisfy his own curiosity, but also to distract Rivkah from killing someone out of boredom, Aemilius leaned over. "Why are they bothering with the sail?" he asked quietly.

"Saves energy, I guess," was the curt reply.

"Every sea is made of drops." Hanno's voice had a sing-song quality to it that had the echo of a babbling brook.

In the near-darkness, Rivkah shrugged. "The sooner we catch him the better. I look forward to making him hurt."

Aemilius watched the black banks as they faded into the distance, then looked ahead to the boat—or where he imagined the boat to be. "We're not gaining," he said quietly.

"He speaks to the water too. It listens to him."

"More than to you?"

"Maybe not, my little scorpion. Maybe not." There was the suggestion of a smile in the voice for a moment, which faded. "But…"

"But what?"

"There's something…" Hanno's voice had sunk down to a whisper.

Rivkah made to speak, but a hard look from Livia stopped her, and they sat quietly in the boat, listening to the gentle lapping of the water on the hull, and the cries of the world in the night. Around them, the banks of the river widened into an estuary, plains stretching away in the dark, dusted by the faintest suggestion of moonlight. On either side, far away, hills loomed, black drawings against the endless grey canvas of the sky.

"He can sail, the bastard," Taurio muttered from the back.

"We knew that," Abrax hissed back.

The river had stopped winding, becoming a broad, Roman road to the sea. Aemilius felt the breeze on his face cooling as the boat picked up speed, pushed along by unseen forces underneath them. Quietly, the directions from Prasta faded as they left the hidden rocks and sand banks behind them.

And suddenly, they were no longer sailing on a river.

They were away.

He still found it hard to understand the horror of the sea, but he could *feel* the ground dropping away under him. He could sense the depth of the water that he was skimming across in only a tiny wooden shell. He found it all too easy to imagine a wall, in a house, and him as a tiny insect at the top of that wall and everything under it as water that would crush him, fill his lungs and cut his life short.

An elbow from Rivkah jolted him back into the present. "Stop it," she said.

"What?" he said, wincing and rubbing his side.

"You were panicking, and you need to stop it. We are all going to die; nobody wants to. If you panic, you'll not only die quicker, but you'll make your life miserable while you're waiting. So stop it." She didn't allow him to get the question in. "Just wait. Learn to wait. We'll catch him soon, or get in range of Abrax lighting his boat on fire, and then things will happen. Think of it as a ride on a horse. Just sit back and wait."

A thought occurred to Aemilius. "I wanted to ask"—Rivkah swore in Hebrew—"no, I wanted to ask—we've just struck out straight into the darkness. What happens to our cart? Our horses?"

To his surprise, she didn't reply with an insult. "We have... people," she said, almost reluctantly. "No legion is made up of just soldiers. There are quartermasters and baggage train drivers and all sorts." She paused. "I don't know all of it, but they do." She nodded towards Abrax and Livia. "They've been doing this for ages. They know someone everywhere."

"So, will he..."

"If we don't return, then someone arrives, settles our bill and takes the things we need."

"But we don't know where we're going!"

"They go to one of a number of secure places," Livia said over her shoulder. "Eventually, everything makes its way back to the Fort. We just need to catch this bastard, skin him alive, ask him a few questions as he dies in agony and then take stock of where we are. If we're far from the cart, supplies and the like, there are places we can go."

"The Hidden Legion has friends," Abrax added.

"As much as any Roman has friends."

"Hand on the tiller, eyes on the sail, mouth shut."

"Or what? You'll play me a song on the flute?" Taurio grinned. "Have I sung you the famous Gallic song 'The Boar, the Oar and the Door' yet? You'd love it. At one point they rhyme 'canny' with fa—"

"I would *bless your fields with rain*, my friend"—to his credit, Taurio knew a threat when one was spoken and shut up immediately—"if you would help me listen to the water by staying quiet. There is something... there is a drop, a drip, a crack in a wall somewhere..."

Aemilius looked around, confused. The open sea had many things, but a wall was definitely not one of them. In the east he could see a faint purplish glow that brought the promise of sunrise, and Donato's sail was still there ahead of them, frustratingly far away, but... walls?

"You're making no sense, frog."

"Shut it, girl," Hanno growled. The flash of anger in his voice made the hairs on Aemilius's arms stand up on end, and he glanced at Rivkah. She looked like she'd been slapped awake, mouth opening and closing like a fish. She looked around at the others, barely visible in the gloom, but nobody said anything. What Aemilius saw, he didn't like at all. Surprise, concern... and fear. This was not how it was supposed to be. They were used to Hanno being calm, confident and happy on the water. This was something different.

And then Aemilius looked at Hanno himself.

Completely unaware of the people around him the water-magus sat stock still, poised like a cat on the hunt. Every fibre of his being spoke of concentration and focus. The air seemed thicker around him, and only the rhythmic, slow movement of his chest gave any life to the figure.

When Hanno flinched, Aemilius felt like he himself had been struck.

He looked to see if anyone else had noticed, but the crew had fallen back into the quiet waiting he'd seen from them before—the professional soldier's rest. Trying hard not to stare at Hanno, Aemilius focused instead on the thin line of the sunrise. He was dimly aware of the suggestion of land somewhere far to the south, but it could just as well be his eyes playing tricks, willing them somewhere safe.

The purple line had swollen and turned a soft, dark blue with a hint of the coming dawn. Aemilius stared at it as hard as he could, keeping his eyes off Hanno at all costs. Up ahead the sail had grown ever so slightly bigger, but Donato was a long way off still.

Around him, the soldiers of the Hidden Legion took their rest. None of them had slept, and he was starting to feel the heavy drag of it, the leaden feeling in the legs and the stomach, when he heard the sound.

It was a new sound, oddly in tune with the waves—Hanno. Groaning softly.

"What is it, friend?" Abrax's voice was deep, calm and reassuring.

"There's something…"

"The crack in the wall?"

"Something…" The words faded almost as soon as they passed the water magus's lips. His breathing was suddenly a bit laboured. "…strange."

"Prasta," Abrax snapped.

"I don't have anything," the bard hissed back. "I could play, but he needs food. Food and water."

"Tell me more." Abrax had managed to shift himself so that he could reach out to Hanno, who looked like a child next to his hulking frame.

"He has magic," Hanno whispered. "He has magic we haven't seen yet. He is too fast. I won't catch him."

"Don't say that," Abrax said. "You are Hanno the Wise! We have done too much and seen too much, old friend. We do not give up. Are you going to give up on me?"

Hanno said nothing, but the groaning had stopped. The small man's spine straightened, and he sat up. A tiny wave splashed up over the gunwale and hit Abrax in the face.

"Didn't think so," the big magus said, smiling.

Abrax turned, and Livia swore, and Hanno gasped.

"The wall..." he hissed.

Aemilius looked down at the water. There was a line of foam alongside the boat. He looked up —and forward— and then his insides turned liquid and the gorge rose in his throat. Donato's sail had disappeared, and instead, from out of nowhere and coming at them fast, was a wave easily twice as tall as the boat.

Hanno's knuckles whitened as he grasped the gunwale.

"Hold on tight," he hissed.

Nobody needed to be encouraged.

Within moments the boat was rising, and rising, and rising, and then they were up on top of a hill in the middle of the ocean, and then they were careering down again, and Aemilius's stomach now lived in his chest.

Once the wave passed, there was another, smaller wave of swearwords from everyone on the boat, but Abrax was first to ask the question.

"What was that?"

As he looked at Hanno, Aemilius thought of how they had mocked him on his first foray into the waves, days that felt like lifetimes ago. *He looks how I felt.*

The water-magus was ashen-faced. "Something cracked somewhere. A dam burst. That's what caused the wave."

"A dam? Underwater?" Livia looked puzzled.

"No—" Hanno waved his long-fingered hands, as if to brush away a fly. "No, no. Not... physical. Something...

has come from somewhere. In the water. He's... summoned something."

This was language they understood. There was an enemy, and the enemy had made a move, and now it was time to kill something.

"Where?" Rivkah was on her feet, blades in hand.

Hanno fell silent and seemed to flow into his own skin, softening his shoulders and his elbows as he felt for the connection with the water. "Far away," he whispered, "but coming fast." He drew a deep breath. For the first time since he had stepped on the boat, his eyes opened fully. "My friends." The boat slowed to a halt.

"Shit," Livia muttered.

Hanno stood, balancing perfectly despite the rocking boat. "An evil is coming, the likes of which I have never felt. We cannot run, for it moves with speed I cannot hope to match. We must meet it here. I will do all I can, but if this is the last time we speak, know this. You have been the water that fed me, the drip that filled my soul. I owe you everything, and will give you everything." There was a silence then, and the only sound was the lapping of the waves against the side of the boat.

"What do you need us to do?" Abrax's face was set in determination.

A coldness sank over Hanno's face. "Stand back," he said, walking slowly to the bow of the little fishing boat.

In a quiet little pocket of his mind, the part that wasn't screaming *you are going to die*, Aemilius marvelled at how the little man could move about the boat like a dancer on a flat floor. There was no movement wasted, no struggle against the forces at play. Quintus on a horse came to his mind, and Aemilius thought of Furibunda, and just as he had decided that his only purpose was to live and find and recover a horse that he had only owned—if he could call it that—for two days, he found, rather calmly, in the swelling of the waves and the thickening of the air, that death had come to him yet again.

A monstrous head easily the size of their little vessel rose out of the waves, about a hundred yards ahead of them, and let out a strange, gurgled, howling cry. Beady eyes set above powerful jaws lined with sharp, curved teeth stared balefully down at them. Aemilius felt the hot shame of urine running down his leg and he stared, crying, at the impossibly thick, curved neck and the suggestion of the body beneath. Thick webbed claws the size of swords surfaced as the beast trod water in front of them, howling again. *It's as big as a house.* He forgot how to breathe and just stared at the thing, at the bluish-green tinge of its scales, the curved maw, the flaring nostrils. It looked like someone had smashed together four types of dog and glued them together with spite.

All of a sudden the eyes rolled back, and its face contorted in rage as it launched itself forward. And Hanno the Wise tensed, straw-thin arms extended to their full length—and then he clapped his hands together.

Aemilius was pushed back by the force of it. Something—the very air?—extended from the magus. He could see the circle of quiet and calm spreading from the boat, forming a bubble around them, pushing... five yards, now ten, fifteen—

The monster crashed into the invisible barrier, howling, clawing and snapping. Half its body reared above the water, and tons of muscle pushed and pushed, crashing it towards the boat. As a child Aemilius had once seen fighting cockerels, birds trained to attack and attack only. The monster had the same single-mindedness, the same absolute will to get at them. The stench of rotting fish wafted over the boat, making Taurio gag and swear.

A familiar blast of heat, and a fireball exploded towards the creature. With terrifying swiftness the thing just *dropped,* disappearing into the roiling water around the little skiff.

"No!" Hanno shouted. "If I hold it, we can tire it out. All it is going to do now is go—"

Aemilius's stomach lurched as the boat rose under them. He made the mistake of looking over the side...

They were caught in a sphere of air, boat and water. Hanno had somehow created a marble of protection around them, big enough to cover the boat from bow to stern along with the water it sailed on. Underneath them, all Aemilius could see was an expanse of bluish-green scales, like an island rising out of the sea, split in half by a row of fins with spikes the size of a grown man. Through the water he could see jaws chewing at the barrier, worrying at it like a dog with a toy, and above them, set far back from the muzzle like an over-bred pitbull, furious eyes that seemed small from here but must have been as large as his head.

In the bow, Hanno shook where he stood, muscles tensed to breaking point.

Abrax waved his hands, drawing heat from the air and fire from the sun, but every time he threw anything at the beast it would simply sink back into the water, causing the boat to lurch. Rivkah stood snarling at the creature, but even she was not so reckless as to leap to her death.

We need help. The thought flooded Aemilius's mind. *Help.* It thrummed through every vein of his body, filled him with urgency. *We need help.* It overwhelmed everything he had ever thought, wanted or remembered. *Please. We need help.*

The monster exploded up from the safety of the water again, showing a deep purple gullet framed by an obscene amount of teeth. It hit Hanno's bubble from the side, tilting the boat and sending the water inside it sloshing back and forth, against the direction of the sea.

Aemilius stumbled, and fell, and stared down at a fish.

That's not a big fish, he thought, dimly aware that his head hurt. *Ooh. There's another one.* Two specks on the scales of the monster. *No, wait. Five. Oh, and some more.*

"Look!" Livia's voice was hoarse.

Behind the monster, the water looked like it was boiling. *Something* was heading towards the creature at speed. The legionnaires stared in disbelief as the churning water overtook the monster's tail and crept up its body. Suddenly the jaws were no longer worrying at the boat in the bubble. Instead the creature twisted this way and that, snapping into the water and flinging out cascades of thrashing, flopping fish of every colour. Orange, white, grey with black stripes. Some were bitten half through, others bleeding, but the waters around the creature did not calm.

"*Hanno! Starboard!*" Taurio screamed.

The water-magus's head snapped to the right and his eyes popped almost out of his head in shock. He just managed to grit his teeth and flick his wrists before something crashed past the boat—

"Is that...?" Prasta gasped.

The ocean was suddenly full of massive, silvery blue shapes, each easily half the length of the boat, pouring past them, under the bubble, and...

Howling and thrashing wildly beside them, the impossible monster started rising out of the sea. Water cascaded off its scales and the enormity of the creature threatened to ruin their minds. It was an island emerging, a mountain springing from the ground, borne on the backs of an uncountable mass of silvery fish pushing up, and up, and up...

Hanno's voice was a hoarse whisper.

"Abrax... one chance."

The tall fire-magus set his feet, extended his arms as far as they went and turned his fingertips to the sun.

The air around them cooled so fast that hairs stood on Aemilius's neck.

And then the sea monster's head exploded in fire. The colossal body twisted and thrashed, swinging the powerful neck back and forth to shake itself free, lurching to get to the cold embrace of the water—but there was nowhere to go. The ocean had turned into a floor of writhing flesh, and whenever it swiped at the silent army with its fearsome claws, sending carcases flying, new bodies surged to fill the gap.

Standing side by side, Abrax and Hanno moved with the beast until the last convulsion ripped through the gigantic frame, the last lash of the neck—and only let it go when the life left its hellish body.

And as quick as they had come, the fish melted away from the sinking behemoth.

They sat in silence, feeling wave after heavy wave rocking the boat as the body of the creature turned slowly over onto one side, the scaled white underbelly rising out of the water as it started sinking beneath the surface. Even in death, it was terrifying. It looked like a composite of three different animals, each blown up to hideous size. From somewhere the breeze returned, and the boat started moving away just as the body turned over fully. The last thing they saw was a leg with webbed claws disappearing under the waves, and then, almost as quickly as the scaled nightmare had emerged, they were back in a world where monsters the size of a fleet of battleships didn't exist. In fact, the only evidence that anything had happened at all was a swathe of dead fish of all sizes—snappers, ratfish, groupers, bream, and scores and scores of tuna.

And then, Hanno collapsed.

Abrax just caught the water-magus with an arm and managed to ease him down to a sitting position—and Aemilius almost yelped when he saw Hanno's face.

The little magus he knew was gone. Instead, an old man lay in front of them.

Hanno's hair and eyebrows were drained of colour, a sharp white against his black skin, no longer smooth but dry and cracked with wrinkles. His cheeks had all but disappeared, making his cheekbones jut out. His body looked broken, like that of a life-long labourer. The arms and legs that had propelled him lightly up a rock only days ago now looked sinewy, tough and stiff. He sat with an old man's hunch and seemed to be holding tremors at bay.

"Oh, frog," Rivkah said, a catch in her throat.

Hanno coughed, wheezed and grinned. "Big old bastard, that one."

"That he was." Livia smiled, but her voice betrayed her and she looked away quickly.

"Do you need to rest? I think we can get this plank to land." Taurio had his hand back on the tiller, and nudged towards the sail.

"I have enough in me to keep our speed, and the water tells me where to go," Hanno wheezed. "I am not letting him get away."

Abrax sat beside the shrivelled magus, who looked even more child-like beside him. "You need to stay awake and alive for me, my friend, because I intend to personally make sure that the songs written to celebrate you make you so embarrassed that you die."

The old man chuckled. "And in Carthage, the water runs uphill."

"I've seen you do some things before, but that?" Taurio whistled. "There were absolute thousands of the bastards. Chuck in a boatload of carrots and some roots, and you would have had yourself a fine stew."

"Yes," Hanno said thoughtfully. "The water told me they were coming... but I did not ask them." Taurio frowned. "Nor did I tell them what to do. When they came, I gently asked the water to steer them... but even so, pushing that much weight would have been far beyond my capacity. Just holding the shield, with that amount of water in it, was nearly enough for me." He thought for a moment. "No, the swimmers knew what they wanted to do. They wanted to... help."

There was still a sparkle of mischief in Hanno's eyes, and for a good few moments they were trained on Aemilius.

THE HEAT OF the day softened as the sun set behind them, and they were cooled by the spray as the fishing boat skimmed across the sea at speeds it would never reach again. Around him, Aemilius watched as the legionnaires took turns manning the tiller, talking quietly and snatching what rest they could. On occasion they would see sails in the distance, or the hint of a coastline, but they were gone as quickly as they appeared. Up ahead he could see the first hints of dusk creeping up from the horizon, rising slowly and dragging night behind it—but there was no sign of slowing down.

"Here," Taurio muttered, leaning over and handing him a small square of hardtack. "Eat it slowly."

Aemilius grunted in reply, and got a nod from the big Gaul. *I am one of them.* The thought was pleasant and warming, in the cooling evening air. Chewing on a corner of the biscuit, he thought about the flavour. It tasted salty but a little bit sweet as well, and he could almost feel it expanding in his stomach. "Where did you have these?"

"I always keep some tucked away for an emergency."

Aemilius looked at the billowing sails and the foaming sea at their side. "Is this an emergency?"

"No," Taurio nibbled on a biscuit. "But I will say that big boar-whale-snake-thing was one, and it didn't seem the right time to be handing out snacks."

"Wise."

"And if more of that is what's in store, you don't want to go in on an empty stomach."

Aemilius nodded. "We could have died, there."

"Yes." Taurio seemed unmoved by the thought.

"And there was very little anyone could do."

"Yes."

"And is that not a problem?" Aemilius found the big Gaul's utter lack of worry infuriating. He glared at him, getting no response whatsoever.

"It is," Livia chipped in, "but not one of our making."

"We are not a water crew," Prasta added.

"What kind of crew are we, then?"

"Riders," Livia replied.

"We go ahead, scout out, deal with what needs dealt with," Taurio added. "And if it is unusual, or nasty, or both, we call in the specialists."

"This little encounter, for example, would have required…" Prasta fell silent, looking deep in thought.

"Alberic and Marius," Livia offered.

"Yes," Rivkah said. "Especially Marius."

"Behave yourself," Livia grinned.

"What can I say? I like his harpoon."

"Clementia would be good," Prasta offered.

"I don't know if the poor thing deserved Clementia," rumbled Taurio.

"Oh, come now, big man. Just because she shot you down—"

"She did *not*—"

"She did," Prasta grinned. "I was there—"

"*Long* story short," Taurio said loudly, "For special situations you want special skills. The Legion has a number of uniquely skilled bastards, of which we are six"—he looked Aemilius up and down—"seven, forgive me—"

"—but the real problem at the moment is that we don't know what we are getting into, and there is no time to send in reinforcements," Livia said.

"Graxus was supposed to support us," Abrax said.

"Some magus," muttered Rivkah. "Couldn't support a rock out of his own face."

"Anyone can get caught in the rain," Hanno said. His voice had changed too. He sounded like he looked: an old man. "The ambush is a powerful weapon,"

"Well—after the week we've had, I'd like to be the

one doing the ambushing," Rivkah said petulantly. "I'm about done with this constant near-death crap."

"Rest, daughter of Abraham," Hanno wheezed. "I am sure our destination will provide plenty of chances to spill blood."

"Oh, so you know where we're going, old frog?"

"I do. When the sun rises, we will be in Alexandria."

Livia turned and looked ahead, her regal profile outlined by the setting sun. She looked majestic and untouchable.

"Alexandria?" she mused. "Well, shit."

XIII

ALEXANDRIA

EVERYTHING HURT.

Aemilius woke up half-curled under the sternsheets, with his head next to Taurio's foot. He was greeted by the sky at dawn, the noisy cawing of seabirds and the fresh, raw smell of salty air. Wincing as he hoisted himself to a sitting position, he looked up—and nearly fell out of the boat. High, high above their heads was the fire of the sun itself, sitting on top of a mountain. A remarkably regular mountain, with even sides, tapering as it rose...

He made a noise that was nowhere near a word in any language.

"Impressive, isn't it? I will say this for the Romans," Taurio leaned on the tiller, guiding the boat to a rickety-looking pier. "When they want something done properly, they do a very good job... of stealing it from the Greeks."

Abrax shot the big Gaul a withering look. "The Greeks crumbled because they were too convinced of their own superiority."

"When we all know that the Carthaginians were the true kings of this little pond."

"If you look at the history—"

"—you find a *lot* of crumbling walls."

The bickering continued, and Aemilius continued to stare. The structure was so much bigger than anything he had ever seen that he had to remember to breathe. It stood on a rocky island in the mouth of the port, with a square base and a broad central tower above which reared a smaller, hexagonal tower, which in turn, impossibly high up, became a round tower with an open gazebo at the top.

"I remember when I saw it first." Prasta sounded wistful. "Feels like a long time ago now."

"You carry your advanced age well."

She didn't even look at Taurio. "Shut up. If you talk, the likelihood that you mess up your one job increases drastically." She narrowed her eyes to stare up at the tiny figures barely visible at the top. "Some say they have a massive mirror up there that burns enemy ships."

"That is an old wives' tale," Taurio huffed.

"Maybe," Livia said. "But I don't see any enemy ships on the horizon, do you? Would you like to be miles from shore when your sail burst into flames?"

The big Gaul focused on easing the boat up against the rickety pier. Within moments the Legion was disembarking, stretching sore muscles and rubbing painful cramps.

"I feel like I haven't moved for about a hundred years," Rivkah moaned.

"Your life is truly a constant swim upstream, daughter of Abraham," chuckled Hanno.

"Oh—forgive me, I didn't—"

"Now help an old man."

One by one they found their land-legs on the pier. The fishermen who went out at first light were long gone, and they had the wooden boards to themselves. To the east a barrier extended like a jawbone to an island just off the coast, forming part of the harbour. The gigantic lighthouse stood in the middle of the entrance to the harbour, a giant, one-eyed sentry. Aemilius thought back to Zeno and shuddered in the cool morning air.

Up ahead on the pier, Livia and Abrax were conferring. Taurio looked around curiously, and Prasta seemed to be annoyed about something. Rivkah was still helping Hanno to his feet. The diminutive water-magus was nothing like he'd once been, turning in an instant from an agile leaper to a shuffling wreck. Livia and Abrax seemed to come to a conclusion.

"Corto's. Let's move," came Livia's curt command.

Too tired to puzzle out what a 'Corto' was, Aemilius took in his surroundings slowly.

Up ahead, out of the sand dunes, rose an imposing city wall at least three times the height of a man. A packed dirt road snaked alongside it, out of a gate with a curved top. To their right a cluster of buildings spread out, flat and low.

"The Necropolis," Rivkah said, not waiting for a question. "Nothing for us there. We're going for the Moon Gate."

Aemilius made a face as if to say *I knew that*, but the others were moving and there was no time to assert himself. Within moments they caught up with other travellers, and they were soon part of a slow-moving stream into the city. The gate was manned by leather-faced soldiers in Roman uniforms, waving people along sullenly, and he noticed a subtle change in his fellow travellers. Livia had sunk into herself ever so slightly and walked slowly, head bowed, hood up. Abrax had similarly lowered his eyeline, and Prasta walked close to Taurio, presumably to elbow him in the ribs if he thought of something amusing to say about Roman occupation. To his side, Rivkah supported Hanno. *So that is how we're playing this. Us tired commoners.* Without a word he stepped to Hanno's other side and made himself useful as a crutch.

Together, the Hidden Legion limped through the Moon Gate and found themselves in Alexandria—built by Greeks, taken by Romans, high seat of culture and education in the Mediterranean. *Nice and straight*, thought Aemilius, and immediately cursed his history teacher. Day after day he had listened to that old stork pontificating on the merits of the straight line, the direct road, the grid layout, and his only revenge, his only refuge was the certainty that he would never remember any of it. Now he was looking down a long avenue that had been, in classical Roman fashion, planned as a direct route into the heart of the city.

This plan had then met with the reality of humans.

It was not long since dawn, but the streets were already lined with hawkers of all kinds. The handcarts of Hispalis paled in comparison to the vibrant explosion of colours on the canopies sheltering a variety of stalls from a hostile morning sun—spices, leather, fruits, beads and jewellery, dried meats and a sea of fabric. Tunics, turbans, and layers upon layers of light clothing swirling around tanned skin.

Aemilius took a deep breath and allowed himself to sink into the scene, like water. He recognised a couple of phrases being shouted, but others sounded almost like Latin but not quite. His grasp of Greek, called 'rudimentary' by his teacher, was doing him all sorts of favours, but the hubbub of the market still verged on the overwhelming. Allowing his ears to attune themselves in peace, he tried to let his other senses catch up. He watched.

Two old, olive-skinned men with white beards arguing heatedly (or having a pleasant conversation; hard to tell) by a stall that seemed to sell dried animal parts.

An old woman, bent almost double at the waist, holding a sack weighed down with her purchases of the morning, weaving between the stalls and disappearing down a side street.

A nimble kid with a thick head of curly hair approaching a stall at speed, ducking down at precisely the right moment and swiping a fist-sized fruit of some sort without breaking stride, then accelerating away from the shouting.

"Places pretend to be different, but they are all the same, really," Rivkah muttered.

"The shape of the bowl of the sea is different everywhere, but the sea is always water," Hanno agreed.

The legionnaires were a welcome anchor of immovability in the chaos. None of them seemed even remotely bothered by all the moving parts around them. The local pickpockets, hustlers and shysters seemed to be giving them a wide berth. *When eagles fly, smaller birds know to shut up.* The thought gave him a little buzz of pride and straightened his spine.

"Oi. Peacock. This way." Aemilius turned to the left and saw that Abrax and Livia were almost out of sight, heading down a side street, followed by Prasta and

Taurio. Rivkah had already turned her back on him, supporting poor old uncle Hanno. He shuffled after them, feeling markedly less like an invincible eagle on his own.

Just a couple of steps into the shade made a lot of difference. They walked from the gentle hubbub of the market into an almost physical silence—the side street was only just wide enough for one cart, or for two people to pass without budging—and the houses rose for three high floors, which cast a deep shadow. *Do they ever get any sunlight here?* Aemilius thought. And then: *Where are we going again?*

The second question was soon answered.

It did not take them long to arrive at a door set into a little alcove two steps down from the street. He leaned in towards Rivkah. "I know I haven't seen much... but this is a hole, right?"

"Yup," Rivkah said, grinning. "Just the way we like 'em."

Livia walked confidently up to the door and rapped on it—three quick knocks, a pause, then another three.

Moments later the door was half-torn off its hinges, and Aemilius took an involuntary step backwards. The man in front of them growled what could have been a question, stepping into the doorway and filling it. His face was a scarred, bashed and misshapen journal of a lifetime of fighting. An almost non-existent neck led straight into a barrel-shaped trunk. Arms thicker than Aemilius's legs ended in plate-sized hands with stubby fingers, one of which was holding a nasty-looking, well-used short club.

Prasta glanced at Taurio with a raised eyebrow. He glared back at her.

The bruiser in the doorway took one look at them, blinked—and then his eyes lit up and his face split into the biggest smile Aemilius had ever seen. A voice like rumbling rocks gave a hearty bellow. "Livia Claudia! On my doorstep! The Gods do hear an old man's prayer."

"Corto! You are as fine a figure of a man as you ever were, and you have not aged."

Somewhere under the bruises and the cuts, the man in the doorway blushed and chuckled. "You are a dangerous woman."

"And you are a wonderful man. In a cruel and brutish world, the best friend—"

"'—is an old friend,'" Corto finished. "Come in, come in." He turned nimbly and made space to usher them through the door.

Aemilius glanced at Rivkah and wished he could say something. There was none of the honeyed artifice about Livia here. Was this a genuine friend? It certainly seemed that way, as Corto bustled about in the near-absolute darkness ahead of them. Very shortly pin-pricks of light flared up over candles in various corners of the room, revealing a small, surprisingly neat tavern. A bar at the far end, a hint of a back room in the shadows. Within moments Corto had dragged three tables together and put out seats for all of them. "Where are you coming from today?" he said, in the practised tones of the innkeeper.

"Hispalis," Livia said.

Corto paused and shot her a look. "Long trip. Eventful?"

"Yes," Livia said, ending a conversation with many more words unsaid.

"Well—you'll be needing food, then!" Corto said

brightly. "Can't have hungry travellers." He swung past the tables, dancing his bulk through the room without ever touching or knocking over anything.

When he disappeared from view, Livia commanded the attention of Taurio, Prasta, Rivkah and Aemilius. "Let's get this over with. I met Corto when he was a wrestler in Rome, fifteen years ago. He was, at his peak, untouchable. We drank together. He got me out of trouble a couple of times."

"And in return?" Taurio said, eyes glinting.

"I fixed several of his matches and made us both, for a time, very rich," Livia answered levelly. "And I warn you gently, Gaul—he is a proud Roman and quite protective of me. So be on your best behaviour and shut your face or he'll make you eat your balls." After a moment's reflection, she added, "…please."

"I am ever so sorry, Your Majesty. I shall know my place and present myself to the majordomo for a flogging at his earliest convenience," Taurio said, grinning.

"Go ram a cactus up your arse," Livia replied, grinning back.

Moments later Corto appeared, balancing three improbably sized planks that landed with military precision on the table.

There was a short silence while the Legion took in what was in front of them.

Hunks of bread that glowed golden in the candlelight.

Cubes of firm, white cheese, arranged in a pyramid.

Thinly sliced meats, ranging from pink to deep red, that looked like they had been carved off just moments before, possibly before the beasts were killed.

A small mound of brown balls of some sort, dotted with green.

On each plank, one bowl of sandy-coloured paste, swirled through with a rich yellow liquid.

Dainty bowls with olives in a variety of colours, dotted with almost transparent slices of garlic.

By the time they had the sense to look up, Corto had disappeared again, only to reappear with three jugs in one hand and a tower of cups in the other. "Wine," he said, almost apologetically. As he slung the cups around the table and arrayed the jugs in front of them, he rumbled, "It is absolute swill and I will beat myself about the face for serving it to you, but it is all I've got. Oh, and—" He dipped his free hand into his tunic, there was a flash of metal and three solid *thunk*s in succession, and in each of the planks, a wicked-looking knife vibrated, short blade buried in the wood. "I forget my manners. For the cheese."

"Corto—this is a *feast*," Livia said.

Aemilius noted Taurio ever so smoothly sneaking a hand onto Prasta's forearm and soothing her back towards the table. Next to them, on the other hand, Rivkah was grinning maniacally and nodding along.

The big man shrugged. "It's not worthy of the company, but then not much is. Tuck in."

And so they did.

The wine was ice-cold and refreshing, watered down a little but not enough to stop conversation from rising in pitch and volume. As they sampled everything the innkeeper had presented, they talked of the state of Alexandria, brought news from Rome and discussed the expansion in Frisia.

Eventually, Corto smiled. "Oh, but I've missed you," he rumbled.

"Likewise, my friend."

"But I also remember that you do precious little without reason, so I doubt this is purely a social call."

Livia smiled. "This is true. We had to leave Hispalis somewhat... quickly, and so we are in need of some help."

"I will do everything I can," Corto said, bowing once. "What do you need?"

Out, Aemilius suddenly realised. The darkness, and the wine, and the talk and the food—and the fact that the only sleep he'd had for two days was under a plank after a battle with a sea monster—had given him the most astounding headache. He rose, a little unsteadily, and mumbled something about just stepping out for a moment. No-one paid him much mind, and he picked his way through the dim tavern towards the door, bumping his shins into stools, tables and crates five times in surprisingly little time. *Either this door is heavier than most, or I am getting weaker*, he though as he levered it open with his shoulder just enough to squeeze through, then felt it push him out into the street.

He was fortunate to come out into the shade. The rising sun had drawn a sharp line of burning white on the opposite wall; he could feel the heat radiating from it. His travelling clothes from Hispania suddenly felt thick and unwieldy, and he fought the urge to peel them off. Leaning against the wall, he allowed himself to sink onto a ledge and just sit for a while. Inside the tavern the Legion was, no doubt, laying plans to smoke out Donato, interrogate him and win the day, save the Empire and fight all the monsters, and Aemilius just felt *exhausted*.

How could these people go on for so long? How could they just... stay awake? In the last two days they had been nearly killed by a flying witch and a creature the size of a small fishing fleet, and now they were sitting around a table eating cheese.

It's too hard.

He felt oddly disconnected from his decision to stand up, and he made no choice at all as to where his feet took him. Away from the tavern. Away from the market. Past a side street crossing this one, past more houses, onto a bigger road.

Carts, lazily making their way into the city.

Women striding from somewhere—and definitely *to* somewhere else—some balancing big jugs on their heads, others with babies strapped to their backs.

A group of men around a collapsed wall: one working, five standing around and arguing about how best to reassemble it.

Aemilius felt his gut fold in on itself, as if he'd been punched.

And then, two moments later, he realised why.

In amongst the traffic, coming from the direction of the city wall and heading towards the centre of town.

A figure in a hooded robe.

Donato.

He couldn't see the man's face, but the silhouette and the way he moved immediately washed the weariness away. He stared as hard as he could at the man, who was making his way as urgently as one could without attracting attention, and calculated. *Corto's is too far away. He'll be gone. What can I do?* It took no time at all to come to a conclusion he did not like at all.

Cursing silently, he stepped out of the shadows and followed Donato, quietly, like a hunter after his prey.

* * *

B*E INSIGNIFICANT*.

As he turned another corner, Aemilius replayed the words in his head. With his heart racing he had thought about what he knew about following people in cities without being detected—nothing—and wondered what he should do. Within moments he had invented a conversation with Rivkah, or some sort of combination of Rivkah and Livia, or possibly all of them, and they had told him, after the cursing and the name-calling, to be insignificant. Act like you belong, like you're supposed to be there, but not like you are important. Become a... a... bedside table. Or a footstool. *But one that moves*, Aemilius thought, *and preferably at speed*. Donato definitely knew where he was going, and was not worried at all about being followed. At one point his target stopped abruptly at a stall, forcing Aemilius to duck into a doorway and improvise the world's most casual leaning position—*I am just resting here, thank you, I am tired from doing an unimportant job and if you ask me to leave I will, obviously, but*—and then Donato was moving again, and so was he.

The feel of the city changed slightly around him. The high-rises for the poor gradually made way for bigger houses with only two floors, and under his feet the ground gently rose. Street vendors gave way to shops. The streets were better maintained. Statues with legends in Greek—philosophers, warriors, poets. And still Donato walked with confidence, taking each turning without hesitation, like he knew exactly where he was going. *Which he probably does,* Aemilius thought idly. *If you're doing whatever he's doing, you want to know where you are going.*

The thought lodged in his head and would not move.

And what is that, exactly? What is he doing? They knew that he had some magic of some sort. And he'd been behind summoning Zeno. He talked to the mormo. He'd brought forth the cetus they'd battled. Even in the midday sun, Aemilius shuddered. He'd felt like a mouse being chased by a rabid dog, and he never wanted to go through that again. Donato was connected to the hydras and the harpies as well. Were the monsters specifically targeting the Legion?

An alarm bell rang in his head, and he realised there was suddenly a lot less cover.

Engrossed in his thoughts, Aemilius had stepped out onto open ground. Behind him he was dimly aware of a row of villas for the wealthy, with gardens, walls and gates. Here, the road was paved, and very nicely so— and it led up a steep hill to a temple with a gilded roof. He cursed himself for not watching the route. Donato was already mounting the gleaming white steps to the colonnades. Picking up his pace, Aemilius strode across the open plaza, as if he was late for a meeting, and tucked himself in behind a group of scholars arguing.

"…but they don't *do* anything!"

"Their mere existence here is an affront to our Gods."

"You just say that because you lost that debate in the square."

"Shut up, Ipastos. Always banging on about that damn debate."

"You can't discount all Jews because you lost an argument once."

"I *didn't* lose, and I can discount who I please, and lots of people agree with me."

And so on their conversation went, bickering as they huffed up the stairs. Aemilius worked as hard as he could to keep an eye on Donato through the crowd, only breaking cover from the grumbling Greeks when his quarry disappeared over the top of the stairs. His heart thundered as he took the steps two at a time, feeling every agonising moment, sure that it would all be for nothing.

And sure enough, when he got to the top, Donato had vanished. A massive courtyard, leading to all manner of alcoves and nooks populated by quiet men with big scrolls laid out on large tables, stretched out a hundred yards to each side. The temple sat in the middle of the courtyard, square and massive, sun sparkling off the gilded roof.

Move.

At the very last moment Aemilius started walking again, just as Donato emerged around the corner of the temple, followed by a squat, old man in priest's robes with thinning hair and a stubby nose. They seemed to be in animated conversation, but it was impossible to hear. Whatever it was, the priest was not happy. Moments later, they ducked in through a side door and disappeared into the temple.

No, the voice in his head said with determination before he had the time to start arguing with himself. *Go back. Get the others. If we come back here, we'll find Donato, or his snub-nosed friend, or something. If you go into the dark, you're dead.*

"Hard to argue with that," Aemilius muttered, turning on his heel and heading back towards the steps. He had come this far, tailed a magus through a foreign city and remained undetected. He was a master hunter, and now it was time to go report on the location of the prey. Coming up to the crest of the stair, he looked down onto Alexandria. It spread out before him, all tiled roofs and winding streets, a testament to human ingenuity and resilience. He could see the Moon Gate, the big avenue and the sea, dominated by the towering lighthouse. Further to the east he could see a large building of some sort—a governor's mansion?

Enough. Standing still made him feel watched, slow, a target. He pushed himself to move, go back down, find his way back to the side streets and the tavern. The steps under his feet were well-worn, and he thought about everyone coming here to seek the knowledge of the scrolls and whatever was in that temple. A cool breeze came in from the sea and caressed his cheek, and for a moment he was just a man—he ignored Rivkah's voice in his head, throwing comments—*just a man*, enjoying a walk in a beautiful city second only to Rome. Sighing, he closed his eyes for just a fraction of a heartbeat—

His foot slipped, his eyes flew open and he flailed to regain his balance. He heard quick steps and felt strong arms grab him, pulling him upright. "Keep moving," someone growled in accented Latin. Aemilius stood on his tiptoes, feeling like he was on a cliff edge. There was unmistakeable pressure on the small of his back—the point of a knife.

The rest of the journey down was a lot less pleasant. Whoever was behind him had an iron grip on his forearm, twisted behind Aemilius's back. One wrong step and his shoulder would pull out of joint in an instant, most likely followed by falling and breaking his neck. *Master hunter,* he thought, witheringly. *Master idiot.* "Please forgive me," he tried. "I am a visitor. Have I done something wrong?"

There was no reply.

He switched to Greek. "Please, sir. I meant to cause no offense."

"Shut up," the man behind him growled. "Over there." The moment his feet hit cobbled ground, the man was steering him towards the nearest houses. The stately homes dotted around the big temple—for whatever reason, on this occasion, his old history teacher decided to remind him of the Serapeum of Alexandria, home to legendary statues and all manner of fine things only equalled in Rome—offered little cover, so Aemilius and his jailor marched on.

"Where are you taking me?"

"Shut up, Roman, or I'll turn your spine into pig-meat." Going down the hill, they came upon a main road, and two twists took them to a narrow and deserted side street. Aemilius was spun round and pushed backwards into a doorway.

The man who had grabbed him on the steps was tall, rangy and gaunt, with tanned skin and a patchy beard. A deep, angry scar extended from his right ear to his jaw, and dark brown eyes stared at Aemilius with undisguised hatred. In his hand was a small, practical knife, held with relaxed ease. "You were sneaking."

"What?" A piteous mewl.

"You were sneaking," the tall man repeated. "You were following. Why?"

"I don't know what you're talking about," Aemilius stammered. "I—I—I don't—"

The man clenched his teeth and shoved him with his free hand.

The doorway was made of stone. The door behind him was firmly shut, as he had felt when his shoulder smacked into it; presumably locked. He had been given nothing to work with by his captor...

...except the time it had taken them to get there. Time

enough to twist this way and that, and ease a hand onto his hip as if by accident, and gently grasp...

"I'm sorry!" Aemilius wailed, bursting into tears and cowering away from the man. "I only did what they told me!"

"Who?" the stranger growled, grabbing Aemilius by the shoulder, spinning him around, and—

It happened so fast. Pushing off the door with his foot, he smashed into the man, wrapping his free hand around the knife arm, pinning it to his side. "The Hidden Legion," Aemilius hissed into his ear as he drove Prasta's dagger up into his ribs, through his ribs, buried his head in the man's shoulder as he heard the surprised cough, the sickly chortle, felt the heat of the man wetting himself and turning soft in his embrace, spasming once and sinking to the ground, becoming suddenly impossibly heavy.

He heard the man's knife scrape on the stones as it fell to the ground, and then there was only stillness and silence.

Aemilius looked down on the man he'd killed—and threw up.

XIV

ALEXANDRIA

HE RAN, FEELING the dagger tucked into his clothes like a burning spur. Every step on the stones sounded like that horrible wet cough when the knife had slid into the chest. He'd left the body in the doorway, blood blossoming on the front of the tunic.

I killed a man.

The knife had just gone in, powered by fear.

I killed a man.

It had been so effortless, too. Just one thrust. He still didn't quite know how he'd thought to pin his attacker's arm, but here he was—running through Alexandria, and still alive. He bumped into an old Egyptian, who shouted something rude after him, but he didn't answer back. There were more important things that needed to happen, and they had to happen fast.

Why do the streets all look the same? He turned in a side street off the main road, cursed, backtracked, kept running. He was in roughly the right area—There! A barrel, a canopy—a side street—and—

Hot tears formed in his eyes when he saw the steps down to the tavern, and he wiped them away far too hard. He was not a child. He was a killer. A legionnaire. He puffed out his chest, released a breath he didn't realise he was holding, then rapped on the door. Three quick, then pause, then three—

The door flew open on the first knock. Taurio appeared in the doorway, grabbed him by the tunic and pulled him in. "Where did you go?" he growled. "And—is that blood?"

"Are you hurt?" Prasta interrupted, bodying the Gaul out of the way.

"No," Aemilius stammered, thankful for the dim light. Through blurry eyes he could see the faint outlines of the others hovering behind her. "I—I—" He swallowed hard to get rid of the lump in his throat. *Legionnaire!* he scolded himself. Deep breath—release. "I found him."

"What?" Abrax hissed.

"Donato. I found him. I wandered to a main road and saw him by chance, and couldn't get you, so I followed him to the Serapeum—"

"Shit."

"—and he disappeared into the temple followed by a priest, so I thought I'd come get you, but someone was watching me and grabbed me on the way down and pushed me into a doorway, and I killed him." The words tumbled out of him, and when the last one landed there was a ringing silence.

Then there was a gentle disturbance in the darkness, and the bodies shifted, and Corto appeared. His mass seemed to swallow all light around him. "Here," he rumbled. "Drink this."

In his hand was a cup of wine. Aemilius accepted it gratefully and gulped it down, sputtering a little when he realised, a little too late, that it was not watered down at all.

"It is a serious thing," said the innkeeper, "to take a man's life, and the first one is the hardest."

"Time is not on our side," Livia interjected gently. "Thank you for your help, my friend. We'll pay—"

"Try." Corto's reply was short, and absolute, and brooked no argument whatsoever. "Now go, and may luck and bastardy be on your side."

"It usually is," Taurio said.

Still shaking off the burning sensation of the wine, Aemilius didn't quite understand what Prasta was doing, but suddenly his tunic was off. He managed a dull "Whu—?" before another piece of clothing slid over his head, fresh and cool. The material felt soft against his skin. Linen.

"Local clothing," she said firmly. "Easier to blend in."

In the dim light of the candles, Aemilius realised that the appearance of the Legion had changed. They were wearing tunics in shades of sand and sun, loosely tied around the waist. Prasta and Taurio had been fitted with full-body outfits and turbans, showing only their eyes.

Hanno sat on a chair in the corner, looking like he might not get up again. The old man noticed him looking and waved weakly. "I would slow you down," he wheezed. "Besides, not much water to play with here."

The heavy door creaked open and the midday sunshine painted Abrax in silhouette.

It was time to go.

They stepped out onto the street, and Taurio was the first to speak. "Hot," he hissed.

"Just right," Abrax countered, grinning. The big magus seemed in his element here. "To the Serapeum?"

Aemilius realised he was being asked a question. "Yes," he stammered.

Without another word, Abrax strode off, leaving the others to fall in behind him and Livia. Aemilius, Rivkah and Taurio brought up the rear.

"I can't believe you followed him on your own."

"Impressed?"

"Not at all," Rivkah replied. "It was an absolutely donkey-brained thing to do."

"What would you have done, then?" Aemilius tried to hide the annoyance in his voice, and didn't do very well.

"Get within twenty paces, throwing knife in the back?" The option was presented as if it was utterly obvious, and that he was a bit of a fool for not having considered it.

"Oh, of course," Aemilius replied with all the sarcasm he could muster. "I am *such* a fool for not having thought of that."

"That's what I'm saying."

"Quiet—" started Taurio. He didn't manage to finish the sentence. They rounded the corner to the main road, and nearly walked into Prasta's back.

A tall, slim, haughty man stood in front of them, dressed in exquisite robes of white and red. Behind him, eight Roman guards had formed a double row: to a man they were nearly Abrax's size, all bulging muscles and hard eyes.

The tall man was currently staring daggers at Livia, who had adopted the relaxed posture of a snake about to strike.

"It is you, isn't it?" The official's voice dripped with contempt.

"I beg your forgiveness, kind sir," Livia said. "I do not know what you speak of."

"Don't be shitty with me!" the man spat, face deformed with rage. "It is you, and you know it!"

"Do I know that I am me?" Livia said calmly, drawing it out. "I suppose we are in what used to be the high seat of Greek philosophy, so... yes?"

The tall man's face turned a fetching shade of purple. "You will be thrown in the hole!"

"I am so sorry, but I can't today. I am quite busy."

"*Busy?* You will hang!"

"For what, exactly?"

"Murder!"

"Oh, but that is impossible," Livia said sweetly. "I haven't murdered anyone."

The Roman official extended a bony finger and pointed at her. "You lie! You murdered my brother in cold blood!"

"I did no such thing," Livia replied calmly. Behind her back she motioned, once, with her hand. *Back up.* "I only held out a very modest knife while your brother ran at me with his pathetic cock out, hoping he'd be able to pin me down for a few thrusts. As it happens, he couldn't. He was a weak man, a cruel man and a rapist. He died on the point of my knife, and the world was better for it. I didn't *murder* anyone. I just did a little tidying up."

"*Arrest them!*"

Rivkah grabbed Aemilius's elbow and pulled him around the corner and back into the side street, and Prasta, Abrax and Livia backpedalled after them. Taurio was already stepping into a doorway, and Aemilius managed to duck in after him before Rivkah shoved him. She gleefully stepped into the middle of the small street, darting backwards and whipping out two knives.

A moment later Livia ran past the doorway towards

Rivkah, followed by Abrax and a thundering herd of guards.

As the last of the guards ran past Taurio, there was a heavy thump, and he ran no more. Aemilius put his foot behind a barrel by the doorway and pushed it into the ankle of a passing guard with a sickening crunch. He collapsed, holding his leg and wailing.

The first of the men had reached Rivkah. If there was a moment's hesitation from three grown men in armour at using violence on a young girl, it didn't show. They charged, and—

She danced around them as if they were standing still.

A low sweep, a spray of blood from a severed tendon. A knife backhanded into a groin. A lot more blood.

The third had to contend with his fellows grasping at him in sudden panic. He blinked, lost sight of her—and two knives plunged into his neck and out again.

A thin hoop of fire appeared out of nowhere around the remaining four soldiers at waist-height, and Livia turned to face them. "I do not, as a rule, want to rob the Empire of capable men. But all of you have chosen to serve as Caius Africanus's personal guard, and you must have known what kind of Roman he is, and I must hang my head in shame at what you must have done for him." She extended her slender arm, fist closed, and made sure the soldiers were watching her. Two of them were crying, one looked confused and the fourth looked defiant.

She pointed her thumb up.

The ring of fire closed in an instant, cutting their bodies in half.

Moving slowly, she knelt by the man with the broken ankle. "Tell your friends that Caius brought this on his men," she said quietly. "Or I will come, and I will find you, and your family, and your friends, and their friends, and I will bring *my* friends. Would you like that?"

The big guard shook his head, crying. Livia rose and looked expectantly to the end of the street. Prasta stood at ease, a length of rope wrapped twice around her wrist and looped round the neck of a terrified-looking Caius Africanus.

"And you," she said conversationally to the ashen-faced official, as if she was sat at a dinner table with an old acquaintance. "You are surprisingly like your brother. Quite happy to be the bully while you think you have the upper hand."

Caius's mouth moved, but no words came out.

"I am not going to kill you, because I think it would give you too much satisfaction to die by my hand. So what we are going to do now, you and I—" Suddenly, a dagger was in her hand. She made sure he was watching the point of it, then moved it slowly, excruciatingly slowly up towards his eye, stepping close enough to bite him. "What we are going to do is this. You are going to go to your villa. You will tell your servants to tell anyone who asks that you are ill. You will be ill for a week, and see no-one. And I will get on with what I need to do, and then I'll leave Alexandria and never see you again, if I can help it. Understood?"

Caius Africanus nodded meekly.

"Release him."

With a flick of Prasta's wrist, the rope whipped up over the tall man's head. Before he realised what had happened, she had grabbed him by the shoulder, spun him around and booted him up the backside. "Off you go," she snarled. "Lucky bastard."

Aemilius had heard the expression before, but he

had never actually seen anyone run for his life. Middle-aged Roman nobleman Caius Africanus almost hit the ground face-first, legs a blur as he flailed to get himself as far away from all of them as possible. He disappeared around the corner almost instantly.

"Do you think that was wise?" Abrax had appeared at Livia's shoulder.

"No. Fun, though," she said. "And besides—he knew the moment he saw me. It was that or the hole for us, and I don't think we'd have ever come out. You'd find"—she smiled coldly—"that we would be responsible for a remarkable number of recent crimes."

"Fair enough," Taurio said, catching up to them. "We are a bit like that."

"Maybe I should have wrung his neck," Livia mused as they crossed the main road and ducked down a side street. "But I just figured, you know. If he were to turn up dead, the governor would probably be glad to be rid of him... but he'd have to make an example. You know what they're like."

"We do," Taurio said darkly.

There was a silence.

"I don't," Aemilius said.

"Oh." There was a sadness to Livia's sigh. "I'm sorry. I can't. Who wants to tell him?"

"I will," Taurio said. "When the Roman Empire takes a territory, they never overwhelm the natives. Instead, they keep them in check with life improvements, on the one hand—aqueducts, roads, order—and cruelty on the other. Professional soldiers. So if, in a big city like this, a Roman noble goes missing, they have to make it clear to the natives that that will simply not stand."

"And so they go from house to house," Prasta said,

voice catching. "And they drag men out of their beds, and they beat the women and children until they find someone willing to blame someone for the deed. And they aren't too worried about finding the murderer."

"They just want you to know that one Roman nobleman will cost you ten—twenty—fifty of your friends and family."

It was not the hate or anger in their voices that made Aemilius feel sick to his stomach. It was the sadness. The inevitability of it. "So... why do you fight for Rome, then?"

"I can't speak for the others," Prasta said, "but I don't fight for Rome. I fight for the people of the Roman Empire. They are not a bad lot, and most of them don't make any sort of decisions about murdering the innocent."

"When she's right, she's right," Taurio muttered. "All Romans are obviously despicable by their nature, but I feel that some of them are worth helping. Just to see if they can get themselves better, as it were."

"You are too kind," said Livia, with only a little sarcasm.

"You're welcome, Princess," Rivkah chipped in.

"The Hidden Legion does not fight for Rome," Abrax added. "We fight in spite of Rome. We fight for the sons and brothers that died screaming in terror in that dark forest, sent to their death by a vain idiot, betrayed by a man nourished by hatred of Rome. We fight, knowing that if our existence were ever to be confirmed as more than a song in the shadows, the Empire itself would march on us and squash us, for it must never be suspected that they are weak."

Aemilius swallowed hard. He had been brought up to be proud of Rome, proud of what the Empire had done for the world, and it was difficult to imagine the source of his father's power and authority as a boulder rolling over the world, crushing everything in its path. So he kept quiet, and allowed himself to be led by Abrax.

Their route was different from the way Donato had gone, eschewing dark, twisting alleys for straight roads. Now that he knew what to look for, though, he was much more aware of the Serapeum towering over them, catching glimpses of its gleaming roof between and over houses. They were out of the poor quarter quickly, and Abrax threaded his way between the stately homes with the easy gait of someone whose feet knew every bump and angle in the cobbles.

"Do you all just know everything?"

"He does," Rivkah replied. "Apparently he studied here, ages ago."

Watching the magus stride through the streets, head held high and robes swirling, towards the seat of education, Aemilius found no problem imagining this. "So—what's the plan?"

"We go in, we take Donato, we get out," Livia answered from the front. "Just before we come to the square, we'll split up into twos—Prasta, you go with Rivkah. Taurio—"

"Watching the baby." The big Gaul grinned.

Aemilius made a face at him.

"Keep an eye on the other pairs. We converge on the temple. Watch out for scouts."

Those were all the instructions needed, and Aemilius got a little thrill when he felt the focus shift. He was getting used to this now—the feeling of the Legion getting ready to do battle. *Does that mean I am one of them? Can I be one of them and still be a Roman?* Lost in his thoughts for a moment, he suddenly realised that he was alone.

Almost alone.

"Coming?" Taurio said, grinning.

The others had somehow transported themselves away, mounting steps to the east and west, respectively. The Serapeum rose above them, gleaming in the midday sun, a steady trickle of scholars up and down the stairs.

Taurio looked up. "Suleviae save us," he groaned. "I don't mind the monsters… but it's all the *running* and the *climbing!* Can't stand it."

"Come on, grumble. A bit of exercise will do you good." Aemilius strode past him, but a hand on his arm stopped him.

"Do an old man a favour and slow down," Taurio muttered, nodding ahead. Six men in white robes had formed a half-circle around a man with a thick, black beard, and were shouting and gesticulating. Another two men came storming to the single man's aid, and before long the groups were shaking fists at each other. "Scholars. I'm guessing someone got a date wrong."

"Maybe," Aemilius said thoughtfully. Somewhere in his head, a couple of puzzle pieces fit together.

Walking past the quarrelling group at a safe distance just as three burly Roman guards walked in the opposite direction, they made their way up the stairs, Taurio leading the way. "It's a beautiful building."

Aemilius noted that once his friend was moving and had set his eyes on the prize, he was not out of breath at all. "It is. Up at the centre there is a big temple— that's where he disappeared into. He may be long gone by now, but I would guess the priest he was talking to stayed."

"It's been a long time since I bashed a holy man," Taurio said with eagerness. "Hate them."

"Why?"

"They go on for *ages*. And they're always so *full* of themselves."

Fair enough. Step by step the stairs yielded to their efforts, and they reached the courtyard without hearts thumping too badly. The temple blazed in the sun, and Aemilius gestured to the westward side.

Replying with a side-glance, Taurio pointed out where Rivkah and Prasta had emerged on the far side of the courtyard, looking for all the world like meek servant-women bringing messages. Completing the group, Abrax and Livia strode in from the west, a noblewoman and her advisor. They closed in on the temple from all directions.

Too many columns. The colonnade sweeping around the courtyard was perfect for skulking and hiding. Aemilius worked hard not to have his head on a swivel, but every shadow held the promise of an enemy. He thought back on Hispalis. *He knew we were coming. Is this another trap?* If it was, at least this time they'd go in and do some damage. After all, they'd smashed through everything thus far... *And only two men had died, with another reduced to a husk.*

The waft of incense stung the eyes. Or maybe it was the smell it was masking.

He stood before the entrance to the Temple of Serapis.

Crossing the threshold, he was surprised to find himself in a cavernous space, lit by open squares in the ceiling. A gigantic statue of a kindly-looking bearded man rose before him on a broad base, palms up in supplication. A titan of peace—Serapis. At his bronzed feet lay a variety of offerings in different states of decay, and a swarm of very happy fruit flies buzzed around at ankle-height. A young priest had drawn the short straw and been stuck on guard duty, overseeing the guests. He cast one bored look at them, then went back to gazing into the middle distance, moving his mouth silently and shuffling his feet. Incense burned from braziers in every corner. Dotted around the room were worshippers—old men, young men, a woman with a hunched back—praying to the God of Healing.

Aemilius drew a breath, and suddenly Abrax was at his side.

"Is that our man?"

He replied with a subtle shake of the head.

"Search the room. Act... respectful. If we don't find anything, we ask the priest."

Aemilius found himself hoping, for the priest's sake, that they found something quickly. He tried to drift around the room with Rivkah in a religious way, but constantly dodging rotten bananas and bad portraits of sick relatives made it hard to look inconspicuous. Luckily, they didn't have to wait long. Nobody had made a sound, but Prasta had stopped at a spot just behind the big statue, almost hidden out of sight.

Slowly, the other five made their way towards her.

She was standing by a raised ridge around a circular hole in the floor, where spiral steps led down and out of sight. The squat, old priest sat with his back against the plinth of the statue, looking peaceful in sleep. Prasta nodded towards the old man and quickly slid a single finger over her throat. *Dead*. Aemilius noted that the man's throat was an unnatural colour of purple, as if someone had very precisely crushed his windpipe.

They looked down at the spiral steps. Livia rolled her eyes. *Shit*.

Without a word Rivkah went towards the hole, dagger at the ready. Aemilius reached out and touched her elbow. Her head whipped round to glare at him, mouthing, *What?*

He glanced over at the priest on duty and held up his hand. *Wait.*

A moment later, the man winced, looked round secretively and then ducked out through a small side door.

Now!

In tight formation, the Legion stepped down into the heart of the Serapeum.

THE DEEP STEPS turned sharply, and the wan light from the temple faded after the first three. Aemilius felt his hands get clammy as he pushed his palms out to both sides and probed the ground with his toes. *After hydras and mormos and sea monsters, wouldn't that be the funniest thing?* he thought bitterly. *Snapping my neck on some stairs in the dark.* But just as suddenly as the light had disappeared, a warming orange glow met him, outlining Rivkah and Prasta ahead of him—and then they were out of the way and he was out of the staircase, standing on beautiful slabs of cool stone in a corridor.

He felt Taurio's big hand on the small of the back, shoving him out of the way in a friendly sort of way. "Invaders don't stop on the beach to admire the view. Move, rabbit."

Taking three steps into the corridor, Aemilius started—*a massive man, coming out of the wall*—then caught himself and regained his cool. He was looking at a statue in an alcove. There were more of them around him—a row of them, set into the far wall, regularly spaced and each rendered in incredible detail. Gods and goddesses of all kinds, half again the height of a man, in armour and robes, staring down on the legionnaires. The hallway was illuminated by hooded lanterns set against bronze plates, which bathed the space in a warm glow.

Prasta whistled appreciatively. "I thought we had our share of them." Asserting quickly that going left would bring them to a wall and another set of spiral steps leading up, the Legion started moving carefully deeper into the Serapeum.

"It's a bit complicated," Livia began as she scouted the room. "But Serapis is sort of a combination of a bunch of old Egyptian gods and a couple of Greek ones. He was supposed to combine people in the worship of one god rather than argue about which one is best."

"Not a bad idea, on the face of it," Prasta said. "Did it work?"

"Not really," Livia said. "Regardless of the number of gods, people will always find ways to hate other people. I reckon we're going this way." She pointed to a small opening, only just big enough to fit Rivkah, tucked in behind a statue.

Taurio groaned. "Are you sure?"

Wordlessly, Livia pointed to a barely visible foot. Someone in the tunnel was very much not moving.

"He does leave a trail, doesn't he?" Abrax mused.

It didn't take Taurio long to drag the young priest out. This one looked pockmarked and sickly, but he also looked like he'd been perfectly able to move around until someone or something turned his throat the purple of a bad bruise. Once the body had been propped up, Rivkah went first.

"It's bigger inside," she hissed back from the darkness. "Abrax, if you would—?"

The gentle glow of a light-orb spilled out of the passageway.

"Fine," Taurio muttered. "But you all go first."

Right, Aemilius thought, ducking into the passageway before he had time to catch up with himself.

Suddenly, the stones felt like they were pressing in on him from all sides. He had to duck to not smack his head, and his hunched shoulders almost reached to the roof of the passageway. Sand hissed under his feet and he only had the faintest glimmer of light to follow—*There!* Rivkah's hand caught him and pulled him out of the passage. *Out of the way, out of the way.* He stepped to the left, forcing himself to take in his new surroundings quickly.

He was standing in a tunnel about half the size of the corridor—still spacious, but much rougher. Where the first tunnel's walls were flat and straight, this looked much more like the trail of some massive burrowing beast. Nobody had taken the time to lug slabs of stone in here. No statues. No lanterns. This was... older.

One by one, the others appeared.

"Oh, I don't like the look of this," Taurio grumbled. "Not one bit. And I hate it when you're right, Princess."

"I know."

Staring hard, Aemilius spotted what Taurio was looking at.

Footsteps in the sand. Several, and new.

Guided by the faint light from the floating orb, they made their way through the tunnel, following the footsteps. Turning a corner, they came upon a straight stretch lined with shelves. Prasta seemed to inch away from the walls, picking a path that was very much in the middle of the tunnel. Aemilius nudged Taurio and nodded towards the skinny bard.

"She hates tombs," he whispered. "Her lot think the bodies of the dead should be burned and scattered over the land. Some of them bury theirs in a hill, and others leave them out to return the flesh to nature and then take the bones, but she thinks keeping them in a stone box means they won't get to the afterlife."

Aemilius glanced at the lids, wrist-thick slabs of stone, and thought how much one of them must weigh, and how it must feel to be trapped under one for all eternity, and very subtly picked a path equidistant from the shelves on both sides.

Another turn, another row of coffins. It felt like the path was zig-zagging away from the temple, sloping gently down. Up ahead, Rivkah extended a skinny arm—*stop*—and then cupped her hand to her ear.

Once the soft swish-crunch of their feet in the sand had stilled, all Aemilius could hear was the blood rushing in his ears... but...

Something on the edge of hearing. A man, speaking passionately. The light globe dimmed to a barely perceptible shimmer. Around him Aemilius watched as the legionnaires shifted.

They didn't need to get any closer to recognise the voice.

It was Donato.

THE APPROACH WAS torturously slow. They moved like hunting cats, every step measured and silent, drifting ghost-like around a corner, then another, until they caught the orange shimmer of torch light, soon followed by the smell of pitch and the sound of... water?

Abrax's orb, already only the faintest whisper of moonlight, winked out of existence, and they stood in the dark, listening.

"...and that is why we must all step forward, brothers. All of us. The order of Serapis is not served by the Romans. They respect none of your Gods. They will allow you your square of worship, but what happens if you take one step out of line?"

There was a low murmur of agreement.

"The Roman doesn't care about you. He waits in his palace, he watches you break your backs and he enjoys the fruits of your labours. He brags about Alexandria—the Bride of the Mediterranean—but he does not treat her well. Your Governor is corrupt."

Another murmur, slightly louder.

"His officials are corrupt."

More agreement.

"His soldiers are cruel. And I see you, and I feel your pain, and I hear you ask—what can I do?" There was silence, the kind an experienced preacher would command. When he resumed, there was a different tone to Donato's voice: cunning, cold and conspiratorial. Like he had leaned in, and invited his listeners to do the same.

"The Roman has many things. He has a mighty army. He has gold and governors. He has historians busy lying about how magnificent he is. But one thing the Roman does not have plenty of... is fear. So that is what we give him. We will help you, and you will make him believe. Make him believe the land is cursed. Make him believe the people of the land are mad, and bad, and rotten to the core. Come to him in the night. Poison his food.

Whisper to his wives. Steal his children. Make him look over his shoulder in the day and sweat in the night."

A loud, echoing cheer.

"Make him dream of endless horrors and see sharp teeth wherever he goes."

Another cheer.

"Make him—"

"I've had enough of this, I think," Livia said quietly. "Abrax—hit him hard. We'll deal with the rest."

Aemilius just about felt Rivkah kneeling quickly next to him before Abrax and Livia stepped around the corner, side by side.

There was a shout—followed by the *whoomph* of something bursting into flame. In the flash of light Aemilius saw Taurio, a short club in each hand, charging around the corner. Prasta followed him, holding a small clay pot in her left and a length of rope in her right. Rivkah came after them, fists clenched.

Aemilius was last to turn the corner.

A natural cavern opened up in front of him. The sandy floor was the size of a large courtyard, maybe eighty yards to a side and split up by a dozen rocks, each half the size of a man. The ceiling vaulted up above them, easily five times their height. A wide river crossed the corner at the far end of the cavern.

A huge, flat rock set against the wall opposite formed a natural platform, and upon this Donato stood, crossing his arms and holding off a rain of fire.

In between the Legion and their prey stood twenty men of various ages, all of whom had turned to the intruders with hatred in their eyes.

"The Roman! He's come for us!" Donato shouted. "Kill them!"

As one they gave a roar and charged.

Prasta swung her arm back—and up—and brought it down with furious force.

The ceramic pot spun and twisted, skipping and skimming across the sand towards the men in front, and exploded on a bearded man's knee, sending him screaming to the floor. Another three faltered and fell, screaming and clutching their legs. Aemilius watched in horror as their skin melted under their hands—but that didn't deter the others. Leaping and stumbling over their fallen comrades, they looked up to see Rivkah standing in front of them, hands on her hips, unarmed. Grinning triumphantly, the three broad-shouldered youths at the front of the mob charged at her, screaming and clutching daggers, hell-bent on murder.

Ten yards...

Aemilius saw, and they didn't notice, that Rivkah had pushed one foot slightly back and braced it against a small stone.

Seven yards...

Her knees bent ever so slightly.

Five yards...

She extended her arms straight back, like a bird of prey.

And even though he should have known better by now, Aemilius couldn't help but think it. *They'll rip her to pieces.*

Three—

Her arm whipped forward and suddenly there was a fast-moving cloud of sand at eye level. Screams as one of them stumbled, as triumph turned to terror. They were running blind, going too fast to stop. None of them saw her leaping, knives appearing in a blink of an eye. Planting a foot on the falling boy's shoulder, she leapt again, kicking him down and sending his face straight into the stone with a crunch as she rose, twisting in the air, jabbing her daggers down wherever she could find purchase.

When he was a little boy, Aemilius had once been clawed by a cat. He remembered complaining bitterly to his mother that the cat, a tiny little thing, could cause so much damage. She'd explained to him that it wasn't actually the cat but himself that he had to blame. "The cat only pushes the claw in," she'd said. "It is you pulling away that causes most of the damage." So when the boys, sprinting, suddenly blinded, felt the point of a cat's claw sink into their shoulders, their reaction was understandable, and the consequences were horrific. The next wave of Donato's disciples was greeted by a spray of arterial blood as the big boys up front spun, ripped the blades across their own necks and crashed into each other, vaulting an airborne Rivkah clean away.

When an army charges, the brave are often followed by the wise, and the remaining men spread out to face the Legion. Aemilius watched as Prasta, Rivkah, Taurio and Livia fanned out to meet them. *Thirteen of them, four of us.*

No—five.

He stepped next to Taurio, who glanced at him. "Stay close to me at all times," said the Gaul. "At all times. Go for the wounded ones."

Up ahead, Donato seemed to be finding defences for everything Abrax was throwing at him, flames exploding and fizzling inches from the magus's face, but it was clearly keeping him occupied. Aemilius watched, stunned, as the rock started bubbling under their nemesis. A wave of water rose from the river and slammed down on the circle of lava, enveloping the dark-haired man in a cloud of steam.

The magical battle was so captivating that Aemilius nearly missed Taurio sidling to the right, feinting at the three men facing him and pulling them to the side—but when he did, he scrambled to stay behind the big man. *What is he doing? Why is he—?*

And then Taurio charged, roaring.

The beat and a half it took the men to realise what was happening was enough for him to get within swinging range. The first club connected with a wrist and the dull crack was quickly followed by a piercing scream and a dropped knife. Heart thumping, running after Taurio, he came upon the young man kneeling in the sand, crying and scrabbling for his knife, and he let time float by and allowed someone else who was also him to stab down, once, in the neck, lowering a knee onto the man and holding him down until his thrashing was half-done, then told himself to *get up, get up, get up* and stay behind Taurio. The big man was swinging two clubs, keeping two knifemen at bay. One of them was already wincing and wielding the knife clumsily with his left, the other arm dangling by his side. Over his shoulder he could see bodies, but there were too many to count. *Learn from the Legion.* The idea whispered past him, and he bent to the ground.

The sand flying past Taurio was enough to distract his opponents for the blink of an eye. They hit the floor, one after another, bleeding from broken skulls, and stayed down. Taurio spun around, confirmed instantly that there was no immediate threat and nodded once to Aemilius. "Good work, rabbit." Then he was on the move again, closing in on two men threatening Prasta.

They didn't stand a chance.

Moments later, it was over and the Legion was standing over the bodies of twenty men, dead or dying. Up on the platform, Donato screamed as the sleeve of his robe caught fire and crumpled, rolling off the stone and onto the ground.

Moving slowly, carefully, the Legion approached and formed a semi-circle around the fallen man, a good twenty yards out. He lay on the ground, clutching his arm and shuddering.

"Talk," Livia commanded.

Donato spat a globe of crimson blood onto the sand and pushed himself up to sitting. "I am impressed," he wheezed, "by your tenacity, Romans." He held up a hand. "No questions just now. I am…"—he looked almost thoughtful, then smiled—"tired."

"Abrax…" Livia's voice was thick with warning.

"In fact"—Donato clambered to his feet, arm clutched to his chest, fist clenched—"I would like to ask you a favour."

His arm. His wounded arm.

No

Wrong arm—

"*Abrax!*" Aemilius shouted. "*His hand!*"

"Mind my children, will you?" A flashed grin, a moment of absolute silence, and then a *snap* as the disc he revealed in his hand broke—

And death came to Aemilius.

The ground under their feet suddenly lurched and boiled with movement. He felt the vice-like grip on his arm as Taurio hauled him onto the nearest rock and watched in confusion as he saw the others do the same. What had moments before been sand and gravel was now a seething mass of snakes in a twenty-foot-wide circle all around them. He turned to Abrax to see the magus flailing, barely keeping his balance on the rocks.

A movement by Aemilius's foot distracted him and he saw the snake as Rivkah's heel came down on its head and crushed it with a dull pop.

"Look!"

Behind Rivkah, Donato had almost crossed the cave. They watched him launch himself without hesitation into the river and disappear from sight.

Taurio's club smacked on the rocks and another snake lost its life. The hissing nightmare roiled below them. Standing across from them on a flat rock ten yards away, Livia supported the weight of Abrax and screamed with frustration.

"Hold them off!" Prasta shouted, folding herself down small and rummaging in her bag. Out came satchels and vials, herbs and a pot of some sort of dust.

By her ankle, Rivkah stomped on another snake that was either crawling or being pushed up the rock by the seething mass below.

Aemilius watched as Prasta whipped out a cloth sack, pouring ingredients into it at speed and shaking.

"Now close your eyes and hold your nose, or you'll never smell anything again!" Without waiting to see if they'd all done as they were told, the Celt threw the bag in the air.

"Promise?" Taurio shouted back before covering his face in the crook of his elbow.

For a moment the constant hiss of the snakes was all he heard—and then the noise changed.

"Safe?" Taurio shouted.

"Safe!"

They opened their eyes and breathed in, and Aemilius really wished he hadn't. He was standing inches above a circus of slaughter. The snakes, frenzied with pain, were attacking each other. A lot of them were writhing in agony, blistered welts rising under withering scales.

"They are disgusting creatures, but that's…" Taurio's voice trailed off.

A familiar rush of hot air brushed past Aemilius's face and a thin ring of fire formed around each of the rocks, driving the reptiles away and offering a moment of safety.

Aemilius looked across to where Donato had disappeared, and just as he was trying to figure out how the magus had evaded them again, he noticed it.

The circle in the sand.

The grains rattling, shaking, jumping…

And then a fresh horror burst out of the ground, drawing itself up to almost half the height of the space. Jaws that would easily fit around a grown cow opened to hiss, and a forked tongue tasted the air past a pair of fangs as big as a four-year-old child. Yellow eyes glared down at them, and the body swayed and slithered as the monstrous creation kept coming out of the ground.

The effect on the other snakes was instant. The ones still alive all slithered to the monster, which was dozens of yards long and somehow still coming. Their numbers had diminished significantly, but there were still altogether too many of them. They rubbed themselves up against the creature, crawling over its massive, five-foot-wide body, nudging it with their heads.

"I guess Mummy's come home," Prasta said, almost wearily. "There are times when I wonder whether I chose the right job."

"Do you have any more of that fancy snake dust?"

"I'm out," she replied. "So do we run, or...?"

"Through the catacombs, in the dark? And lead that thing into Alexandria?" Livia replied.

"Didn't think so," she sighed. "Abrax...?"

The fire-magus was standing but only just, looking like he had aged by another ten years since they entered the chamber. He drew an intricate pattern with his hands, and a line of fire grew out of the sand, a barrier between them and the vermin gathering around their God. The giant snake hissed at them, swaying, but it did not approach. Instead, in a horrifying spectacle, a group of the smaller snakes formed a line as wide as its trunk, and started moving slowly, deliberately towards the fire.

"No..." Rivkah muttered. "They're not going to..."

Yes, they are. Aemilius watched in terror as the smaller snakes lay their bodies down onto the fire, so that the monster might cross unscathed. The stench of burning flesh filled the cave, but the giant snake was now heading towards them.

A *whoosh* and a fireball the size of a man's head shot towards the snake. It exploded on its scales, leaving a blackened mark, and the beast shrieked and reared its head, but then it resumed its advance.

"Well, it's been fun," Taurio said. "But this might be the end for us. Oh, and there's a wave coming as well. That's just great."

The water in the river had risen up, a water-snake to match the creature, and it was indeed coming at them at twice the speed of the nightmare beast. Rising to the very top of the dome, it condensed into what looked like a giant drop of water, which hung for half a breath and then fell—almost gently—onto the snake's head, buckling the muscular body and driving the horrid head into the ground. The creature thrashed, but moving through the suddenly wet sand was much more heavy going—and the river kept rising, washing water along the scaly body, dragging it down.

Aemilius turned to see a familiar shape, all skin and bones, leaning up against the entrance to the cave. "Hanno!"

The diminutive magus waved weakly.

Rivkah screamed something in Hebrew, leapt off the rock and charged towards the worm.

The monster reared, shook itself and blinked—but no matter what it did, its body was sinking in the wet sand, a prisoner of its own weight. It twisted this way and that—and then suddenly yanked as Rivkah jammed two daggers under its scales. Hissing furiously, it cast about for the source of the attack, but the girl was already moving, skipping across—

The snake lunged, and Aemilius yelped. *Nothing that size should be allowed to be that fast.* The monstrous jaws opened wide, teeth glistening—and its head smacked into the ground where Rivkah had been. The river was flowing into the cave, turning everything the snake's body touched into quicksand. It kept sinking into the ground, and no matter how it twisted it couldn't get loose.

"Abrax?" Rivkah shouted, bloodied daggers in her hands. "I just need you to bring the bastard down."

The fire magus looked on the brink of collapse, but— hands moving like lead—he cast one last spell.

A crown of flame wrapped itself around the beast's head. It twisted and snapped, but the only way to escape was to go down—and when it did, the crown followed. Gradually the snake's head sank to the ground, and Aemilius gasped as Rivkah, more demon than human, leapt towards the flames, slid under that crown of death, landed on the snout of the beast, and jammed her daggers in, one in each eye.

As one, the snakes in the cavern all reared.

Rivkah was thrown from the beast, twisting in the air to land on her feet, screaming as her knee smacked into a rock.

The sea of reptiles stilled instantly as the life blinked out of them.

The abomination spasmed once, twice… then toppled over, like a dying tree, and crashed to the ground, sending up a spray of wet sand.

And then there was silence.

After a while, Livia spoke. "I've seen some things," she said quietly. "And that was definitely one of them."

The ground beneath the rocks sparkled where fire had melted the sand into glass, crested with dead snakes, coloured with their blood. The obscene form of the monster was sinking out of sight before their eyes, with the occasional wet, sucking noise. As they watched, more water appeared under the fallen head, and it too started to sink.

"I have never been happier to see a frog," Rivkah said. "What happened? I thought you were nearly dead?"

"I was. I got bored," Hanno said from the cave-mouth.

They picked their way carefully across the sandy floor, alert to snakes that might have a final twitch in them. When they got to the followers of Donato, the Legion eased up a bit. The would-be terrorisers of Rome were all stone dead. As they passed, pinpricks of corpse-fire appeared on the men.

"So what was this, then?" Prasta asked, looking back at the bodies. "A… recruitment drive?"

"Striking fear into Rome," Livia said. "I wish he'd realise how unimaginative we are. Rome does not fear things, it smashes them."

They'd gotten to the cave mouth, and Abrax conjured up a point of light to show the way.

"Hard to smash the shadow in the night," Taurio said. "I hate to say it before I've caved his face in, but he's got a point. You can win the war, but if you can't keep the peace—Whoa, my old fish. Are you well?"

In front of them, Hanno faltered. "I am well as a well," he said, one sinewy arm outstretched. "Just a little…" Taurio ignored him completely and lifted the diminutive magus in his arms like a child. Aemilius followed, allowing himself one look back at the cavern, growing dimmer behind him. He made out a hint of the outline of the giant serpent under the sand. He saw the sparks of corpse-light in the fallen men. He shuddered and tried to shake off the death, leave it behind, and walked into the catacombs, past the rows and rows of sarcophagi.

When they stepped out from the narrow passageway into the lit corridor, Taurio broke the silence. "I am surprised that we've been able to go in and out uninterrupted—"

"—apart from the twenty men we just killed," Prasta interjected.

"Yes, yes." He feigned annoyance. "But you know what I mean. It just feels very…"

"Quiet," Livia said darkly.

"Yes."

Once again the Legion settled, wearily, into a battle-ready stance. Rivkah went up the spiral staircase first, quick and light on her feet. Aemilius expected to hear the sounds of knife-death the moment she disappeared out of sight, but there was nothing. Instead she hissed, "Clear."

They filed up, all in order, and it was.

No worshippers.

No families.

And no priests.

Taurio looked at the others. "So," he said. "What do we think?"

"We haven't done anything wrong." If Abrax was worried, his voice did not let on. "We are but simple worshippers. We were in the temple. If any priests challenge us on that, we can say that we got lost. At worst, Corto supplied me with enough for a reasonable 'donation to the cause,' as it were. But we avoid making ourselves the centre of attention. Do we agree?"

A general muttering of consent, and the Legion moved towards the doorway. "Do we split up?" Prasta scanned the other doors.

"Not safe," Abrax muttered. "We don't know what's waiting for us."

Aemilius saw the shadow of the figure by the window disappear, just out of the corner of his eye, just a moment before the voice boomed.

"Come out now, unarmed! All of you!"

Livia rolled her eyes. "Hades's hairy ball sack. I am sorry. I genuinely thought he'd stay down. I think he'd be happy with just me, though."

"Just you try, Princess," Rivkah growled. "If you so much as *think* of making some sort of noble sacrifice I'll hamstring you, gut you and strangle you with your own shit-cord."

Livia looked away for a moment, and Aemilius wasn't

sure whether she was hiding a smile or a tear. Then—
"Right. Let's go and see what he's brought, shall we?"

They stepped out into the courtyard.

AEMILIUS HAD NEVER seen that many soldiers at once.
There had to be at least a hundred of them, maybe
two hundred, all armed and ready, all identical in
their armour. Behind them, anticipating a welcome
distraction of violence, a crowd three times their number
had assembled.

"Looks like they've sent half a guard company," Taurio
said with approval.

"I've still got it," Livia said.

"Were you worried?"

"No."

The man in front, a chiselled, sun-baked guard captain,
stepped forward and barked at them. "Livia Claudia,
you are charged with the wilful murder of seven Roman
guards—"

"Seven? We only killed—" Rivkah counted on her
fingers. "Did we kill them all?"

"I suspect the one we left alive didn't do so well," Livia
muttered. "Happens to guards who see the Governor's
deputy piss themselves."

The guard captain continued. "We have you surrounded,
there is nowhere to run to, and if you try anything we'll
happily pin you to the wall and turn you into pig food."
He gestured to the rooftops, where two groups of six
soldiers crouched, crossbows aimed squarely at them.
"Do you yield?"

Livia was about to step forward and speak, when
Aemilius hissed behind her, "Wait."

She paused.

"Rivkah," he muttered, making sure his lips could not be seen. "Will you try something for me?"

An intense quiet, but no rejection. *Let's hope this works.*

"Step forward and listen for my voice. You're a victim. But…" He whispered the rest and just about caught the sideways glance from the most dangerous girl he'd ever known, but she stepped forward nonetheless.

"I have been abused!" Rivkah shouted in Hebrew, not betraying for a second that she was taking the prompt from Aemilius. "I, daughter of Abraham, was set upon by three—no, five—Greek scholars, who beat me upon the head and face, and would have forced themselves upon me!"

There were angry shouts from behind the imposing row of Roman soldiers.

Moving slightly to the side on Aemilius's orders, Abrax stepped forward, voice booming in fluent Greek. "The little street-rat lies! This is just another Jew trick! No self-respecting and cultured man would touch her with a stick!"

"Oh, you didn't say that in the alley, you creep!"

Somewhere behind the Romans, a fight was breaking out.

"No—don't fight!" Livia shouted, sounding every inch the commanding governess. "Leave this to the guards!"

"There goes the Roman!" Abrax bellowed at her. "Trying to control our every move!"

The soldiers were well-drilled, but there was the hint of heads turning here and there as the crowd began to swell behind them. "Stand your ground!" their captain shouted. "And you! Shut your mouths!"

"I will speak!" Rivkah cried. "I am just a little girl! A harmless little girl! A tiny, harmless, innocent little girl! Sons of Zion—do you not have mothers? Do you not have wives? Do you not have daughters? Do you want some old creeps to be able to lay their hands on them whenever they might wish?"

"Oh, so all Greeks are old creeps, is that it?"

"Don't deny your reputation!" Livia shouted.

"Do you *hear* her?" Abrax bellowed.

Six separate fights had now broken out behind the Romans. While they watched, two of the fights merged to become one sprawling melee. Punches were thrown. Aemilius watched as one old man in robes whacked a young man in the head from behind with a heavy roll of papyrus. The shouts rose in volume and pitch.

The guard captain stared at them with hatred. "Take them!" he commanded.

Two young men tussling lost their balance and fell into a soldier, who swivelled and struck one of them with the pommel of his gladius, and somehow the sound was louder than seventy men shouting, and suddenly there was a riot.

Aemilius looked quickly at the crossbowmen. "Temple! Now!" he snapped, and was astonished when the legionnaires all ducked in after him. He sprinted across the floor to the door opposite, bursting out into chaos. The eastern courtyard was an ebbing, flowing free-for-all. People kept coming up the stairs, and the Roman guards were quickly outnumbered.

"Steps?" Aemilius shouted.

They responded by running past him.

At the top of the stair, they saw that somehow the fight had spread down to the square below. Behind them they heard the guard captain barking formation orders, and as they carefully picked their way down the steps, they were treated to the spectacle of every single combatant scanning them on their way past, concluding that they were neither friend nor foe, and leaving them be.

Once on the ground, they made their way swiftly across the square and disappeared down an alleyway, and let the riot sweep them to safety.

XV

ALEXANDRIA

THE MORNING SUN had not yet warmed the gentle breeze from the sea. The birds squawked happily overhead, and in the distance Aemilius could just about discern fishermen heading out for the day.

There had been no feeling he could remember like that of waking up after the sleep he'd just had. After making their escape from the riot, they had ducked into the safety of Corto's tavern, followed the big man down into the basement and emerged into an enclosed courtyard, and then to a big apartment with a number of small bedrooms, the purpose and provenance of which was not discussed in too much detail. They had beds, a table with a jug of wine, and a door with a lock, and Aemilius crashed into his bunk and was asleep in an instant.

They had spent a day and a night in hiding, waiting for the thundering knock on the door, but from the sounds of it the Roman authorities had their hands full with a couple thousand angry Jews and Greeks desperate to rearrange each other's faces. Taurio had sagely pointed out that in such situations crimes did sometimes get committed, and the more crimes that got committed, the more likely people were to forget or ignore minor things. Aemilius thought killing a handful of Roman guards might not be considered 'minor,' but he kept that to himself. There was no reason to keep being negative. They had not caught Donato, but they had slain his creatures and saved a whole lot of people from certain death. The fact that those people had then tried to kill each other was, Livia explained, not really their concern.

What was their concern, however, was to get back to what the legionnaires called the Fort, and report to the mysterious 'her.' This was to be accomplished by a friendly ship to Sicily, and that was how Aemilius found himself standing on the beach ten miles west of Alexandria's city walls, looking at the sky and breathing easy for the first time in a long time. The others were dotted about the beach. Abrax, who had looked tired, drained and significantly older even after a long sleep, stood on the highest point and looked out to sea. Livia stood with him. *Getting their—no,* our—*story straight, probably.* Prasta had managed to scrounge some supplies to organise, and near where she'd laid out their provisions Taurio had fashioned himself a makeshift fishing rod and line, which he was optimistically lashing at the sea. Rivkah lay on a stone, a study in inactivity.

Aemilius pushed himself to move towards the last member of the Legion, currently sitting on a stone with his eyes closed and his feet in the water. He needed to ask a question, but Hanno beat him to it.

"It was you, wasn't it?" the little man said.

Aemilius faked his best surprised face, then stopped

when he realised Hanno was definitely not looking at him. "What do you mean?"

"You know."

I do. Steeling himself, Aemilius decided to go for it. What was the worst that could happen? *He could drag me into the sea, or shove a puddle down my throat, or—*He interrupted his own runaway thoughts. "I don't know. Maybe."

"Hm." Hanno seemed to find this mildly amusing. "But you are here to ask me about magic, yes?" When Aemilius faltered, and the magus added, "You have, for instance, shown no interest in my soup recipes."

"You have soup recipes?"

"Several, as it happens," the magus replied, sounding a little wounded. "But ask me about magic." He paused for a second. "I command you. Or beg you. Whichever calms your waters."

He took a few deep breaths, then plunged in. "What is—? No, how—? When...?"

Hanno smiled. "Breathe, and think, and ask one question."

Aemilius did as he was told. "I have been thinking about the conversation we had, and I was wondering—can you really *learn* magic?" The words burst out of him, followed by a rush of blood to the face. *Why do I always have to sound like an eight-year-old brat?*

"I should hope so," Hanno chuckled. "I know a lot of things, and I had to work for every single one of them. Next question—your head is thick with them."

"How do you do it?"

"Much like with anything else. You start with the first lesson, and learn that one, and then you move onto the next one."

Aemilius made a face at the old magus. *No—not old*, he reminded himself. *Just… unhelpful.*

"Now ask the next question." Hanno's voice had acquired a subtle note of… command? No, instruction.

Here we go. "Could…" Aemilius hesitated for a moment before he found his bravery. "Could *I* learn magic?" And then the words were out, and panic surged in him. "Because I am never going to be able to take out the eye of a monster snake in a somersault, and I can't throw a man across the room like Taurio, and I definitely can't charm any governors, and killing makes me a bit sick, and I could maybe be good at sneaking, but I don't know, because I just feel like I got lucky, and—"

A bucket's worth of water hit him in the face, tasting of salt. When Aemilius had shaken himself and managed to open his eyes again, he found that Hanno was looking at him. There was no hint of judgement in the big, brown eyes, incongruously youthful in the wrinkled, old face. Instead, there was curiosity.

"Magic? …you? You'd have to stop talking first," he said, smiling a little. "And you'd have to listen. Can you do that?"

Aemilius nodded, wide-eyed.

"Good. Then let's talk about magic." A wave touched Hanno's foot and crawled up his shin, nudging his knee like a friendly dog. The old man stuck his hand in the water and smiled as it faded back down into the sea, then rolled his shoulders and winced. "There's magic in everything. For me, it is the water. For our bald friend it is heat. For her"—he glanced towards Livia—"it is what happens between people. Some scholars get very busy and angry arguing about what is and isn't real magic, but the way I see it—if I don't understand it and I can't do it, it might as well be magic."

Aemilius nodded. The questions surged forward, but he held them off. *Don't talk. Listen.*

"Finding magic is not hard," Hanno continued. "Finding *your* magic?" The old magus smiled. "… harder. And before you start searching you should know that magic is not free. In the stories we only see the thunderbolts and earthquakes. We never hear about the headache after, or the three days throwing up, or"—he gestured to his white hair—"this.

"Magic costs, and you should never forget it. Some things cost a little less when you get better at them, but I spent almost everything I had on defending us against that horrid creature. I panicked, lifted far more water than I should have, and thinking back there must have been something more clever that I could have done. I survived, for I am Hanno the Wise, and when I get three days to myself I will think of what I will do the next time I am battling a beast like that, and it will hopefully cost me a little less—but as for magic, I would not be able to do much more in my current state. If, say, we met another of those on the way back—"

Aemilius shuddered.

"—I would have to choose."

"Choose what?"

"Do nothing, and die… or do something, and still die." Hanno smiled, but this time it was a harder smile. "Magic costs, and sometimes it costs a lot. You have to learn, and learn cleverly, and always be humble, and ask nicely."

"I… could do that."

"Maybe so." Hanno looked him up and down. "You

are not as dumb as you look, which is fortunate. Tell me about the fish."

"Uh…"

"You called them."

He tried to remember. The malevolence in the eyes of the cetus. The infinite depth of its hell-maw. The boat rocking back and forth despite Hanno's best efforts.

"I just had a, uh, thought," he stammered.

"And what was the thought?" Hanno was gentle but insistent.

"We need help." As he said the words, he remembered the moment, the smell of salt and death in the air, the screaming in his head… and the sensation of being one of many, and the weight of the water pressing on him and the power in his body.

"Ah!" Hanno smiled. "Good. And then what?"

"What do you mean?"

"Don't think about your answer, but speak immediately. How did it *feel?*"

"Like I only had one thought."

Hanno clapped. "Excellent!"

Aemilius stared at him.

He continued. "You cleared your mind. You did not demand. Instead you made a simple request."

"I asked nicely," Aemilius said slowly.

The old man beamed at him. "See? Quick thinker, excellent tutor. You asked very nicely indeed. And even though a *lot* of water-dwellers answered your call, you didn't *control* them at all. You didn't push them. You didn't use them badly."

"What would have happened if I did?"

"You'd be dead," came Hanno's matter-of-fact reply. "You would have collapsed on the spot. You would have aged by four or five lifetimes in the blink of an eye. The only reason you are alive is that you did magic without knowing."

"I... what?"

Hanno looked at him and chuckled. "Oh, you didn't realise? That's so lovely. No, you did. And what's the absolute best thing is that it suggests to us where your magic lies."

"I can command tuna?"

Hanno smiled. "Did you get to Hispalis on a saddled fish?"

Aemilius blinked. "I can speak to horses and fish?"

"I have met a fair few people in my time with magical gifts, and I will say that that would be the fourth strangest combination I've ever heard. Shall we try to see if there are other animals that will listen?"

Despite the warmth of the morning sun, Aemilius felt a chill. This was all moving rather faster than he thought it would. "Uh... Yes, uhm... What do I do?"

"Start by looking less terrified," the old man said, smiling as he levered himself to his feet. "And close your mouth. And breathe. Now—we are going to ask nicely. Think of an animal."

"A... bird?"

"Birds are good," Hanno said. "They see, and they fly, and when they shit on our heads, we are thankful that the cow has no wings. And what should you remember?"

"Learn cleverly, always be humble and ask nicely."

One chalk-white eyebrow rose and Hanno tilted his head appreciatively. "The river knows where it is going!"

Aemilius remembered one of his more scathing tutors, and owned his words. "I can learn if I want to."

"Good. Now, think of a bird and ask it to come sit with us."

"What kind?"

"I don't know, do I?" Hanno smiled. "I only occasionally try to talk to birds, and they rarely listen. Very little water in them. Just remember—one thought only."

Aemilius closed his eyes, tried to clear his mind and immediately thought of all the different hand-things Abrax and Hanno did. *What do I do with my hands?* He opened his eyes again, to find Hanno studying him intently.

"That looked like a little more than one thought," he said gently.

Nope—just one, but a really loud one. "Sorry," Aemilius mumbled. He closed his eyes again, tried to think of a bird, any bird, and found out that he had actually never seen a single bird in his life. Never at all. Did they have hands? Who knew? Frustrated, he opened his eyes again.

Hanno smiled. "It is quite hard," he said gently. "That's why, generally, few people do it, and very few of them do it well, and almost all of them die quite messily."

One more go. He eased his eyes shut this time, and tried to imagine a feather, and when he did it was long, and a dark, lustrous brown, fading to a tan white towards the tip, and he imagined another and another and another, and he saw that it was a wing and it was a strong wing and he followed the line of it up the neck to the eye, the amber eye that saw all down the rip-scythe beak, and he whispered, "Come here now," and added, "...if you wouldn't mind." And he saw the eye and he felt like the eye saw him, and he blinked—

And it was gone.

He sighed and opened his eyes. "Has a flock of birds appeared behind me?"

"No," Hanno said, smiling. "But our ship has. It is time to go, young Roman." When he saw the look on Aemilius's face he added, "Don't give up on yourself." His eyes twinkled. "I won't. Now be a good pup and help an old man." He reached out a sinewy arm that looked like it could snap in two with a change of the wind, and Aemilius reached out to support him, and they turned towards the beach, where a rowing boat that could fit at least ten people comfortably had settled ashore, and three muscular sailors were waiting to take them aboard. Out in the bay a big-bellied Roman merchant-ship bobbed gently, and beyond it two lighter liburnes, looking menacing even at a distance.

Aemilius boarded the rowing boat in a daze and allowed the gentle movement of the sea to lull him into a stupor. He was about to go to Sicily, and then ride all the way to Umbria to go to the Legion's Fort, and he had done magic once accidentally, and he couldn't do it again and nothing about his life would have seemed even remotely plausible to him a week ago. He watched the cargo ship grow bigger as they approached, climbed up the rope ladder after the others, did what he was told and settled down out of the way, watching with detached interest as the sailors scurried back and forth, raising sails and barking incomprehensible orders at each other. He felt the push of the wind a moment after the cloth snapped, and they were off.

He did not look back at Alexandria, or the Lighthouse, or the Serapeum on the hill.

So he did not see the big, brown eagle circling high

overhead, powerful wings spread out as it eased down to the spot it wanted, searching for the source of the voice that had commanded it.

ACKNOWLEDGEMENTS

As with all the others, this book would not have happened without the love and support of **Morag**, who is and remains the Best Wife, and without whom I would have finished far fewer things in my life. This one is for you, as were all before, and all to come. Other people are allowed to read them, I suppose—but they are mainly for you.

My agent and one-man cheerleading squad, **Max Edwards**, deserves all manner of thanks for everything he has done through the years, and chiefly for his relentless enthusiasm. If we run out of fossil fuels I have a solution to the energy crisis. We are on a long walk, my friend, but I am quite enjoying the scenery.

My **lovely parents** and my dear **brother**, ever-patient and over-qualified super-readers who are never anything other than unreasonably positive and supportive about this writing nonsense. I promise—eventually, something I write will make it onto Netflix.

My editor and brother from another mother, **David**

Thomas Moore, who I aspire to become half as clever as when I grow up.

Chief Gladiator **Michael Rowley**, for ideas, approval and encouragement.

The **Secret Experts**, whose support and expertise have been much appreciated. All the precise and accurate bits in this book are theirs, and all the embarrassing inaccuracies are mine.

The **Quartermains**, the **Groves**, the **Englishes**, the **Jilkses**, the **Yius**, the **Holmeses** and a host of other dear friends who have bought, read and patiently listened to me talk about my nonsense through the years.

Thank you, thank you, thank you.

Snorri Kristjansson

ABOUT THE AUTHOR

A teacher, a stand up comic, former cement packing factory worker and graduate of the London Academy of Music and Dramatic Arts, **Snorri Kristjansson** also writes things. Sometimes they are books (mainly about Vikings), sometimes they are films (mainly not about Vikings) or silly stage plays (you probably don't want to know, to be honest).

He now spends his days working with words, eating cakes and teaching drama.

🐦 @snorrikristjans
🌐 snorrikristjansson.com

FIND US ONLINE!

www.rebellionpublishing.com

/solarisbooks   /solarisbks   /solarisbooks

SIGN UP TO OUR NEWSLETTER!

rebellionpublishing.com/newsletter

YOUR REVIEWS MATTER!

Enjoy this book? Got something to say?

Leave a review on Amazon, GoodReads or with your
favourite bookseller and let the world know!